JOURNEY
TO THE
STARS

'I was born under a wand'rin' star.'

ALWYN DOW

Order this book online at www.trafford.com
or email orders@trafford.com

Most Trafford titles are also available at major online book retailers.

Print information available on the last page.

ISBN: 978-1-4907-9945-2 (sc)
ISBN: 978-1-4907-9946-9 (e)

Trafford rev. 01/17/2020

www.trafford.com

North America & international
toll-free: 1 888 232 4444 (USA & Canada)
fax: 812 355 4082

INTRODUCTION

'In February 1954 President Eisenhower met with aliens at Holloman Air Base. They were said to be Nordic or Alien Green in appearance.'

This is an actual extract from T.Good's Pentagon memoir published in the UK Daily Mail on 12 May 2014. However, although this extraordinary meeting has been disputed by some, JOURNEY TO THE STARS follows the potential consequences of such a meeting as experienced by Kiwi Grant and Duke Morton (MI6 and CIA) They have been sent by the 'Deep Cover Unit' to investigate such strange phenomena with potential links to 'earthbound' terrorism be they Racial or Islamic. An ultimatum has been sent and time is running out for them and the even Planet Earth itself. The book begins with a clandestine meeting in a back room off Bond Street in London.

1

AFRICANA

'The lamps are going out all over Europe,'

No, t.his is not a reference to Sir Edward Grey's speech in 1914, but a comment on the power cut that took place one hundred years later in June 2014. The cut was sudden and international, and many wise heads were at a loss to determine the cause. However, in a back room off Bond Street in London, officers of DCU Operation Scorpion thought that they knew the answer. These were Tom Franks and Hilary Tucker and they had recently received information from Paul Ward, a retired agent that such a scenario was imminent, and now he was missing. Their office was in complete darkness and as they looked out of their window the air was still, and there was not a sound to be heard in this usually frenetic metropolis.

'It seems eerie.' said Franks.

'Yes, almost unworldly.' she replied, as emergency sirens split the night air. At this he smiled, and they both began to laugh rather uneasily.

'I've got Jo Grant and Duke Morton waiting outside. They're in the dark in more ways than one,' he said with a grin. 'I think that they had better get down to Bristol as soon as possible to find out what's happened to Ward. I'll bring them in and explain shall I?'

Tucker nodded and he went to the door and ushered the pair into the room.

'Sorry about the short notice,' he said, 'but actually we've been expecting a power cut for some time. However we believe this one to be sabotage by the group that we call Cerberus and we need to nip them in the bud before they can go further. Please take a seat if you can see one.'

Then, just as they did as he asked, the lights came back on and he looked at his watch. 'Precisely one hour,' he said, 'seems like another trial run. Come in and I'll tell you more.'

When they had settled down he told them that Paul Ward was a retired Civil Servant now leading a normal comfortable life in Bristol, but he had been a British agent during the African apartheid and UDI crises, When he was there he had come across the racist organisation known as Cerberus, but now, after many years 'out of it' he had told Whitehall that he had reason to believe that they were undergoing a renewal with much wider ambitions. He had said that he was compiling a detailed dossier with names and an 'incredible new development' that he would send within weeks. He had also implied that strategic power sources would be hit very soon. It had not arrived, and now he was 'missing' and the DCU wanted to know if there was a connection between his disappearance, Cerberus and the recent blackout. It would be a 'missing persons' police case initially, so Kiwi would be asked to liaise with the local force while Duke remained as backup.

They only had a few days to get ready and while there was much to be done but there was still time for socialising. This usually occurred in group settings of colleagues or friends at the 'Left Bank' French night club or even the Old Ship Inn, but this particular night was different, 'St Valentine's Day' of course. Maybe it was the music, maybe it was the wine, but soon Kiwi found herself back in her flat and flat on her back, with a man in her bed. Hours of delight ensued until their desires were satiated and exhaustion overcame them both. Only then did she pause to take stock. 'So this is what they mean by a one night stand,' she thought rather ruefully as she looked across at Duke's form spread across her bed.

'An hour ago I was drinking champagne and now look at me. Well that's that; never again.' She soon drifted off to sleep, but the thought in her mind, between doing somersaults or snorkel diving was not 'never again' but 'when again and please again.' As it turned out she didn't have to wait long at all because, as dawn broke she felt a nudge in her ribs from the man in the bed.

'Did you hear that?' he murmured.

'Did I hear what?' she responded.

'It's Prince. They've got him. Listen.' He reached over her tumbled form and turned up the volume on the clock radio next to the bed. 'Listen,' he said again.

Kiwi muttered, 'I'm listening,' from under the covers.

The announcer continued 'It will be fine today with a few outbreaks of rain.'

'Damn' he said, 'Come on get up and come downstairs for the TV news.'

'What, for the weather forecast?' she muttered.

'No, it's Prince. They've killed him.' he continued, 'I knew they would sooner or later'

Kiwi was still half asleep. 'Prince who might I ask, and Prince of where to boot?' she responded and tried to hide, but he was determined, threw the duvet aside and there she lay (blonde today) but stark naked and bare.

It's funny how a natural urge can suddenly take over. The killing of Senator Joshua Prince of California would have to wait for a while.

✳✳✳

Later at breakfast he went into more detail, insisting that a political conspiracy was going from strength to strength in the world and no one was doing anything about it.

'He was on to something about aliens from a planet called Gonda, that I've never heard of,' he said, 'and he thought that they were linked to a radical Aryan group in the States and despite all the government denials he just wouldn't let it go. I don't go much on all that ET stuff myself but he thought it was important enough to lose his life over.'

Kiwi thought otherwise, and tended to think that there might be something in it. She knew that such ideas were not entirely new, and respectable papers like the New York Times and Washington Post had carried stories of UFO sightings for decades including 'a fleet of UFO's' in 1952. Duke went on to say that on the 8th December 2010 a cigar shaped object had been sighted launching OUT of the Pacific in Los Angeles Bay. This phenomenon had been seen by many including the Senator and he'd been asking questions about it ever since (of course this tended to convince Kiwi even more, but she knew that Duke was sceptical about such things).

She admired his zeal for 'causes' and it was one of the things that had attracted her, but sometimes she thought he that didn't see the 'big picture' especially when it came to 'those little green men out there in space,' as he put it.

Anyway, green or grey she was now getting ready for work, and first impressions could be important. Franks had arranged a meeting with Inspector Matlock and she was already running late. 'It's all Duke's fault.' she thought as she smiled to herself.

❊❊❊

Inspector Matlock from the Bristol Central area police HQ was in charge of the missing person enquiry.

'I'm told it has an African connection' he said rather disparagingly, 'but they usually end up as local affairs in the end, so we are probably wasting your time anyway.'

Kiwi had become familiar with many of the regional Police stations over a period of time and had met Matlock and other officers before, but usually such cases had been about immigration issues, or cases that involved International drug or arms smuggling, not missing persons.

'Well sir,' she replied, 'now that I'm here I suppose we'd better look into it don't you think?'

He grunted his assent and just said, 'Well we've got enough to do already but you can have that desk over there.' saying which he pointed to a dusty corner with a very dirty window in the corner of the office.

'Thank you sir,' she replied pleasantly taking her bag to the seat in question. She realised she wouldn't get much help from him. Next she opened her briefcase and took out her papers, opened her lap top and began to read her instructions from Tom Franks.

Top Secret Africa DCU Operation Scorpion

Any case related to past issues during apartheid in South Africa must be treated with sensitivity and any case that involves the UDI situation in Southern Rhodesia at that time must be handled with care. This is because we have reason to believe that such white supremacist movements have not gone away altogether but now form part of a wider world conspiracy, not only to achieve their earlier stated aims but to undermine democratic governments throughout the world now, in order to achieve the Aryan supremacy that they and others have failed to accomplish so far. There are many names given to this clandestine organisation and one of them is 'Cerberus' We know that it has a number of bases throughout the world, together with an organisation modelled on a contemporary Roman Empire with a leader known as 'Alpha' The lower ranks such as Beta, Gamma and Delta follow the Roman equivalents of Magistrate, Consul and Governor. DCU created 'Operation Scorpion' to deal with this threat and we have followed its activities in many areas. In addition there is now a wider stage as we have recently had indications that they are not acting alone. This aspect is TOP SECRET and concerns links with extra- terrestrial groups thought to be from the planet Gonda. It may be that they have a common agenda but in any case the implications are serious. Many will not believe this analysis but we can't take chances. Details on Gonda will follow but your concern is to investigate Cerberus for now. The missing man is Paul Ward and he had been an important DCU officer in Africa working on 'Operation Scorpion', but he had more or less retired. However, he had recently reported that he had suspicions about local figures who may be Cerberus agents in his community, but he didn't specify who or how. He promised to send a dossier and alluded to imminent attacks on power infrastructures but it has not arrived and now he's missing. We need to find him if possible and establish if there is any connection. It may be nothing but it could also be the start of a trail that will lead us to Alpha, so follow every lead and be vigilant.

Kiwi closed her lap top thoughtfully, remembering how Duke had suggested a similar conspiracy in the States that very morning. Not only that but she was actually quite receptive to the idea that 'we are not alone,' and stories from her home in New Zealand sometimes backed this up. After all, the original Australasian archipelago had been called 'Gondwana' and her Gran often claimed to 'hear the spirits.' On the other hand she thought that she'd have a job convincing Duke, whom she knew to be sceptical about non-Christian interpretations of space.

When such issues had come up before, she had even quoted the Bible back at him when he seemed too wedded to 'traditional' views in which earth was the centre of the universe and not a mere speck in it. Her favourite one was Genesis 15 in which the Lord spoke to Moses and said, 'Look up to the heavens and count the stars if you can. Such will be your descendants.' Kiwi thought that God might have meant the antecedents too, because anything else was illogical in her eyes. However Duke believed in Catholicism and accepted the supernatural as real. If her reasoning matched, well that was well and good, but where differences occurred, it was always Faith and Biblical revelation for him. He quoted the New Testament in which Jesus had said that, 'No one comes to the Father except through me.'

'And how do aliens fit into that scenario?' he had asked.

'What about Hindus and Moslems and other world religions, not to speak of those who have no religion then?' she had responded.

'You're so lucky when you say that it's all nonsense,' he had replied, 'to be honest I sometimes wish that it were.'

Kiwi remembered this line from 'Brideshead Revisited,' explaining as it did the burden and responsibility of being a Catholic. Fortunately the matter had not been a major problem up to now, but she had an uneasy feeling that he might be unreceptive to any ideas on that score and so, if Franks was right this could well be a problem for the future.

∗∗∗

Matlock was peeved that she was late, commenting that he expected his officers to be prompt at all times.

He then continued. 'I've called you in especially as the Super said that Ward, the missing man worked in Africa at one time. I don't think that's got anything to do with it as I said, but take it from me we'll have more Government people down on us like a ton of bricks if we don't put it to bed soon. I know that you have to report back to your other masters but when you're here you work for me. I want you to work alongside the team but only under my direction. Is that clear?'

Kiwi agreed, but she decided to keep a private ILO dossier as backup. She'd learnt not to trust all police officers.

The Inspector then called a meeting of all the staff and began to outline the case in some detail. He had spoken to Mrs Ward on the phone and gleaned a few facts as follows. Apparently Paul Ward had telephoned his wife Lorna from the 'Cup Cakes' tea shop at about 6pm, but he had not yet come home. By eight o'clock she had begun to wonder what to do. Firstly she went down the garden to his work shed and then to their narrow boat 'the Laura', which was always moored at the bottom of the garden, calling out as she went along, 'Paul, are you there? Where are you? Come out; come out wherever you are' she continued in a sing- song tone as in 'The Third Man', when Holly Martens located the shadowy cat, then the feet, and then the face of the inscrutable Orson Welles in the lamp-light. Next she had walked around the park opposite their house, and then she had visited all the neighbours, but he wasn't there and no one had seen him that day.

It was getting late, she had said, about 9pm when she had started making phone calls. Just a few friends, and of course the Bakers and the Glovers who were supposed to have gone to the Cathedral for an ecumenical meeting with him. Mike Baker confirmed that he had been with them but they had gone off shopping and didn't see him after the meeting. Lorna was rather worried by this time, and all her other calls, including the local hospital and the AA, had been fruitless. The Glovers were out so it was past midnight when she had decided to call the police.

'Not 999, that would seem to be too dramatic' Matlock said, 'So she called me as I was a friend of her husband, and I advised her to wait until the morning and phone again if he didn't turn up. She had indeed phoned again at about 8am as there was no sign of him. I then assured her that I would come round at once and bring WPC Jo Grant with me. He may turn up at any time of course but I suppose that we'd better go through the motions. I don't want this turning into a major crime or international incident if I can help it, so I don't want anyone talking to the Press or anyone else for that matter. Let's go Constable.'

Lorna saw the silver Audi pull into the drive and recognized it as Matlock's car because he sometimes picked Paul up for golf or bowls or a day out at Bath Rugby. There was a second person, a woman, with him. Neither was in uniform. She opened the door before they had a chance to knock or ring the bell. 'Come in and forgive the mess' she said as she led them into an impeccable lounge that overlooked an impeccable garden at the back of the house. The curtains were a plain blue and the wallpaper a very traditional stripe with photos neatly spaced along the walls. Kiwi noticed that they seemed to be set out in chronological order with school/university on one wall, followed by wedding/children and then quite a few of the pair on Safari in Africa.

'Please sit down.' Lorna said, 'is there any news?'

'I'm afraid not' Matlock replied 'By the way this is Constable Grant from the station.'

Lorna turned with a smile. 'Oh hello, pleased to meet you, can I get you some tea or coffee?'

Kiwi looked at the Inspector, but he frowned, so she answered 'No thanks Mrs Ward, we are just here to ask you a few questions, the quicker the better and we can get on with finding him.'

'That's right' said Matlock, 'let's get started then. Just tell me about yesterday.'

Lorna hesitated 'what do you mean; everything?'

'Yes I mean everything' he replied, 'every little thing. Start at the beginning and take your time.'

'Well' she said 'I'll have to think. Let's see now. I got up to clean my teeth, it was probably about seven then I went down to make a cup of tea. He was getting ready to go to the Cathedral for a meeting of 'Bristol Churches Together.' He went into the shower, took rather longer than usual as I remember and then joined me in the kitchen but the toast had gone cold and he complained so I just said, 'You must be meeting someone special today, you've been ten minutes in the shower, but he just laughed;' she paused, then continued, 'but isn't all this rather trivial when, after all we should be looking for him shouldn't we?'

Matlock sniffed 'Not at all. We don't want to miss anything do we eh constable?'

'No sir,' Kiwi replied dutifully, 'but may I ask a question sir?'

The Inspector frowned as he had done earlier, and was wont to do when he disapproved of something, even though he didn't always know why. Actually he tended to like centre stage.

'Certainly Constable, carry on, don't mind me.' He laughed, but it was more of a snigger.'

She knew his brusque Yorkshire style by now but she continued 'Well, Mrs Ward, did he have any other plans for the day as far as you know?'

'No, he was only going to that church thing' Lorna replied, 'nothing else that I was aware of, but he didn't always tell me everything unless it was really important you know.' She had suddenly become even more anxious and looked at Matlock for some kind of relief from this line of questioning.

He duly obliged and said, 'Tell me, did anyone else go with him to the meeting?'

Lorna was relieved at this easy question and answered straightaway, 'I know that Mike and Diana Baker were going, they're Methodists you know, and then David and Liz Glover, strong Catholics they are, were going as well. Paul and I are C-of E but I suppose that's what this ecumenical business is all about isn't it? Although I must say you wouldn't think so if you listened to Liz Glover. She always thinks that the Catholics have a direct line to God, so they must always be right. It's surprising that we all seem to get on so well, but this time I couldn't go anyway so I told Paul not to get into an argument. Mind you he rarely did, he liked to get on with everyone. Would you like their numbers?'

'Yes thank you,' he replied, 'and do you have a recent photo please and do you mind if we have a quick rummage through his study and your room if you don't mind. This is just to help us find him you understand.'

Lorna agreed but accompanied him to the master bedroom, hovering about and looking very nervous and helpless.

Meanwhile Kiwi moved into the study. There were files everywhere in a very small room and most pretty obvious by their titles such as Golf or Holiday but one took her eye and it was marked DAR. It was locked, so she made a note to ask Lorna for a key later if Paul didn't turn up quite soon. There was also a steel cabinet with five drawers each marked H1-H5 and she decided to ask Lorna about this as well. The cabinet was also locked. The room was orderly and she thought it probably reflected Ward's character. Lorna on the other hand was emotional, not only as befits an anxious wife but sincere deep down. Kiwi had noticed how she was trying to suppress the tears that were welling up in her eyes, like little lakes. These were not crocodile tears; there was a real and sincere grief in the streaks that trickled down her face.

Eventually Matlock led them all downstairs and after thanking Lorna they drove back to the station and bid goodnight.

Kiwi now only had a short stroll back to her flat where she had arranged to meet Duke, picking up a Chinese meal on the way home.

He pounced as soon as she opened the door.

'Mine all mine,' he shouted taking the packages of crispy duck, chicken fried rice from her. 'I love you too,' he added with a big grin.

He was incorrigible but Kiwi was a little preoccupied with the events of the day so she simply bowed and made a suggestion 'Duke San,' she said adopting the Japanese greeting, 'If master put food in oven, geisha will shower and reappear in kimono for Saki.'

He smiled. He was hungry, but not that hungry and a few glasses of rice wine often brought pleasant surprises. He'd had quite a few in his short life and here's just a few of them.

Firstly he should have been called Nick Morton. His family came from the 'white' side of New Orleans and admired the pioneering work of the ODJB (The Original Dixieland Jazz Band) led by Nick La Rocca. His mother was Irish and insisted on a Catholic upbringing for her son and unlike many in Louisiana they were not prejudiced in any way and this went for music too, so when they heard the maestro Edward 'Duke' Ellington, an embryonic Nick became an honorary Duke. Tall, dark, slim and good looking in a 'Tom Cruise' way he sailed through college with honours and became a foreign correspondent on the Boston Herald, a job that took him to trouble spots in the Far East, Middle East, Africa and Russia. However he was not just a follower of the Flag, frequently asking the question, 'Why don't we sort out our own backyard first?' He especially had in mind the racist and religious fundamentalism of the KKK and others in the Deep South. This got him into some trouble with his bosses at the paper but almost as a perverse consequence he was approached by the CIA. They told him that they had enough 'fanatics on board' and they needed persons with empathy as well as skill. 'We want you to get inside the enemy's skins wherever they are.' he was told. As cover and after training, he would be sent to the UK as Arts Correspondent for the Observer in Bristol.

Work was important of course but after that first mad passionate night with Kiwi, things began to change, or did they? He could never quite be sure with her. They led their normal separate lives as far as their work was concerned, but in private they enjoyed every moment of a delicious intimacy that neither had known before. A day would not go by without love on the menu if only in the form of a little note or email at lunch in the office. Back in her flat, or his, love could be quiet and reflective and frequently it was passionate.

Kiwi sometimes thought that they were in 'lust' not in 'love' because she wasn't sure what 'love' meant, whereas she definitely knew about lust because she felt it from her neck to her knees. For most of the time though she just followed her instincts and appreciated him for whom he was without asking too many questions.

Duke on the other hand thought that he was the luckiest man alive, and asked no questions at all for fear that she would change her mind at any moment. Sometimes though he was confused by her apparent ability to know what he was thinking, and this could be very disconcerting.

Was she just amusing herself at his expense? Actually for all his macho-bravado at times he was very traditional when it came to sex. There had to be, let's say, something special; if not love then a very deep affection perhaps. He was not into one night stands either.

⁂

Matlock had arranged to see the Bakers the next day at 11 am. He took Kiwi and another young constable Harry Lee with him to make notes. Harry called himself the 'accidental oriental' following the decision of the Avon and Somerset police to embrace equal opportunities, a move not welcomed by his Inspector in any respect.

When they arrived Mrs Baker showed them into a very grand sitting room. The walls were covered in paintings of life in Tanzania, Kenya and Zambia including a series of prints of wildlife by David Shepherd, including Zebras and Lions with a backdrop of Mt Kilimanjaro. There was a corner dedicated to the East African Safari and on the walls there were Zulu Shields and Assegais complemented by carvings of elephants and Kiwi began to realise why this was a case for her role as an ILO.

There were signs of Africa all over the place but was this linked to Ward, she wondered? Yet strangely on one wall there were a also number of Picasso prints, rather out of character with the rest.

Matlock did not seem to notice this but she did. She had already observed that Mrs Baker was a good deal younger than her husband. Was this wall a statement of her independence in a house where everything seemed to reflect his interests? She would have loved to see their bedroom, or might it be bedrooms, she wondered.

'He won't be a moment' began Mrs Baker, 'He's out with the dogs, I'll go and make some coffee.'

'Thank you, and thank you for seeing us at such short notice' replied Matlock as he looked around the room. 'Not short of a bob or two' he whispered, 'Last of the British Raj I should think, and I wonder if that Shepherd print is one of the original; limited editions and all that?'

He liked to show his cultural knowledge, (no simple Sheffield cop he), but she knew him all too well. She had him down as a bully with a chip on his shoulder and one who must be humoured lest sparks fly.

Just then Mike Baker entered the room or, one might say, marched into the room, with a big Ridgeback at his heels.

'Sit, sit!' he commanded.

Kiwi looked at Lockhart with a smile, as if the command applied to them as well, but he was not amused.

'Good morning Mr Baker' he began, 'As you know we've come to see if you can help us about the whereabouts of Paul Ward who hasn't been seen since Thursday, and you and Mrs Baker were with him on that day. We are wondering if there is anything you can tell us about the day itself. Any small detail might help.'

Baker sat down with the big dog sat at his feet. 'Hound of the Baskervilles' thought Kiwi, but looked at her boss dutifully as Mrs Baker returned with a tray of coffee which she poured into four cups. Meanwhile the Inspector had noticed that Baker had edged himself to sit next to his WPC, knees touching and arm outstretched.

Diana Baker seemed oblivious to this but Matlock decided to make good use of what he saw as a 'soft sex' target. Wouldn't Baker be more likely to open up to an attractive blonde? Sam Matlock was a patient man, he was prepared to wait for as long as it took and to use any ploy to get results and he knew that the best information was obtained if small talk could be allowed to melt the ice.

'Well, it's such a lovely day,' he began 'I wonder if Mrs Baker would mind showing me round the garden. I love your roses.'

Diana agreed enthusiastically and they went out through the French windows leaving Kiwi with the ever hopeful Baker. Unfortunately for him they were not quite alone. Harry was still there but diplomatically looking the other way. In the sitting room she began to put him at ease.

'Now this is Constable Lee,' she said,' I hope you don't mind, he'll just be making notes for the record if that's all right. Now tell me sir, how well did you know the Howards?'

Baker thought for a while and then replied, 'Very well indeed. We worked together on Government projects and the like in Africa but we couldn't get on really, not with his attitude you know. He didn't even support the Springboks when they came over here.'

Kiwi let that comment pass for now and made some notes. (Racism=Cerberus?)

Actually she was not making copious notes but drawing a picture of a rather silly dog. This strategy had served her well over the years.

It gave her time to think and, to a degree, it unnerved her 'target'. After a few minutes she got up, studied her notebook and walked behind him so that he would have to turn his head to reply.

'Right then that's clear enough' she muttered so quietly that he had to ask her to speak up, 'Sorry sir, clear enough, I said, but tell me about the day, what happened on Thursday?'

Baker thought for a moment and replied rather testily, 'The 'memsahib' and I we were together all the time, all day. We went to the meeting and I went shopping together, then we came home together that's all there is to it.'

Kiwi realised it was time to change the subject so she suggested that he might tell Harry more about the Safari Rally. 'Yes, thank you, I do understand; just routine questions.' she said, 'Perhaps you could tell Harry a bit more about the Safari Rally, he's very interested in cars.' She really had no idea if this was true of course but she trusted Harry not to let her down.

'Yes of course,' Baker responded somewhat mollified. 'Let's start with this photo shall we?'

The picture was of an upside down car in a ditch and Harry laughed.

'I can't quite see what's happening there. I can tell that it's not a Mercedes or a Nissan Bluebird but not much more' he said.

Baker just smiled and replied, 'Hold on and I'll tell you.'

'It was June, It was hot and dusty, there had been no rain for months and I was a chief rally marshal. The photo of that Toyota was taken at my checkpoint and it never should have happened. They were out to win at any cost and were sponsored by a large American conglomerate called Chemico with corporate stickers all over the car as you can see. The driver Alan Steadman was killed but the other driver Jan Smoot survived, saying that they had had no brakes since the last checkpoint. Steadman had refused to stop because they would have lost too much time. I then went to inspect the doomed Toyota in order to make my report. There it was on its' side, crumpled and forlorn, a beautiful machine reduced to scrap in seconds, another tragic accident it seemed but my engineer Albert Müller called me over to where he was inspecting the brakes. 'Not wear and tear sir,' he said, 'they've been cut right through with a hacksaw. Look you can still see the teeth marks.' It was quite obviously sabotage, but by whom? Well that was the first surprise, but nothing prepared me for the next as I rummaged in the wreckage and came across a waterproof package tucked under the driver's seat. I might not have done so but his seat had been thrown forward revealing a small brown box and an envelope inside the package. At first I thought it must be his personal belongings put there for safety, but when I opened the box I was dumbfounded.

It was diamonds! Hundreds of them shining and twinkling in the fading light. I opened the envelope and read a very formal letter. I recognised the logo as that of the South African Government at 179 Kruger Street, Pretoria and it was addressed to RS (whom I took to be Steadman.) and it was marked Urgent and Top Secret.

The Office of the Interior 179 Kruger Street Pretoria

Collect Girl's Best Friend from contact KEY at Kigoma Hotel on Lake Tanganyika and carry with you to end of Rally at Nairobi. Deliver to Mrs Green at 39 Delamere Close. Do not open.

Well, what was I to make of this? It seemed like smuggling, but why the official South African Government heading? In my innocence I suppose, I couldn't understand why South Africa needed to smuggle diamonds. Didn't they have plenty of their own? I told Müller to keep it quiet until I could get some advice. Eventually an ambulance arrived to take Smoot to hospital and to remove Steadman's body, and soon after a team delegation led by a very tall American came to inspect the situation.

'I'll take responsibility for moving the car.' he drawled in a Texan accent.

'I'm General Dallas, MD of Chemico. It's our car and I'm taking it away now.'

He then signalled to a tow truck to move into position but Müller stopped them.

'I'm sorry,' he said, 'that would be illegal and we must wait for the Kenyan Police. They might be here soon.'

I knew this to be unlikely but I backed Müller up as I didn't know what else to do, short of mounting an armed guard.

'I'll give you a receipt,' he motioned to his drivers to couple up to the stricken vehicle. 'Now give me your names so that we can write and thank you for your cooperation and maybe there'll be a reward.' he said with a laugh.

I wondered if he knew about the diamonds and had made the assumption that they were still on board, but I didn't feel like telling him. Anyway they were soon gone, taking any evidence of the tampered brakes with them, and all I had was a receipt. Well, not quite all. I still had the diamonds and they didn't. I'd heard of Chemico as being a major fundraiser for the Smith regime and their ideas for another 'apartheid' state and that suited me fine, but I didn't take kindly to being pushed around, so I decided to keep the diamonds for the time being.

Eventually I presented a full report to the Safari Directors and handed in the letter and the diamonds. I was given a commendation for 'responsible service' and then told not to 'make waves old boy.' I did persist for a while, telephoning to ask what had become of the diamonds and the investigation into the brakes. They said that the diamonds were unlike any found in South Africa or anywhere else as far as they knew, so they had been sent to NASA for investigation. My ears pricked up at this. Why NASA? Was there something about space rockets or meteorites or even more unlikely, were aliens involved? I wanted to know more but I was stalled at every turn. Apparently the brake evidence had gone missing as well. To cut a long story short I never did find out. Then I came back to the UK, met Diana and, as you can see, we now live happily ever after.

Kiwi wasn't so sure about that, and she thought that there was more to this than meets the eye. To be perfectly frank they did not seem to be a well suited couple at all. She had also noted Baker's and Ward's East African connection and Franks had advised her that Ward had reported some 'local' suspicions recently. But was there something more significant given Baker's remarks about Ward? Could race be an issue here after all? She knew that he had implied that when he had said,'With his attitude about the Springboks you know' And now the locked file in Ward's office seemed to make sense. DAR could only mean Dar-es-Salaam in this context but what was the full picture and did the locked cabinet have secrets to reveal as well? And where did the spectre of Cerberus fit in, if at all? On the other hand she had a good feeling about Baker. He seemed to know nothing more than that with which he had to deal at the time. She had studied him closely and decided not only that he was as frustrated as his wife, but that he was an 'ingénue,' almost incapable of deception, and that's not a very helpful attribute if one has something to hide she thought.

Meanwhile Matlock and Mrs Diana Baker had been getting on very well. Mrs Baker talked endlessly about the garden and the roses while he listened patiently

'Tell me what you remember about the day.' he said.

'There was coffee when we got there at about eleven o'clock' she replied, 'we had a talk until about one and then broke into informal groups at small tables where sandwiches and a soft drink were served. We finished at about two thirty and then Mike and I went shopping.

'Does he like shopping?' Matlock asked, seemingly in a rather absent- minded way, but it was actually his key question to determine if they had spent all of the afternoon together.

'I suppose he couldn't get out of it this time.' Diana responded and laughed rather nervously.

'And did you do a 'Ladies shop' if you know what I mean?' he continued.

'Yes I did actually, because I don't get into town so often these days. I went into Marks and then I popped into Cup Cakes for a coffee before getting home about five. He likes me to stay at home you know. When I do get a chance he usually goes off somewhere and we meet up later.'

'And is that what happened on Thursday then?' He was closing in and his quarry was responding well.

'Yes, we said we'd meet back at the house about six but he didn't turn up until after seven.' Here Diana paused, 'Is that all now? I rather think we should be going in, he won't like me to talk to you for very long.' She seemed to be getting rather anxious, so Matlock touched her hand reassuringly.

'That's fine, you've been most helpful' he said with a smile, 'Let's go in then.' Baker had gone off with the dog again so the three of them bid farewell to Diana and left.

Back at the station Matlock was looking quite pleased with himself.

'It seems they were not together all day Thursday. After some shopping they split up and he didn't get home until seven. They both had a few hours on their own. What did you two find out?'

He listened while Kiwi summarised their findings then said. 'Good. Well done. Now I want you and Charlie to put your notes in a File marked Baker, keep them brief, none of that Rally rubbish, all red herrings in my opinion. The answers lie here in Bristol not up the Limpopo. Then put the rest in a storage box.'

Kiwi and Harry assembled their reports.

'I may as well chuck my lot out.' said Harry.

'Not on your life,' she replied 'Let me have a look at your notes Harry. Evidence is evidence. We just don't know where it might lead and I've got a hunch that there may well be something we might need later. Keep it all and by the way please give me a personal copy; but don't tell the Inspector.'

She had an uneasy feeling about Matlock, cheery one minute and rude the next. She had also got the impression that he knew more about Africa than he was saying. There were the 'Shepherd' prints and now the Limpopo. Was he protecting someone and if so who and why? Franks had said that Ward had 'suspicions' so maybe he had shared these with Matlock with a view to gaining evidence on Baker or someone else. She might have found some confirmation of her suspicions if she had known a little bit about his background, but she didn't.

❖❖❖

Sam Matlock was an imposing individual; tall with a faintly olive complexion a prematurely bald head and probing eyes earning him the nickname of 'Bald Eagle.' At family gatherings other visitors often remarked on the way that his relatives all seemed to have that same appearance and even his two boys were 'chips off the old block,' if a little less so. His manner was one of caution mixed with confidence. He frequently moved his head from side to side as if something was waiting to take him by surprise, and he'd be ready for it, and his boys reacted in much the same manner.

On the one hand he was a rather tough and somewhat ruthless police officer, but on the other hand, according to his friends, he was an exemplary father of his two boys Samuel and Stephen on whom he absolutely doted, as well as being a considerate and loving husband. He seemed to lead his life in compartments and adapted his personality to each. At work he was efficiency itself and he was strongly tipped for promotion, but he was not the same man at home. He celebrated every birthday and special day with his family and nothing was too good for them. Matlock's 'domestic' character was tuned in to his family life and it would seem that nothing could disturb it, but if we are to gain more of an insight into the Inspector, we might reflect on an occasion when his guard slipped and his 'work' character intruded on a day out at an Animal Park.

They had set off through the Wolves enclosure and past the Lions when suddenly the traffic stopped. A few moments went by, then a few more and then more. Matlock had looked at his watch.

'Come on, get a move on.' He had said but they did not move. 'What the heck's going on?' he continued, now sounding rather concerned. 'We're going to be late for the concert if we're not careful.'

Mrs Matlock and the children started to play a game of 'I Spy' but after a few more minutes he said, 'I'm going up there to see what's going on.'

'No dear, you can't. Look, it says "You must not leave your car under any circumstances" so we'll just have to wait, won't we?' she replied.

'Not on your life' he had muttered and, taking his walking stick, he got out of the car and strode down the road until he was out of sight. She was rather worried, and more so when he didn't come back for a while, but soon the boys spotted him.

'Daddy, Daddy… here he is! Daddy, Daddy! Look Daddy they're moving.'

They immediately set off again and, after a while, when the boys were pre-occupied, she said, 'What was that all about back there?'

'Oh, nothing much,' he replied, 'some Baboons thought they ruled the roost around here, and no one would take them on.'

'So what did you do dear?' she asked.

'Well, I looked them in the eye and told them who was boss.' he said with a rather grim smile.

'Thank goodness you did.' she replied She patted his arm but, as she did so, she noticed that the sleeve was speckled with blood.

She drew back, momentarily fearful to ask questions so she just whispered. 'Don't forget to change shirts when we get there. That one's got rather grubby.'

Later she wondered if all men have that capacity to turn from peace to aggression in moments, where anyone, absolutely anyone, can wound or kill given enough motivation,. and could it ever be right?' She looked across at her husband in his clean blue shirt and held his hand. She loved Sam and trusted him implicitly. She knew that he had been 'protecting' his family, and she supposed that was a good enough reason for any good husband and father.

❊❊❊

Kiwi's doubts about Matlock would have to wait for the time being. He wanted to start more enquiries about Ward in the City centre.

Maybe these would uncover something but Mrs Baker hoped not. There was something that she had not told them on their visit, and she never would if she could help it. She had a deep secret and no one must ever know. Her life and her love depended on it.

A fly on the wall might have observed the following...

On the day that Paul Ward went missing Diana Baker had also been at the Cup Cakes tea room. She was feeling anxious and very nervous as she sat at a very small table deep inside the restaurant. She wished she could go deeper inside, but then David might not see her. She looked aimlessly at the Guardian crossword on the table but could not concentrate. Glover always did this to her. Why did she let him? Why? Why? He had told her to be there at three thirty, which allowed an hour after the meeting finished. Well, it was now four thirty, and she was starting to wonder when suddenly there was a tap on her shoulder.

'Hello darling' a voice said.

Her knees went weak. It sounded just like her husband's voice for a moment, but no, it was David. A shock ran through her whole body and she flushed a deep pink around her neck. He reached over, slightly under the table and touched her hand.

'Do you think it's going to be all right then?' she asked.

'It certainly is,' he replied, 'all booked' He was smiling and she felt safe, longing to be in his arms where she had felt so much alive, as if every time was a first time. It was only two weeks ago and she could not bear to wait another moment. She was glowing; Mike would never, could never understand and she knew that her life with him was over.

Unfortunately it wasn't only Mike that she had to worry about. She knew that David was devoted to his wife and family and that he was always fearful that their affair would be discovered. She hadn't told him how she knew it, but she had a very strong feeling that her friends were already aware. Women's intuition maybe, but why had Lorna Ward and Liz Glover stopped chatting when she had entered the hairdressers? Was she going paranoid?

❊❊❊

As mentioned, Matlock had already set up a 'low profile' house to house search of the most immediate areas. He wanted it kept that way so as not to alarm Mrs Ward but now he wanted a more serious scrutiny. He therefore decided to ask questions about the missing man in the Bristol City Centre and had divided the immediate vicinity of the Cup Cakes tea room between his officers with Kiwi to start there. As she approached she experienced that delightful aroma of coffee beans roasting, a temptation closely akin to the smell of Fish and Chips, but much more agreeable she thought. She could see that it was very busy; but nothing could have prepared her for what she found inside the tiny restaurant. The place was full of French and German pensioners, Japanese tourists, Chinese students and others at every table, on all three floors.

She cornered a young waitress holding a tray.

'May I see the manager please?' she asked politely.

'The manager busy. Not possible. Come later' was the predictable reply but when Kiwi showed her warrant card she ran away and Mr Lorenzo soon appeared.

'Oh hello Constable, we're very busy today as you can see. Let's go through to the office. Will you have a coffee?'

They had got to know each other quite well despite that unpleasant business over some illegal workers.

'Thanks Jorge, black please' she said.

'Well how can I help?' he asked.

Kiwi came straight to the point 'We're asking questions to see if we can locate a man who went missing yesterday. This is his photo. We know that he went to the Cathedral in the morning for a meeting but he didn't come home that night'

There was a pause and then Lorenzo said 'Yes of course, of course. I know him. That's Mr Ward, we know him quite well. He often comes in with his wife, but yesterday? I don't know. I'll ask Tatiana, she was on duty.'

He stepped out into the corridor and called out in a loud voice. 'Tatiana! Tatiana! Come up here please.'

There was a moment's silence, broken immediately by the crash of falling crockery, after which Chinese and other voices seemed to rise to a crescendo, and then Tatiana appeared looking flushed. Lorenzo asked her if she remembered Mr Ward being there yesterday.

She seemed scared but said 'I think so. Just as we closing. About six, go to meeting, he say. Can I go now? Much work to do.'

Kiwi was pleased at this outcome, it was a lead of sorts and she was grateful.

'That's very helpful' she said but as she left she was wondering who Ward may have been meeting and why, and would he have wanted his wife to know, because she hadn't mentioned it.

After their interviews with the Bakers, Kiwi thought she might be on to something. Diana was a very attractive young woman and Mike was, well, maybe he was past it, she thought, 'I wonder if they do it?' she thought to herself, 'maybe she has a lover, maybe, but a lover's got to be special, I mean tingly and all that; like Duke and me. Yes like that, when you just can't stop. Or can you? I mean if it's not right? What if someone else is involved? Should you stop, or more to the point, should you start if you're not free?' She wasn't thinking about the morals of the situation, but of the practical implications in Police work where betrayal could so often lead to murder.

She paused in her reverie and considered how lucky she was, and even luckier when she got home and Duke suggested a visit to Weston-Super-Mare for the evening.

He made it sound like a real adventure with extravagant promises of sunny skies and maybe sightings of dolphins, but of course it rained, and it was donkeys not dolphins that amused them that day. They had paddled for a while and then as the sun went down over the pier he drew her close and kissed her on the cheek.

She said nothing as he stepped back, but, placing her fingertips on her lips, she said, 'Here please'.

Once more he drew her to him gently, but this time with an urgency that made her gasp. They kissed with a passion that startled yet thrilled her, oblivious to the fun fare in which they were standing.

'Look at them Mum!' said a little boy, tugging his mother's sleeve,'

Yes dear,' she said, 'I think they need to cool off with some ice cream don't you? Come on let's go and get some!'

But Duke and Kiwi were still locked in an embrace, and ice cream was the last thing on their minds....

Back home she stretched out on her bed thinking. Was she right about Diana? Had she sensed the 'Heart of the Matter,' just in her very brief visit to the Baker house? Diana was undoubtedly a young attractive woman, with (to put it kindly) a bit of an old duffer for a husband but so what? Did she have a lover and what's more to the point, how might they fit into the case? The Bakers and the Glovers were the last to see Paul Ward so let's start there she thought. So what kind of man was David Glover, and what kind of woman was Diana Baker? She knew that they were involved with 'Bristol Churches Together' but was this moral crusade just a cover up when Cupid came calling. Finally she gave up, lay back on her bed exhausted, only to hear the phone ring.

It was Matlock. 'They've found him' he said grumpily; 'and where have you been all evening? You'd better come to the station right away and we'll both go up and break the news to Lorna. Perhaps we should take WPC Drew with us and leave her behind as some sort of support if she needs it. She's had a baby and probably knows more about these emotional things than you do.'

Once more Kiwi ignored this slight, noting that it hadn't occurred to him to mention the more appropriate word 'comfort' either. Yes he was a hard nut all right.

They immediately went to the Ward house and broke the news and, just as he had described this was a most traumatic mission. Lorna fainted and Kiwi was actually quite glad that WPC Drew was there as well.

Later she joined her colleagues in the outer office while the Inspector was on the phone in his. He then strode out looking grim with more details.

'They found him at the sports centre, with a knife through the heart.' he said. Apparently the Bristol Beavers gymnastics team had gone to use a vaulting horse in the gym but couldn't move it, and when they took the lid off they saw that there was a body lying crumpled up inside. Naturally there was a lot of fuss and the Paramedics and the Police had been called. A driving licence on the body was in the name of Paul Ward.

'We'd better get down there Constable' said Matlock, 'we don't want anybody messing with the evidence do we?'

'No sir, I mean yes sir' said Kiwi. She had never got used to dead bodies.

When they arrived at the scene the Coroner was still there.

'What do you make of it Tom?' asked Matlock in that most familiar friendly tone that he used when he wanted something.

'Strange case this one' came the reply but Professor Tom Greene was not drawn into the Inspector's familiarities; just making this matter of fact statement. 'The murder weapon was a knife straight through the heart from the front and he knew his killer, knew his killer yes, but, and this is very strange, the victim's face has also been cut, in a number of slices on both sides. Oh yes, and what's more, he was dead when the cuts were made, and they probably weren't made until a little later. No blood you see, no blood, no heart beat no blood do you see?'

'I think we do Professor' said Matlock, 'thank you very much, that's very helpful. Come on, let's go Constable, we've got a lot of work to do haven't we?'

'Yes sir' said Kiwi 'but where shall we start, it all seems so strange, macabre even don't you think sir?'

The Inspector was back on professional ground again quickly 'Evidence, evidence that's what we need. We'll just have to question everyone again' he said tersely. 'Let's get on with it. We haven't got time to waste you know.'

The next day a suitably refreshed and red haired Kiwi joined him at a meeting in Superintendent Powell's office to discuss the dramatic turn of events. The Super had decided to set up two teams, one under

Matlock to follow up the immediate connections and another one under Inspector Jean Curtis to look into his work colleagues, wider family and friends.

'Let the dog see the rabbit, I always say. No point when you can't see the wood for the trees is there? A stitch in time saves nine I always say. Good, good. Just let me know if there are crossovers but I'm sure you'll manage. I know that you'll get on fine.' And with that he dismissed his two top officers with a wave of his hand.

They both mumbled, 'Thank you sir' and left.

Matlock turned left in the corridor and Curtis turned right.

She smiled at him and said, 'Good luck Sam.'

'Police work isn't good luck,' he replied tersely.

He had little respect for Curtis, but this sentiment was based on his prejudice against any of those he considered to be in their jobs due to 'all that nonsense about equal opportunities' be they women, gays or racial minorities.

He had observed the rise of 'Feminism in the Force' with alarm just as he had misgivings about 'positive discrimination' of any sort. He was a middle aged, somewhat conservative police officer, and was much more comfortable with a world where women made the tea.

Now it seemed that it might not be long before he reported to a woman, or even a black superintendent who couldn't cut the mustard, and maybe both! Time to retire then, he thought. Up to now he quite liked working with WPC Jo Grant because she seemed to be the traditional sort. He summed her up thus, 'Comprehensive school, Police College, respectful, co-operative and efficient within her own limitations.' Small and attractive, she didn't seem like a police officer at all, and that suited him fine. But what was she doing with red hair today? He felt somewhat unnerved by this and didn't know why.

Curtis was a different case entirely, 'Jumped up Les. I wouldn't be surprised' he thought. Tall dark and slim, University First Class Degree, fast tracked to promotion and 'not up to it' was his opinion. He was wrong about both.

Later Jean Curtis was called into Powell's office again.

'Come in Jean, do sit down.' he said.

'Uh-Oh something's up' she thought but just said, 'Thank you Sir.' and sat down.

'Funny business, police work,' he said, 'just like the buses, nothing for ages and the two along at once.' He smiled and waited for her response.

'Do I take it Sir that we have another missing persons case?' she asked.

'Bang on Jean.' he replied, 'a tourist has gone missing from a Coach Trip. They had a day out doing the sights and then he went out for a walk before dinner. He didn't return to the hotel that evening and he's still unaccounted for. I want you to pick it up and see if there are any connections and get WPC Grant onto it, she seems to have time on her hands. Oh and tell PC Lee to keep an eye on her. Matlock says she's not entirely to be trusted.'

'Yes sir, I'll see to it right away.'

As it was late she left a note for Kiwi and Harry Lee to check out the file and report to her as soon as possible, asking them to make arrangements to meet up in a room at the station to read the 'Missing Persons' report as soon as possible. The file was on the desk with other papers so Kiwi picked it up and began to read.

> Walter Müller. Man aged 85. He is a tourist on a visit with his wife to Stratford on Avon and The Cotswolds and Bath and Bristol accompanied by her nurse.
>
> Herr Müller was enjoying his trip. He had said that Frau Müller should wear a toga at the Roman Baths and how nice she'd look in a smart uniform. He'd said it seemed like old times, when they were young together. She wanted a short rest so he went for a walk about 6.30 and didn't return. His passport confirmed German nationality and marital status. Included were several visas from African countries in the 1960's but no further entries after 1980.
>
> End.

The point about Africa interested Kiwi greatly. Could there be a link to Ward's disappearance and could the two cases be connected in some way? It certainly seemed likely, so when they had finished reading the report she made an appointment for them to see Frau Müller the next day. On her own initiative she also made up her mind to take Duke along not only as he spoke fluent German, but also because she felt that there might be a link to Cerberus here. Matlock had shown some impatience with the idea of an African scenario and so far she had managed to keep that aspect out of the missing person's cases. She therefore decided that this would be on a 'need to know' basis and Curtis and Matlock did not need to know at this point in time.

As it happens she was not the only one to seek allies at the hotel where a small frail looking lady was waiting; but she was not alone.

'They told me I could have a friend with me' she said, 'I don't always remember things clearly. Will that be all right? This is my companion Frau Brand.'

The other woman was probably in her late fifties, dressed in a simple black dress with pearls around the neck. Her dark hair was tied back in a bun, which made her look rather like a schoolmistress or a warden in a prison.

Kiwi spoke first. 'I'm afraid our German is not very good so may we all speak in English?'

'Of course,' replied Frau Brand. 'Just go ahead and we'll try to help, but don't tire her please'

Harry began with the police report that they already had and, to be truthful, the ladies could not add much to the existing file. Frau Müller did say that her husband did not like to be away from home for long but she had persuaded him to come on a 'Holiday of a Lifetime.'

Kiwi was curious. 'So where did you normally go on holiday then. Was this to be an unusual kind of adventure?' she asked.

'Well we had a wonderful time in Austria last year, unfortunately Albert said he had no wish to visit England but I changed his mind.'

'Had he said anything on the journey and had he ever told you why he didn't want to go to the UK?' Kiwi persisted, 'Didn't he feel safe here?'

Frau Müller looked at her friend and was about to speak but Frau Brand spoke first. 'I think that's enough for today.' she said.' I can see that she's getting very tired. Come back tomorrow please but perhaps Albert will have returned by then.'

With that she took Frau Müller by the arm and physically lifted her from her chair. 'Come' she said, and guided her out of the room.

'Strange' Kiwi thought' Frau Brand seems more like a watchdog than a companion'.

The next day she decided to make a surprise visit to the hotel and they were in luck because Frau Müller was alone in the conservatory with no watchdog in sight. She seemed strangely free and began a long story for their benefit.

'I want you to understand,' she said.' You are so young, just as we were. You are so proud of your pretty uniforms, just like we used to be. I had a white blouse, full blue skirt, socks and heavy marching shoes in the 'BDM' and Albert was so smart in his neat uniform of the Hitler Youth. I don't think you could ever understand what it was like. How wonderful it all was before the war. Where did it all go wrong? I ask myself that question every day'

Kiwi felt that this kind of background might well lead to some clues about her husband, especially as Frau Müller obviously thought that it might.

She reached over and held the old lady's hand. 'Just tell us,' she said, 'tell us what it was like, and why it was so wonderful. Tell us in German,' she said', I know that will be easier for you and my colleague will write down what you say.'

She looked across at Duke almost expecting a frown but he nodded and just said,' Yes go ahead please.'

Frau Müller now actually looked rather relieved and said, 'Yes I will, I must. I'm tired of all this secrecy after so long with Albert always looking over his shoulder. Please listen to me as I tell our story.'

Kiwi had given Duke the opportunity to back out of this task because she knew his sentiments well. His father had been one of the first US troops into Auschwitz and had taken many explicit photographs at the time. Naturally Duke was very young at the time but, as he had told Kiwi with tears in his eyes, those pictures had haunted him ever since. On the other hand he confessed that they had also been a major factor in formulating his view of the world when it came to politico/moral issues.

'I hope that I would have resisted being part of the Nazi terror if I was there,' he said, 'but how can one be sure how one would behave until that day comes?'

These events had scarred him, but they had moulded him as well, creating a moral stance very much in keeping with his mother's firm guidance in the Catholic faith.

Now Frau Müller began her story:

I know that it was before you were born back then from 1936 to 1944, but try to imagine it as it was at the time in Munich at Christmas. It was snowing, sleigh bells were ringing and everyone came and sat around the kitchen table. Those were fine family days but after the war started it all changed. Albert came home from the war for Christmas in 1944 but to my horror, said that we must leave at once.

That night as we lay in bed he said, 'My darling, if you are to come with me you must be told everything' I lay there beside him listening to his heartbeat, I loved him so.

'Tell me then,' I said.

'Right.' he replied.' I have papers in my bag for an Albert Müller and a Frau Magda Müller. That's us we are now the Müllers. The 'Organisation' has provided us with a new identity and tickets for a flight to Buenos Aires the day after tomorrow.' He paused and then continued, 'I've tried not to bother you with my army duties.' he said, 'but now you have to know. Well, after Dunkirk I served on the Eastern Front with the SS. We had some dirty work to do there I can tell you, but nothing prepared me for my next assignment. I was wounded, as you know, so they sent me to Poland, to a place called Auschwitz, a prison and work camp. Most prisoners died there.' He paused.

He could see that I was shocked, 'Then did they die by accident or disease?' I asked.

'No,' he had said grimly, 'Prisoners were worked to death and then killed, or just selected to be gassed when they arrived. I was a guard. I'm so sorry, I'm so sorry. I thought it was my duty and I only acted under orders do you see?' He grasped my hand so tightly that I thought it would break.'

Yes dear I understand,' I whispered, 'I understand and I do love you so.'

Kiwi looked at the frail old lady and smiled.

'It must have been really hard for you to accept this mustn't it? After all you weren't under orders were you? How did you feel about it?'

Frau Müller responded in a rather puzzled way as if she had asked a rather stupid question

'No it was easy' she said. 'I loved him you see. I loved him.'

Kiwi paused and wondered. 'So this was love was it? No doubts and unconditional. A marriage of minds as well as the rest, in other words an impossible dream; but here it was.' She shivered as she tried to place herself there at that time and place and she wondered how she would have responded. For her, love was a choice and up to now she had not thought that it would close down all options in this way. The thought made her feel uneasy, and she now began to doubt her capacity to love, ever. But then there was Duke, what about him?

It was all too difficult, but now she had to listen to the rest of Frau Müller's story that the old lady continued as if in a hurry, saying that Frau Brand wouldn't like to see her talking to them.

'She's one of 'The Organisation' you know,' she said, 'They have 'looked after' us for years, in South America and then when Albert went to work in Zambia. I hope that this has been of some help. Please find my Albert. He gets confused sometimes.'

Kiwi agreed that there was not much more to be gained at present so she and Harry took their leave quietly by the back entrance to avoid Frau Lang the 'watchdog.'

Harry had said that 'all that old stuff wasn't much help' but she disagreed. Frau Müller had mentioned Zambia; once more East Africa was centre stage and she felt sure that there must be a connection with Ward. The trouble was that the whole thing was like a jigsaw for which she had some pieces (that didn't fit together anyway) and nothing like the whole picture at all, The whole scenario was very frustrating and in some other circumstances she might have found it completely overwhelming, but to be honest she was still thinking about love.

❖❖❖

Now that it had become a murder investigation Matlock decided to pay the Cup Cakes tea room a visit himself. He never entirely trusted anyone else to do a decent job unless they fitted his stereo type of the Anglo Saxon male. He was keen to get on with it before Jean Curtis got more leads than he had, and he was very pleased that she'd been side-tracked on that other case. Before they went up he noticed a man sitting in the corner and decided to ask a question on the off chance that he might know something.

'Sorry to trouble you Sir,' he asked, 'we are making enquiries about the Paul Ward case and wondered if you were here and remembered seeing him on the day he went missing.'

He was rather taken aback by his immediate answer.

'Yes I did, and I was thinking of coming in to report it but I got tied up in office and it slipped my mind' he said with an apologetic smile.

'Well sir' said Kiwi 'What exactly do you remember?'

'Well, just that he was here but, as he was leaving he seemed to bump into someone who was coming in or just passing by, I couldn't tell which.'

'I don't suppose you saw who it was?' she asked hopefully'

'I did as a matter of fact. It was Lambert you know, the one with the loud voice. He shouted something and then they went off.'

'One last thing sir' interjected Matlock, 'did they go in the direction of the Leisure centre and did they go together?'

'I'm afraid you've got me there, can't say I really noticed.' he replied and that being the case there was nothing more to do than to take his details in case further enquiries needed to be made so they left him at his table and went into the office.

'We'll have to follow up on that' said Matlock, 'now let's look at some of these files.'

They sat at the desk and began to search for other clues that might be worth pursuing, especially, he thought, credit card receipts and the like. There might even be a paper trail, showing who was there on that Thursday so he and Kiwi started to go through a mound of disorganized paper and receipts in every drawer and, it seemed, on every floor space. There were receipts going way back, some more than a year, but after about an hour she found it.

'Eureka! You'll never guess what I've found' she called out in triumph, but Matlock was irritated by the way she expressed herself.

'I've told you before Constable, we're not in the guessing business. Evidence, evidence, that's how we work. Anyway, what have you got?

She savoured the moment before she spoke,

'Well, I think this counts as evidence Sir, I'm sure of it' she said coolly, as she passed over a receipt before she continued, 'That's a Barclaycard receipt for a Mr D Glover for £13, and a Cup Cakes receipt for a table for two, one coffee, one Bun and a mineral water, and this is the invoice also for £13 and timed at 16.30.'

It was Matlock's turn to be stunned, 'Well, what do you know? Crafty devil, well, well, well indeed. Looks like our Mr Glover has some explaining to do.'

Kiwi was quick to reply, deliberately giving him some of the credit because she had noticed that he would take it anyway, 'Yes sir, you're right sir but do you think we might run a check on his card before we speak to him? See what else he's been up to maybe?'

He now looked at her with some irritation, 'I suppose so.' he said reluctantly, 'Get on with it then.'

Although it was late she decided to check the data base when she got back to the office and, typing in the necessary passwords and codes, she soon had access to the Glover Barclaycard account. There were numerous dining bills, some shopping receipt, a subscription to a bowls club and a weekend at the Hotel Miramar in Bournemouth for a Mr and Mrs Glover dated 20th March. She turned each receipt over carefully asking each one the same question. This one was for the subscription. 'Now what are you hiding you bad little receipt. What are you keeping so secret?' she looked again and again, turning it over and over, and then it popped out at her. The subscription receipt 'gave in' and she could now see clearly that it was dated Thursday 1 April and was from the Bristol Bowls Club at the Leisure Centre where the body had been found on that day. The same day Mrs Glover had gone to Bournemouth?

She was so pleased with her work that she decided to wash her hair when she got home. Maybe she'd be a brunette tomorrow.

The next day Matlock picked her up on the way to the Glovers. She wondered if he would say anything about her hair but he didn't. Actually he had noticed and preferred the black to the more 'stunning' red, but he'd learnt to be circumspect around women.

'They always take things the wrong way.' he often bemoaned.

She had told him about her latest discoveries and he couldn't wait to see what Glover had to say. They arrived at about 11:00 and Liz Glover offered them coffee around the kitchen table.

'Sorry to trouble you' Matlock said, 'We are just following up a few leads about Ward. Just formalities you know, come to think of it we needn't bother you both, perhaps you could show Abbie your lovely conservatory that she was admiring as we drove in.'

It was his usual ploy but vice versa this time and Kiwi was ready, 'Oh yes Liz, will you please?'

Mrs Glover responded at once 'Of course, yes, of course, it's just through here. Bring your coffee won't you?'

They walked out of the room and Matlock waited for a moment before coming straight to the point.

'I might as well tell you now David, that we have reason to believe that you haven't told us the entire truth, and I strongly advise you to do so before we go further.'

He spoke in his most officious tone. Glover made as if to speak but the Inspector put his hand up, as if in a traffic policeman's stop sign, and continued.

'We have found out that you were at Cup Cakes last Thursday and that you weren't alone, we know that you went to the Leisure Centre to pay a sub. And we also know that you spent the weekend of 20th March in Bournemouth at The Hotel Miramar. Now, is there anything that you would like to tell me about all this before I call Mrs Glover in?'

David Glover had gone a deathly shade of pale white with some red blotches on his face, he was shaking and his top lip quivered.

'No, no please don't do that. She doesn't need to know does she?'

'Maybe not, if you've nothing to hide,' said Matlock coldly, 'but you must answer some more questions first. OK? Then I'll decide whether Liz needs to know or not. After that the matter will be between the two of you of course. Now answer me this question and we might get somewhere but you'd better tell me the truth. Who was with you at Cup Cakes?'

Glover was silent for a moment but Matlock did not let up.

'Shall I ask Liz if it was her then?' he asked rather menacingly, getting up as if to go to the door.

'No, no that won't be necessary. I'll tell you but it mustn't come out, it mustn't come out please, please' Glover pleaded.

'I can't promise but I'll try' the Inspector responded 'Now who was it?'

Glover could hardly speak, and then he croaked rather than spoke the words as if he was choking, 'It was Diana, yes Diana Baker and at the Hotel if you must know' and, saying this, he slumped into a heap, his head between his arms on the kitchen table. 'I'm finished, I'm ruined, my life is over. I'm so sorry, so sorry' he mumbled and wept and wept; his shoulders shaking nervously.

Matlock went over to him and touched his elbow rather sharply.

'There will be time for all that later.' he said, 'Go and freshen up now so Liz won't know what's been said. I'll go and get the Constable and then we'll leave. It's up to you then.'

Matlock then walked into the Conservatory smiling, 'That's all settled then,' he said, 'nothing to worry about Liz, we're leaving now.'

They walked out together to the car and, before he started the engine he turned to Kiwi with a grin and patted her knee. She pulled away sharply but he just smiled mischievously and said,

'You'll never guess, you'll never guess.'

She knew that he was playing with her but she still asked, 'What?'

He spoke slowly and dramatically, 'Our Mr Goodie Glover has been having it off with, with, with' Here he paused for the most dramatic effect, 'the lovely young Mrs Baker.'

She feigned surprise. Let him have his moment she thought.

'Do you think that we should tell her that we know?' she asked.

'Not yet' he replied, 'I'm still not sure what this has got to do with Ward's murder. Probably Glover did it. I reckon Ward saw them, Mrs Baker and Glover, together at Cup Cakes but Glover also saw him, followed him and killed him. Any whiff of an affair and his marriage and his carefully cultivated reputation would be over. Perhaps he warned him, but then got wild and killed him. What do you think?'

Kiwi stayed silent. She thought that this theory had too many holes in it, not least the knife, where did that come from, and why make the scars afterwards.

He ventured another suggestion, 'How about Baker himself then? There's something about him that is so, well, so honourable, if you see what I mean. What if Ward told him about his wife's 'affair,' Baker would not want anyone else to know would he, so maybe he killed him to keep him quiet?'

Once more she kept quiet, 'Sorry Sir,' she said, 'I've really no idea.' She actually thought there might be more to learn about Ward himself, and she hoped to do that when she next saw Lorna.

That meeting had to be deferred however when she got a message from the Superintendent to see him first thing next day.

He was alone in his office when she tapped on the door. He motioned for her to come in, and then unusually got up to greet her with a firm handshake, and then most unusually adopted Christian name terms.

'Thank you for coming in Jo' (as if she had a choice) he said, 'The fact is that this is rather awkward. You see we've heard today that that missing German Herr Müller has been found, knife through the heart and scars on the face. Looks like a copycat killing to me but there's another point. MI6 have been on to me and they want to come down and speak to the ILO and that's you so I'm taking you off the Ward case. (The DCU was a closely guarded secret). And another thing, there's some Interpol involvement and they're sending the CIA as well. He must be an important fish. Matlock told me that the fuss over African connections has all been a false alarm so this new one will be best for you and I hope you don't mind. Sam said that you weren't getting anywhere and that he'd rather work with WPC Ann Drew, you know, the one who was transferred to us last week from Wells after her pregnancy leave. He said that having the baby seemed to make her more relaxed, nice girl don't you think? Anyway you'll be working under Jean Curtis on this one although of course the cases might be linked.'

'Well?' He waited as Kiwi wondered what to say.

'Very good Sir' she replied rather demurely, 'I'll get ready for them and pass my Ward papers over to Ann. I've just got one or two things to tidy up sir thank you very much sir.'

Kiwi's term 'tidy up' meant a great deal more. If she had wanted to elaborate she would have said 'follow my instincts.'

With that she stood up and left the room bowing graciously to the Superintendent; but inside she was seething. She had no intention of abandoning the Ward case entirely and all the more so because Matlock obviously wanted her out of it. She'd had her doubts about him in one way or another but now they seemed to be confirmed. Fortunately the Super had agreed that the cases might be linked so that would be useful cover. It was only next door to the office of

Inspector Jean Curtis and with a few steps Kiwi was there. Jean welcomed her with a smile.

'Come in Jo.' she said, 'here's PC Denning's report. He found the body and stayed on until it was moved. Here, take a seat and read it.'

Report: PC Denning

It was 12 midnight as I patrolled my usual beat along the waterfront. I had just crossed the river at the Bristol Bridge and was turning into Baldwin Street when I saw a man sitting on a bench in the shadows. I approached to see him more clearly and shone my torch. He didn't move and I noticed that he did not blink either. He seemed quite elderly so I got closer to see if he needed help. My first words were, 'Can I help you sir? There was no reply so I proceeded to the bench and nudged his shoulder. It was then that he slumped sideways and I noticed a dagger protruding from his chest. I immediately called for backup and forensics were soon on the scene and the coroner about an hour later with Inspector Curtis. She found papers on the body relating to a man that she knew to be missing, (Herr Müller) and the Coroner confirmed probable death by stab wounds to the chest with multi lacerations to the face I went with Inspector Curtis to give the bad news to Müller's wife at his hotel. WPC Drew went with us to stay behind, but her companion said that it would not be necessary adding that the British police are fools and had done nothing to protect him. (Signed PC Denning.)

Kiwi read the report and passed it back to Jean.

'Do you think that we have a serial killer on the loose then?' she asked.

Jean thought for a moment before making her reply, 'Too soon to say I think, but there's as many differences as there are similarities don't you think? It's only the 'modus operandi' that is the same. Everything else is different, but isn't that the very nature of a serial killer' she added, 'the very randomness of it I mean, but maybe our friends from MI6, Interpol and the CIA will give us some clues.'

She went on to say that their 'guests' would not arrive until after the weekend so she suggested that Kiwi did some research and

'Try to steer clear of Matlock' she said.

As mentioned earlier Kiwi had no intentions of deferring to Matlock and WPC Drew over the Ward case. She had got the impression that he wanted her off the case and her flaming red hair was not the only reason. Maybe she was treading on toes and maybe those toes belonged to Baker. Maybe Matlock thought that he was protecting Lorna Ward but at present she was not sure, so she decided to make an appointment to see Mrs Ward before the Inspector got an opportunity to stop her.

At the same time it occurred to her that she'd almost forgotten about 'Cerberus'. The supposition had been that Ward's murder might be linked to that in some way but she'd yet to find a connection.

She had telephoned ahead to make the appointment and she duly arrived at eleven o'clock the next day. Lorna greeted her ay the door looking rather tired and wan.

'Sorry,' she said. 'I've been up all night. Please come through to the lounge, I've just been going through some old photograph albums and things.' As she said this she steadied herself against a chair and Kiwi moved forward to help her.

'Are you all right?' she asked, 'Perhaps you need to sit down for a moment. Let me get you a glass of water,'

'Oh no thank you,' Lorna replied, 'I really am fine, just a little tired that's all. Please go through to the lounge and I'll bring us some coffee.'

Kiwi thanked her and as she went in she noticed that there was a photo album on nearly every table and chair. Some were labelled, and some were not, there was, 'Holiday in Greece' and Sarah's Wedding, and 'Our New Home' and many others. She did not like to pry but here before her eyes there seemed to be a lifetime of memories and she instinctively suspected that some answers to Paul's murder might lie in these archives. She didn't know which, but she was determined to find out. It seemed churlish to intrude on Lorna's grief but she knew that she must.

'We can leave this you know, if you like,' she said sympathetically.

'No,' replied Lorna, 'I don't know how useful it will all be but I'll tell you when I've had enough and you can always come back again can't you? Just let me tell you in my own way.'

Kiwi agreed and said, 'Well, first of all tell me about Paul's friends and work colleagues. Anything that comes to mind and anybody he didn't get on with.'

'I'll try' said Lorna 'but you wouldn't say that if you knew him' She went on to say that he got on with everyone, then paused and toyed with a biscuit, as if unsure what to do with it before continuing.

'Of course we have been quite close to our neighbours Alan and Alma Johnson,' she continued, 'and then there's Jim Lucas. He's got a telescope and a kind of observatory in his garden and Paul used to go there sometimes with Sam Matlock. He told me that he rather hoped that they would see something phenomenal one day but they never did. We also used to spend a lot of time with the Gooding family until that unfortunate business venture about the boatyard. We play Bridge with George and Sue Hamilton, then there's the Glovers, nice people but a bit on the religious side for us, and the Bakers, he can be argumentative you know, and then your boss Sam Matlock. Paul told me that he went to the Masonic meetings because the others all went to the Round Table and joked about some of the Masonic practices. Then there's Colonel Burton, and his wife. They're old friends from Africa but we don't see them much these days. I can give you his address book if you like. There's probably more in there.'

Kiwi refused this offer but encouraged Lorna to go on, 'Tell me more about Gooding. What was the problem there?' she asked.

Lorna said that she didn't know much but apparently Paul had provided expertise and Gooding the money for a canal boat repair business in Bristol soon after they got back to the UK, but it went 'pear shaped.' Paul had told her that Gooding knew nothing about boats and had fiddled the books. There was a big row and Gooding had left the area.

Here she paused again and nervously considered the biscuit once more.

She obviously wanted to change the subject as she seemed to realise that her earlier remarks about her husband 'getting on' with everyone did not sit comfortably with Gooding.

Kiwi realised that she was struggling so she gently eased the conversation elsewhere. 'I noticed that you mentioned coming back to the UK,' she said, 'Was that anything to do with those African photos that I've seen on the walls?'

Lorna seemed relieved and pleased to change the subject.

'Yes, I'd like to let tell you about Africa. You see I hadn't been out of Europe and it was very exciting when Paul got a job in Dar,' she said

Immediately Kiwi's ears pricked up having seen the file in Peter's office as well as the photos.

'Did you say Dar?' she asked.

'Yes I did' Lorna replied,' We all called it Dar, for Dar-es-Salaam you know, we were out there in Tanzania in the late 60's during the UDI crisis for about 5 years.'

'I only know a bit about that from school,' Kiwi lied. 'In fact I don't even know what UDI means, and it was all a bit before my time if you see what I mean. I'd be really interested if you've got the time to tell me about it.'

Lorna smiled, moved to a book-case and selected a book that she handed to Kiwi. 'Here read this.' she said.

The Rhodesian Unilateral Declaration of Independence

The background to UDI began in the wider world of African affairs. It was Harold McMillan's 'Wind of Change' speech in South Africa that crystallised the situation on the African continent, stating, as it did that African affairs must soon be handled by African nationalists, in majority governments. This had already become the case in many African States but the situation in Southern Rhodesia in 1965 remained unsettled and a white minority ruled there albeit as a 'self- governing colony' under British control. The Government in Salisbury (Southern-Rhodesia.) under Ian Smith, wanted independence but the British refused this, using the term 'NIBMAR' (No independence before majority rule). In the ensuing years fuel supplies from the South were blocked, so essential fuel to the copper belt in Zambia were supplied by road from Tanzania. Consortia from across the world took part and this became known as 'The Hell Run'.

Kiwi had finished this small section by the time that Lorna came back.

Lorna smiled and said, 'I hope that's all a bit clearer now. Good book I think, but it doesn't tell the whole story, not at all, nor how bad it was for us. Here's the coffee, get comfy and I'll tell you all about it.

'Paul was Managing Director of Brice, one of the main transporters of those essential fuel supplies to the copper belt but I know that he worked closely and secretly with the British Foreign Office as well. It all seemed fine at first' she began, 'then Paul told me that there had been an incident at a farm near Kariba on the Zambia/Rhodesia border. He didn't say exactly what had happened but that it would be safer for us if we left.

Later there was a report in the Press that an attack had taken place on a lonely farmhouse and a Mr Green and a Mrs Lock and her two sons had been cut to death. I couldn't see why this involved us and I was rather upset at the time because we had a lovely house on the beach and I ran a sort of animal sanctuary. He did tell me that two of our drivers had been accused of the crime and had then been found shot dead (execution style) in the following weeks; but he didn't elaborate further. He said that it was better for me not to know. The 'Hell Run' was always dangerous of course and some drivers were killed when their trucks ran off the road, but shootings were rare. Paul had explained to me that the RSF the Rhodesian Security Forces would sometimes hijack the fuel if they could and then people could get killed. His instinct on this seemed to be right however because before we sailed for home a director of our company had been shot at his farmstead near Nairobi and another was knifed in the street next to us in Dar. We got out just in time.'

Kiwi had been intrigued by this harrowing tale but now she knew that she must get some hard evidence if this was to be connected to Ward's murder. Fortunately she remembered that there were locked files in Ward's office so she politely asked to see them. Lorna agreed and soon she was back in the study, this time with the keys. Firstly she unlocked the locked drawer and it revealed many papers about Ward himself with documents revealing a senior position in the Home Office. She soon got a pleasant surprise as she opened another folder. This was simply marked 'Cerberus Bristol' and to her astonishment and delight it gave details about Ward's proposed dossier investigation into the amorphous organisation 'Cerberus' that Franks had referred to.

Cerberus Bristol (Provisional Findings by Paul Ward)

> Because of the long time lapse between my active service and now, this report will contain details of both. I do not have firm evidence about my suspicions as to the extent of Cerberus or alien activity in the South West at present but I am certain of it especially with regard to attacks on power stations here such as Hinkley, but also in London and elsewhere in the world such as Kariba and Niagara. It will probably be a coordinated operation with other vested interests such as Chemico in the States, but although I have no details I do have the names of individuals and places that may be implicated when a wider investigation can occur. A useful name to follow up is my neighbour Jim Lucas who is a member of SETI and we've studied night skies from his garden with Sam Matlock for some time. He has alluded to a planet that he calls Gonda but only a few specialist researchers like him seem to have heard of it.

There were then many appendices and a separate file that contained a list of current activity. In this file Ward had placed a note stating, 'See cabinet for full details of Africa and other world-wide scenarios.'

Kiwi realised that she might not get another chance to see what these files contained so she made copious notes of places and names before thanking Lorna and finally leaving the premises. She was wondering what the Superintendent and Matlock would make of this explosive development but she decided not to tell them for now. She was also thinking that Duke might help if he was assigned to the Müller case.

When she got home he was seated at the table with a large bundle of papers in front of him. She had noticed recently that he had his 'feet under the table' in more ways than one, and she was not quite sure that she liked it. Yes, she liked him around and especially when cuddled up at night, but where would it all end she wondered. For now she put these thoughts out of her mind and concentrated on the papers. She knew what they were instinctively.

'Have they given you the Müller case?' she asked,

'You bet they have,' he replied, 'It says here that I have got to work closely with you. Let's start right now' saying which he stood and helped her off with her coat, snuggling gently from behind.

'Now-now,' she said, 'I just can't wait to see what you've got there and I've got some news for you as well.'

His face dropped.

'Not pregnant are you?'

She smiled and shook her head; and he looked relieved. They opened a bottle and then began to exchange their stories.

He began by telling her that Müller was indeed a wanted Nazi war criminal and that the Wiesenthal organisation as well as 'Mossad' had been trying to track him down for ages and it was possible that they had caught up with him at last.

'I've got a lot of time for Wiesenthal,' he said, 'that man never gives up in his search for justice. I wish I could be more like him.'

However, he admitted that none of this explained the cuts on his face and the 'copycat' similarities to the Ward murder that Kiwi had told him about before. She now took over and produced her notes from Ward's office referring to names and places in the 'Africa' dossier and there it was; Müller's name listed as an Engineer working for the same Brice organisation that Lorna had said that Paul was working for. She then went on to explain Ward's work on Operation Scorpion.

'Do you think that they were both killed by a contract killer then?' he asked.

She thought for a moment but it didn't make sense. If the files were correct Ward was an investigator bent on exposing the group but if anything, Müller was a fellow- traveller. It just didn't add up.

'If you do have to work on this,' she said, 'I think its best that you stay behind the scenes. Matlock is no fool and he might wonder why you are getting involved. And he's not a man to be trifled with.'

Duke smiled and just said, 'Nor am I, so watch out!' He paused and they looked at each other at the same time and in the same way.

'Time for bed.' they said simultaneously.

'Me first,' laughed Kiwi as she made a dash for the bedroom, with Duke not far behind her behind.

❖ ❖ ❖

She was not surprised to be called into the Super's office the next day with a very irritable Matlock beside him. There was not much to say, except that she had just been tying up some loose ends at the Ward house and that it wouldn't happen again.

'It had better not,' said Matlock with that malevolent attitude in which he excelled.

The Super now introduced three other men in the office.

'This is Franks and Oliver from MI6 and this is Danton from Interpol. I've told them that we will give them assistance in their enquiries.

Everyone shook hands and Matlock said he'd find them an office to work in. Kiwi momentarily retrieved her battered reputation with Matlock by telling him that she was 'off the Ward' trail and now would be questioning Jim Lucas. He had already supplied a firm alibi for most of the week around Ward's disappearance having been in Corfu with his wife and family, but police business has procedures so he had to be interviewed anyway.

She decided to make an appointment to see him at 8pm, citing prior appointments during the day. In this way she hoped that she would be able to find out more about the SETI connection that Ward had alluded to, and maybe even get a sight of the Lucas telescope. As it turned out Jim Lucas was only too pleased to show her his pride and joy in the garden. It looked suspiciously like an ordinary garden shed, but once inside it revealed itself to be a miniature laboratory. There were posters of the heavenly firmaments on each and every wall, and many models of spacecraft and the like set out on benches. There were a few small telescopes but the main one was set up on a kind of chassis that moved back and forth for different angular settings, and above it there was a small window through which the nose projected into the night sky.

Jim explained many technical aspects but Kiwi was more interested in his targets than his telescopes.

This is all so very fascinating,' she said, 'but is it all just about star gazing or do you seriously expect to find signs of life up there.'

Jim seemed puzzled for a moment as if her question made no sense at all but he pulled himself together and replied.

'Well Jo, I know that not everyone is a space nerd, but I can assure you that I'm not alone, and I don't just mean in space, no. there are thousands if not millions out there who are members of SETI and other research institutions. There have been sightings of UFO's for millennia but now we are much more organised and we are able to collate and share our data. I do hope to locate alien life soon and that's not down to faith alone. I could give you many examples of unexplained phenomena but here are a few. In 1986 Japanese Airlines JAL1628 was followed by a UFO over Anchorage in Alaska, at Niagara Falls in 2008 a UFO was sighted and in 1992 a fleet of submersible UFO's was spotted off the California coast. It's not all America though, the 'Topcliffe' sighting in 1952 was at an RAF base in Yorkshire and at KasputinYar in the USSR in 1948 a report was made of a cigar shaped craft following a Soviet plane. These few are just the tip of a very large iceberg but we are hopeful that our persistence will pay off and we might be able to locate a source from which these UFOs come. I firmly believe that it might be Gonda but I have no proof. Let me tell you why I believe this so strongly.

'There is a story common to Nordic and Antipodean legends that the first inhabitants at the North and South poles were from a distant planet, maybe Gonda. They had arrived following the global warming there and their research missions had identified earth as a likely new home. As you may know the Zimbabwe Craton and the Great Rift Valley go back many millennia and it is likely that this was one area that they were attracted to, not only for 'breathing space,' but also for a major energy source that they knew to be there, namely diamonds. There is said to be the largest diamond depository in the world deep beneath the 'Kaapvaal Cover,' an area that crosses many African political boundaries and includes the Serengeti Plain, the Ngorogoro Crater and even Lake Victoria itself. Some say it is half the size of all South Africa. At that time our planet was under one of the very first ice ages and the Gondians made their home in these cold areas for centuries. However the tables were turned when Earth itself started to warm up and other creatures began to thrive. Eventually they had to give up and return home, but before they did they had interbred with forms of human life and many of their progeny remained behind and their descendants are still with us today as hybrids. They are not easy to recognize being Nordic in appearance with some subtleties that only an expert might recognise. Now they wish to return, but overtures to governments on earth have been rejected so they are making common cause with Cerberus. However, there are differences as well as similarities so I'm not sure that such a liaison will last.'

He smiled and asked Kiwi if that answered her questions and she replied that it certainly did for the time being With that she took her leave and went home fairly sure that Jim Lucas had nothing to do with Ward's disappearance. But Gonda was another matter entirely and she decided to make an appointment to see Franks and Tucker with Duke to clarify the position. Was this all speculation, or were these details already known to MI6 and the CIA? She needed to know.

It must be said that Kiwi's request was not welcome in MI6 and CIA corridors. She and Duke were seen as 'field officers' and aspects of national or international security were not for them. In the familiar phrase, such things were on a 'need to know' basis, partly for reasons of security but also because of their safety.

In this case however it might have to be different as Franks knew Kiwi's determination very well.

'We'll have to tell them.' he said to Tucker, 'If we don't she'll find out anyway or make my life hell.'

Hilary Tucker smiled, 'Can't you control your agents?' she asked, 'I'm sure I'd have no trouble with Duke, but I must admit he hasn't quite got her flair. So in a nutshell I agree. Let's bring them in and tell them everything.'

Now Franks looked worried, 'Do you think that we should tell them about our top secret overtures then?' he said.

'I'm afraid we've got no option,' she replied. 'Let's set up a meeting.'

✿ ✿ ✿

It was only a matter of days before the four of them assembled in a back room of the 'Dog and Duck,' a well- known hostelry just off Whitehall. Franks explained that it had to be in such a nondescript place to convince 'them' to come. Polite conversation ensued before they were told that a visitor had arrived, and soon after a figure entered the room. This was a man of about forty, slightly built, well over six feet tall, and prematurely bald it seemed. He wore a dark grey business suit and carried a briefcase that seemed to be made of a number of different leathers that were moulded together. Actually Kiwi thought that it looked like the skin of a Lizard but she didn't say so.

The man was greeted enthusiastically by Franks and Tucker, shaking his hand and addressing him as 'Gregory.'

'Mine's a pint.' he said before it was time to introduce Kiwi and Duke with a polite handshake as well. Later she was to confess that his flesh felt damp and 'creepy crawly' and she suspected that he was 'not of this world.' but Franks continued as if he was a member of any local golf club.

'Good to see you Gregory,' he said, 'Our friends here would like to know how you think the 'talks' are going. Please give them an update as far as you are able. They have important work to do and we'd like them to have an idea of where they have got to so far.'

Gregory spoke in rather halted tones. Duke thought that he sounded like a cross between a Norwegian and an Australian if you might imagine that, but he spoke clearly and very much to the point.

'I am what you might call an interlocutor in this matter' he said, 'Talks of one kind or another have been going on for some time between your governments and those whom I represent but agreement is hard to come by. That is why we have made an arrangement with Cerberus because we share some mutual goals. However now we realise that we might achieve these in a more peaceful manner if we can get a little more c-operation from you. You see, we are only trying to buy time before 'other territories' open up for us and that is why an all-out conflict here would be counter-productive. I will keep the talks going as long as I think that there is hope for a peaceful outcome but Cerberus must never hear of these initiatives because they will take action on their own.'

With that statement Gregory left the room and the meeting was over.

'I hope you are satisfied now,' said Franks, 'Please don't ask any questions. I want you to decide just who Gregory might be but it's worth more than my life to say so. Anyway it's given you some idea about the importance of our venture and the need for total confidence at all levels. Now go and get some sleep and try to act as if nothing has been said.'

Kiwi laughed, 'That's a tall order if you get my meaning,' she said, 'but I think that we know what you mean. In other words it's business as usual and 'keep our powder dry.'

The matter was quite clear as far as Kiwi was concerned, but Duke still had many reservations about the very notion of any kind of alien on earth, especially one who seemed to enjoy a pint in the pub.

Nonetheless there was still more research to be done with his CIA colleagues who were occupying an Estate Agent's office for cover. 'Sorry madam, that house is now off the market,' was a familiar response to a curious client. It's pretty well known that CIA resources are without parallel on a worldwide basis so it didn't take long for him to track down a certain 'Walter Müller.' in the records. He was named not only as a wanted Nazi criminal but as a leader of 'a shadowy group known as 'Cerberus'.

Duke was pleased that this seemed to tie in with Ward's records, but when they did so there was very little else to go on, and as for a killer and a motive, well he thought, we seem to be up the creek without a paddle. However Kiwi wasn't finished yet and she trawled through Ward's papers for more clues.

'Here are some names and some places that I noted,' she said, 'Mme Colbert, Colonel Burton, Joe Rome, Albert Müller, Mrs Green-Gonda, Anya Stein, Charlie Swann, Tom Spooner and Captain Lock. There is the Kariba Dam and a Simba Farm and these link up with Africa, but I also found references from across the world including St Malo in France, Bridgewater in Somerset UK, Otago in NZ, Los Angeles Bay in California and even Tallin in Estonia on the Baltic Sea. I don't know if any of these mean something but I'm going to stick to the Zambezi trail for now and I'll send these details back to HQ to see what they make of them.'

There were still too many loose ends and they seemed to have reached another impasse, so she decided that it was time for some lateral thinking and she decided to follow an earlier instinct.

'Don't tell me I'm mad,' she said 'but I want to do some background checks on Matlock'.

'What did you say? Do you mean the Inspector?' he said incredulously.

Kiwi just cuddled up to him on the sofa and smiled. She knew what she was going to do and why. Meanwhile Duke had business back at the Estate Agents so she just said, 'Find us a nice house.' as he left.

Now she could sprawl out in front of the fire with her notes all around her and she was determined to make some sense of the affair. She decided on a process of elimination with Mike Baker first. She had noted that there may have been some old scores to settle, and he hadn't properly accounted for his movements on the day. Furthermore there was that funny business about the East African Safari diamonds that she had written about in her report. She dug out a copy and read through it again. This time she noticed something unusual that no one had commented on so far. Why was the note of instruction from Pretoria all written in lower case except for KEY, who was to be the contact? Matlock had told them not to worry about all the small details but she had been trained well and knew that small details might make a big difference. As for why Baker couldn't find out more about the diamonds, Kiwi thought there were very many vested interests and political intrigues around at that time which might ensure that the full story would never be known. However there had been references to General Dallas and the American company called Chemico and their possible links with Cerberus. She wondered if Baker had been persuaded to work for them as well. She began to make notes but there wasn't much to go on. 'Apply pressure. Threaten him with Mrs Baker! Where did he go on the Thursday when Ward went missing?' Now, what about Glover? Was he a man with a guilty conscience about an affair, or maybe a murder? And now there's Müller of course.

By the following morning she was refreshed and ready to start again. What about Ward himself and why did he get himself killed? She smiled at herself. Nobody gets himself killed does he? They are, well, they just 'are' murdered. But there must be a reason. Another love affair maybe but no; She had seen Lorna Ward's despair and listened to her touching account of their life together. No, that can't be it. What then? Africa, Africa. The answer's there, but just where? And just who? Think, think; if there was a connection was there an oil connection? Someone had finally caught up with Ward after all those years, someone who would have never given up, someone, maybe, who had lost his wife and children in that bloody murder at Kariba. Was that it? Matlock had told her not to bother, but Kiwi had a mind of her own. She decided to go to the Library to review the newspaper accounts at the time and, if she got into trouble, she'd put it down to experience, but she had to find out. She soon found them on microfiche.

The lead story in The Salisbury Times on 8th Dec.1967 (The voice of the Rhodesian Nation) was much as Lorna had said, but names were given to the murdered families. It was a Mr A Green and his wife as well as a Mrs J Lock and her two sons, Samuel and Stephen of White Rose farm Kariba who had all been murdered by intruders while Captain S Lock was away from the farm serving with the Rhodesian Security Forces. The police were making enquiries and 'an arrest was imminent', the paper said. Kiwi looked again and froze, 'Lock!' she muttered under her breath. Could this S Lock be Stephen Lockhart?

And then it struck her that the mysterious 'Lake Tanganyika' diamond contact had been called KEY! Surely not this as well! A lock and a key would made things so easy to remember. She recalled how it was a simple ruse like this that allowed the code breakers at Bletchley to break the Enigma code. Or was this just one more silly little coincidence? However, it did seem to her that some of those pieces of the jigsaw that she had noticed could be beginning to fall into place. Matlock had known about the David Shepherd East African paintings at the Bakers, he had spoken of the 'Limpopo' river and 'watering holes' He was a Yorkshire man hence 'White Rose Farm' but most strange of all, macabre even, were the names of Captain Lock's boys who were killed, Samuel and Stephen, the same names of Matlock's sons here in Bristol.

She shivered. She knew she was in above her head but who could she turn to with these suspicions, because that's all that they were? She was shocked, she was scared and she really didn't know what to do next. She was too tired so she decided to go home and crash out on the settee. She went to sleep and didn't wake for twelve hours.

In the morning she became a blonde again, hoping for better luck.

The next day was another review meeting, this time with Matlock and Curtis both there. The Superintendent laid down the order for the meeting. First it would be the Ward case and then, if they had time, that awkward Müller affair. He obviously thought that it was low priority, in other words, not a murder enquiry, as yet.

'Jean' he said, 'will you start please, Ward case first.'

'Thank you sir,' she replied. 'Clean bill of health on my side I'm afraid, except a Mr Gooding who had a small business venture with Ward. Put all his money into a dodgy enterprise renovating canal boats and lost his shirt. Blamed Ward, it was only last year but we haven't tracked him down yet. Family all in the clear we think and there weren't any other social or business problems.'

Now it was Matlock's turn and he began briskly.

'Firstly I'd like to introduce you all to Don Washington from 'Investigations PLC.' You probably know them from all their advertising about domestic debt but they're much bigger than that. In fact they are one of the biggest security operations in the States and the Super has authorised me to use them on a short term basis to help us get to the bottom of these incidents. They are part of the world wide Chemico operations if you want to know about their credentials, and you can't do better than that can you?'

He looked across at the Superintendent who nodded his approval as the man stood up.

'Please don't mind me.' he said, 'Just remember that I'm here to help in any way that I can and you can trust me to keep a secret.' With that he sat down as Kiwi took a hard look at him.

She didn't much like what she saw. She remembered the Chemico link from Baker's testimony and trust wasn't a word she would have used herself. He seemed a bit like a copy of Matlock and one of those was enough for anyone. And why had he been employed at all and why now? She hoped that the Inspector hadn't got wind of her suspicions about him and her reservations about the case, because that could be fatal. However, although all this was making her feel rather nervous, didn't it rather suggest that she was on the right track after all?

'Welcome to our little team Don' Matlock continued, 'What have we got to go on so far then?'

There were three other officers besides Kiwi and WPC Drew reporting to him, and Sgt Tom Martin spoke first.

'Report on Mrs Howard Sir. I could find nothing. It's a wrong MO unless she had an accomplice. Not likely Sir. Everyone says how close they were.'

Matlock sighed as if all that was a complete waste of time.

'Who's next?' he said impatiently.

'May I Sir?' It was Tom Blandish, who proceeded to give a more detailed forensic report concluding that it had seemed like a very professional job adding, rather dramatically, that the beating had taken place after death.

'A 'crime of passion' perhaps then.'. interjected Inspector Curtis but Matlock was having none of it,

'It could be lots of things,' he said rudely, and then added 'I suppose that you could be right though, it doesn't have to be a man does it? A strong macho woman could do it easy couldn't they?' he said looking at Jean as if she fitted the bill nicely. 'Now did you find out anything more at the Wards?' he said turning toward Kiwi. She looked at him closely. She hesitated. She was seeing him in a totally different light for the very first time. She knew him to be a surly Yorkshire man but now, was he a cold-blooded murderer as well? Could she keep her cool or was she going to give the game away by some carelessness at this stage? Luckily she was able to pull herself together and speak confidently with a smile.

She told him that she had heard that Baker and Glover did not seem to have good alibis because she thought it wise to leave the door open in that direction for the time being but nothing else she added. She did not want to alarm him nor give him an inkling of what was on her mind. The Superintendent now took over.

'Good, good, so far so good but do try to make some more positive progress won't you? Working as a team all right? Good, good that's what I like to se. Now is there any progress on the Müller case then?

'There's some evidence that he was on the Nazi Hunter lists under one name or another, but as far as we can tell, they hadn't managed to track him down so far. Maybe they did but we can't be sure.' Jean replied.

The Superintendent seemed pleased, 'Good, now remember we don't want an International incident here. Just let's be sure of our facts.'

Time was passing by and Kiwi wanted to share her thoughts with Jean but she was worried. How could she explain her suspicions? Luckily she stopped her in the corridor and solved that immediate problem.

'How's the case really going then?' she asked.

Kiwi responded thoughtfully,' I've got some ideas but no proof, as yet. The trouble is that I can't find a motive for the life of me, unless....' she stopped and then continued, 'well nothing really. I don't really know how to say this but I think that Matlock's involved, one way or another. He's covering up for someone I think and why has he brought in Don Washington?'

Jean was silent for a moment then said, 'I'm sorry I really have no idea, but If I were you I'd watch it girl. That man's dangerous.'

Kiwi was grateful for Jean's understanding but added, 'Yes that's what I think and now there's two of him.' At this they both laughed as Jean left.

The next day she got a call from the Super to meet Jean Curtis and Sam Lockhart in his office.

'Report of a break in' he said, 'Well, actually more of a break out.' he continued and laughed at his own joke.

His three officers all looked bewildered until Matlock broke the deadlock and asked the Super to explain.

'Don't you get it man? Come on one of you young girls. Come on think.' He sat back with his hands folded over his portly stomach and looked very pleased with himself until he decided to put them out of their misery. Apparently routine investigation that had continued at the Ward house had revealed nothing untoward in the house, but a wider search in the sheds and down in the boatyard revealed a most surprising find. It could easily have been missed but it was PC Lee who noticed that the 'Laura' seemed to be tipped off 'her' mountings and a further investigation revealed a large hole in the side but no sign of entry.

'Now do you get it?' the Super crowed, 'Break out-side not in-side do you see?'

The three looked suitably chastened and it was Matlock who spoke first

'That sounds like the ham fisted work of Mr Gooding, Paul Ward's ex- partner in the boat business. Who else would want to just damage a boat? Maybe Ward was out but he found him later. We'd better put out an APB at once.'

It seemed like the police had a real lead at last with motive and method all in place but what about opportunity and where was Gooding? At this point Matlock made a strange request and asked the Superintendent to transfer 'Jo' back to his team to find Gooding. He explained that WPC Drew was ill and he felt that a woman's touch might be needed if the case had to be explained to Gooding's wife and family.

iwi thought that this was a lame excuse and immediately recognised that far from sending her on 'other assignments,' Matlock had indeed grown suspicious and wanted to keep an eye on her for some reason. This pleased her because it seemed to confirm her suspicions but it also frightened her. However she didn't have a choice and when it was discovered that Gooding was staying in Bristol at the Ibis hotel he soon had a visit from them both. He explained that he was on a business trip and that his family were at home in Taunton. He was asked when he had last seen or been in touch with the Wards but he said that it had been years and he did not particularly want to see them again.

'We understand that you parted on bad terms.' said Kiwi and Gooding agreed that there had been some problems. She persisted, 'Isn't it true that you made the company bankrupt?'

Gooding denied this with some vehemence, 'Not me,' he said, 'that was all down to Ward and his stupid designs. High cost materials as well. He had no idea and it was my money on the line.'

Matlock now intervened with a question, 'Would it be true to say that you hated Ward then?' he asked.

Gooding agreed that there was no love lost between them but Matlock continued.

'Did you hate him enough to kill him as well as damage his boat then?' he asked menacingly.

Gooding was taken off guard and immediately denied anything to do with either scenario adding that if anything further was to be said he insisted on a lawyer being present. On hearing this Matlock simply stated that he could get one at the station because he was going to be arrested on suspicion of murder.

'Read him his rights Constable.' he said with some satisfaction and turning to Kiwi he added, 'I told you the answer was close to home.'

She nodded as if to say that he was right after all, but it was not what she was thinking.

What she was thinking was that if Gooding killed Ward why would he be involved in the copy-cat Müller murder and what were the implications of the facial scars? She didn't say much but she knew that there must be a connection somewhere, but where?

However, against her train of thought, it didn't take long for forensics to place Gooding at the scene of the boat in Ward's garden. Fingerprints, footprints and even a receipt for a hammer from a hardware shop dropped in the bushes and paid for by Gooding's credit card, were all part of the incriminating evidence. Matlock had got his man and Gooding pleaded guilty to aggravated damage. Evidence for the murder would turn up later he assured everyone. And maybe the Müller murder was just a rehearsal for the intended victim he said. It all fitted into place and the force could begin to concentrate on other issues in the town he added. The Super agreed, although of course he had to keep the cases open. He also managed to persuade MI6 that an International Incident had been avoided and he congratulated Matlock on a job well done, much to Kiwi's irritation.

She was forestalled it seemed, but she was not one to give up without a fight. She had always been a little afraid of Matlock but this was different. She'd never liked him, but he was her boss. No. it was more than that. He was somewhat strange, she thought, not just a bit schizophrenic but more like a curled up cobra waiting to strike. Up to now she had been loyal and co-operative, maybe not always obedient, but that was her way. Now she was out on a limb. Say nothing and wait for others to investigate? But they wouldn't would they? She was the only one who could make it stick but she needed confirmation of the name connection otherwise it was all supposition.

Was Sam Matlock of Bristol the same person as S Lock of Kariba and, if so, when and why did he change his name? There was only one thing for it, she would have to go through his files to see if there was a paper trail of some sort, but even as she thought this, a shiver ran down her back. If it was he, he was a vengeful and ruthless killer and she knew that she would have to be very, very, careful. She would wait until this coming weekend when she knew that Matlock would be away with his family on a visit to Portsmouth where they had a holiday home. She would then arrange to work on Sunday and use the opportunity to look in his files.

※※※

The days dragged by, but it was soon Sunday and she was in the office, alone for now. She didn't have much time before somebody else might come in so she moved quickly to the filing cabinet in his office. She knew where his keys were, in the desk, yes, there... Now, which key for the cabinet? Yale, Yale, that's it, now turn, turn, click, that's it I'm in! Now, first file, second file, which one? Let's see now. Not staff or Holiday Club but Personal, yes Personal. Yes, Personal SL, yes that's it.' Her hands were shaking as she opened the file. 'No it can't be. Damn! It can't be, Damn!' But it was. The file was empty 'Damn it's empty, Damn, Damn, Damn!' She was nearly crying with frustration.

'But, hang on a minute.' she muttered as she stopped in her tracks, 'There's a note, let's see now, what does it say?' She read the note. It said simply, 'Taken home to update.'

She sat back. She was exhausted. 'What to do? What to do now?' she thought, but then she noticed a bunch of keys at the bottom of the drawer, two bunches in fact.

'Office keys and House keys I shouldn't wonder. Now if I can get into the House tonight I can return the keys before he gets back. Well, in for a penny, in for a pound I suppose. There's only one thing for it now. There's going to be a break in!'

She laughed at the thought, but realised that this would indeed have to be her next step. However, she had decided on one other tactic before she went down the 'Burglary' route, and that was to check out the Register of Births, Marriages and Deaths in the Bristol Central Library.

An initial search on the computers was not forthcoming so she asked for access to the 'micro-fiche' records and there she found what she was looking for, a birth certificate in the name of Samuel Matthew Lock, born Sheffield in 1936'. She realised of course, that this did not prove anything, but now she felt more confident than ever. It would be easy and convenient to jumble up Christian names and surnames to create a new identity. The problem was that it was all supposition and just that gut feeling she had. She could not take her suspicions to anyone without some evidence, and the only way to get it was to see what was in the files at his home. Once more she had to wait for an opportunity when he would be away, not just from the office but from his house as well.

She knew that he sometimes took his family to Portsmouth, where he had a cottage, Usually he and his wife collected her brother before setting out the next day for the coast so, when he said that he was off to Hampshire again for the next weekend, she decided to make her move. 'It's now or never' she hummed quietly to herself.

❖❖❖

Saturday morning came and she began to set her mind to the burglary. First thing was her hair, a brunette definitely, not so noticeable she thought. However at this point Duke arrived unexpectedly and came straight into the bathroom, grabbing her from behind as he liked to.

'What's this?' he said, 'I just fell in love with a blonde and now she's a brunette again.'

She smiled but then she began to shake uncontrollably, turning to put her arms around him. At first he got the wrong idea but soon realised that she was sobbing on his shoulder.

He picked her up gently carried her into the bedroom and covered her with the duvet as he sat beside her.

'What's up darling? Is it me?' he asked softly.

Now she was laughing hysterically as she grabbed him closely. Then, as tears of laughter and relief ran down her face, she told him of her plan. He listened to her for an age as she outlined her reasons for such drastic action, and by the end he told her that he would go with her.

'Not on your life, definitely not.' she said, 'this is my baby and only mine. I don't want you involved.'

'It takes two to make a baby and I'm coming.' he replied.

She didn't want to argue, and in a way she was relieved.

She now began her preparations for the night.

'Now, what does one wear for a burglary?' she thought, 'Black perhaps. Yes. Mask? No. Too dramatic, but a Black Hat, which covers face and hair, seems like a good idea; and a scarf. Yes and a crowbar? No, I don't think so but black gloves? Yes, and trainers. Good, I'm ready or as ready as I'll ever be.'

She paused as she looked in the mirror at her disguised appearance, holding a glass of Scotch in her hand.

'Not bad, not bad at all.' she said, holding up the glass to this mysterious mirror image. 'Cheers! And good luck Kiwi. You won't let me down will you?' She could see Duke behind her in the reflection.

'And nor will I.' he said.

Midnight came soon enough as they tiptoed out of her back door and started to jog across the back fields to where Matlock lived.

'Excellent' she thought, as they stopped to view the house from a safe distance. There were no street lights and that was fortunate for their purposes; but there was a party going on a few doors down. She thought about waiting until the noise subsided but decided that, on balance, and he agreed that it would be best to go now, straight up to the front door with an excuse if she was seen. But what excuse? She hadn't thought she'd need one so didn't have one ready. 'I'm going anyway,' she decided, and walked confidently up to the front door as Duke hid behind a bush. She tried the first key. No it didn't fit. Now the second.

'It opens' she whispered to back as the door opened and they both squeezed inside the front door listening for any sound.

Her mind tracked back to think of some excuse again if she was spotted, but then she stopped and nearly laughed out loud. 'What use would any excuse be when we're dressed up like a pair of robbers?'

She decided that it was time to move and, as all seemed quiet, they tiptoed up the stairs guiding the way with a small torch and not risking any main lights. She had already decided that, if she was going to find anything, it would be in the study and she looked around on the landing

There were four doors, two open, one the bathroom, and the other a child's bedroom, so she moved towards one of the others and opened the door. Yes, it was the study. A computer, a desk, files of many kinds, and bookcases on every wall. She shone the torch around, picking up the labels on each cabinet before opening each one carefully. She checked every file in all the cabinets but could not find what she was looking for. She called to Duke to stay at the top of the stairs to keep a look out and carried on her search.

'Damn, damn, damn' she muttered under her breath, 'Where are you?'

She shone the torch around again and this time it picked up a box – file that was labelled 'Lock', tucked in amongst some history and DIY books in a bookcase.

She took the file down and opened it carefully. Inside were five folders each, marked with a letter of the alphabet. These were Y, CV, K, B, and CG. She opened the first one in the torchlight. The file was entitled YORKSHIRE and it contained old family photographs, certificates, letters, school reports and other miscellaneous papers in the name of S.M. Lock. Sue put it down and picked up the next. It was marked CURRICULUM VITAE, and inside were official papers from the police and the army as well as photos and other papers. The file included a section marked 'Rhodesian Security Force code name KEY' and a comment, 'Decided to call myself Lock for security reasons'

The next was K and in this section there was a detailed description of the KARIBA Dam and the cavernous power station that had been carved out of the rock supplying 70% of Zambian electricity. A rail link passed over the nearby Victoria Falls and this carried 90% of Zambian trade including imported oil and exported copper. Matlock observed that it was not only a critical lifeline but also a very good choice for operations later. 'We will need the power, and my instructions are to accommodate our guests from Gonda and hide them in the depths in their special pods when they arrive,' he had noted.

The next file was B for BRICE, Ward's employers, oil transporters and breakers of the Rhodesian blockade on the Zambian copper belt. She wanted to study it straight away but, before she did, she looked to see what was in the fifth file but then she heard a noise. Was it the sound of the front door opening? She listened again, yes, there it was again; a noise, this time the click of the front door shutting.

'Oh God, he's back, he's come back! Go and hide under the bed quick' she whispered, 'Now what shall I do? Oh no! Is he coming up?'

She strained to listen for any sound, and there it was again, another sound, and this time a definite creak of a stair. 'I must hide but where? Put the file away quick, quick, that's right. Now hide here, yes here, under the desk, tight but, yes, it's a squeeze but I'm in.'

These were her thoughts as she lay there petrified as the footsteps got closer and closer. They seemed to go into one of the bedrooms, and then into the bathroom, because she heard the sound of the chain. Then the door of the study opened and light flooded in from the hall. She bit her lip until it bled, she was shaking in her cramped hideaway but all she could see were a pair of legs and shoes moving into the room. 'What was he looking for and why now?'

The legs moved around for a while and then sat down, exactly where she was hiding under the desk. There was a musty smell of sweaty socks and trousers, and it was as much as she could do to stop from being sick there and then all over those shiny shoes. What then? They stayed there for what seemed like a lifetime, before they got up and walked out of the room. She listened raptly and, yes, they were going downstairs, and was that the sound of a car starting up? Yes it was, she was sure of it but she couldn't move. Fear and cramp had left her immobilised, and she had to wriggle painfully to escape from her hiding place but as she did so she realised that she was not alone after all.

There, seated in a small chair across the room sat Don Washington.

She froze and looked desperately for a way out, but there was none. What's more he was holding a pistol and it was pointing at her. He smiled rather graciously as if the gun was an offering rather than a threat.

'Well hello Miss Nosey Parker,' he said, 'Matlock told me it would only be a matter of time before you'd do something stupid and now you have. Breaking and entering is a crime you know and it might not be surprising if you got injured resisting arrest would it?'

Kiwi wondered if she could stall him long enough for Duke to hear what was happening, so she just said. 'OK it's a fair cop, as you Yanks say, but I warn you not to hurt me because there would be tragic consequences for you. Your name is in my file and you'd certainly be suspected if anything happened to me.'

Washington laughed as if such a notion was ridiculous.

'With what evidence then?' he replied, 'I can assure you that I established a cast iron alibi before I came here. Now I'd like you to turn around and make your way to the garden. We don't want any blood in here do we? I always like to keep things neat and tidy just as I did with that 'Mr Persistent' Senator Prince in the States.'

Kiwi's life was flashing before her, but she was trapped and just had to follow his instructions, making her way out of the study and into the hall. She had just reached the stairs when she heard a loud thump behind her, and as she turned she saw Duke standing over an inert Don Washington.

'I think I've killed him.' he said rather forlornly. 'I just meant to knock him out but he's dead I think. I couldn't bear to think of him touching you and hurting you.'

He began to sob hysterically. 'I've never killed before' he said, 'I'm so very sorry. Please God forgive me'

There was little that Kiwi could do except to comfort him until he had calmed down. Now she had to take charge, pointing out that they still had a job to do. She knew that it would be hard on Duke but she pointed out that they would have to move the body out of the house, and maybe take it somewhere that it might not be found for some time. He seemed to realise that she was talking sense, so they carried the body down to the lawn and hid it so that they could pick it up later.

They then returned to the study to complete the job. Fortunately the files were still there in a heap on top of the photocopier. She discarded the Y for Yorkshire file that was still there. The B for Bristol file was missing, as she had guessed, and now she held the vital K and B files in her hands. Of course she must read them, but what if she was wrong and he did come back. Photocopies of course, and there was the copier right here.

She began her work and it took nearly an hour to copy both files. She put the originals back, placed the copies in her bag, and got ready to leave. Then it struck her that she needed the originals if charges were to stick. She would have to take a chance that the files might not be looked at for some time so she must take the originals, and leave the copies in the file. It was then that she realised that she had forgotten the file marked CG. She opened it and what she found was more than she had hoped for.

Chief of South African Operations
Captain S Lock (Delta)

These are your duties as a sworn official of Cerberus and you must recite the oath of loyalty below every day. You will lead our operations to disrupt power sources to the Copper Belt and elsewhere, and arrange for our bases to receive our guests from Gonda when instructed.

THE OATH This land is ours. It is not theirs.

The name Cerberus is never to be used in public or discussed with others and our relationship with Gonda is to remain top secret.

When necessary, meetings are to be held in the name of a reputable social or political (not military) pressure group of our own design. For example in South Africa we have chosen the 'Zambezi Citizens' as providing the right non-racial and distinctly local emphasis that is necessary in those communities. Likewise the 'African Far Sight Rangers' will provide training opportunities under Colonel Burton that should not excite suspicion. Our aim in Africa is to work with others to secure white hegemony on the continent as a forerunner to a controlled world order across all continents, and we shall soon be in a position to involve our partners from Gonda fully. Their needs are very limited, fresh deep water lakes for sanctuary, and diamonds for their energy source and we have plenty of both. Officers are to be sworn by blood oath to secrecy and loyalty until the day dawns for our glorious future to come.

The success of Operation Trust will be up to you and other leaders like you.

She was dumbfounded, here it was at last, confirmation about links to Cerberus but she still wasn't sure how and why the murders were part of the same puzzle

She looked across at Duke, 'Help' she called out rather weakly, 'wait until you see this.'

He came over and quickly read part of the file. 'Wow,' he exclaimed, 'I'll copy these to go with the others but we'd better get a move on hadn't we?'

He quickly checked the rooms and then they crept downstairs and out into the night. They collected a car and returned to move the unfortunate Washington to a secure spot before returning home completely drained.

When she got inside the door she suddenly felt tired, not sleepy-tired but emotionally exhausted. She flopped immediately into her favourite chair and was asleep in seconds, and then wide-awake in minutes, totally refreshed. Now she opened the files and, fortified by a large tumbler of malt whisky, she began to read and make notes.

It was all there, much more than she had dared to hope for. Matlock was indeed Captain S. Lock whose family had been murdered at Kariba, and whose campaign of revenge for this had been planned down to the last detail. Not just the planning, but the recording and outcome of each one was there.

It was a plan but it was also his testament to the justification of each murder. Somehow she had known that it would be like this. She had noted, over many months, how indifferent and dismissive he had been as the two cases evolved. It seemed that he lacked any compassion, because 'to care' in these cases would have meant an admittance of guilt, if only to himself and this he was not able to do. He did not deploy his conscience if he had one, because, in his eyes he was the agent (or angel) of righteousness in all that he did. She took out her laptop and began to type, slowly as she noted each incident and date, and then faster as if the story would escape if she did not pin it down.

She decided that she'd have to go through it all with Duke in the morning; but there was time for that.

'Thanks for looking after me' she said. 'I could do with a big hug and a long sleep now... Yes, that's right, just there' she murmured as he massaged her neck.

He noticed that she was asleep so he carried her gently to the bedroom and shut the door.

He then went into the lounge, sat down and began to shiver and shake uncontrollably until he too fell asleep, and he was still sleeping when Kiwi left in the morning.

She had had a good nine hours and when she went back into work she was pleased to hear that Matlock would not be coming into the station until the end of the week. This gave her the chance to hand the file and her suspicions over to Jean Curtis. She knocked on the Inspector's door.

'Oh come in Jo can I help you' said Jean.

'I just thought you might like to see this before I hand it over to the Super.' replied Kiwi, and with that she placed the files on the table with a full rationale that pointed the finger directly at Matlock for Ward's murder.

Jean read the Kariba file quietly, looking up occasionally as she did so. When she had finished, she picked up the file marked B for Brice and began again. This file contained a detailed account of Matlock's plans and action since the murders in Kariba, starting with the attempt on Wards life back then. There followed some press cuttings of unsolved murders in the Salisbury newspapers with red ticks in the margins. There was also an article about the 'Tragic Death in Dar-es- Salaam' of the former Director of the Brice Oil Company in a boating accident off the coast; also marked with a red tick in the margin. This was followed by a section marked, 'Ward the Criminal,' which contained full details of the murder plan right down to the time, place and weapon of choice. It concluded, 'Revenge is Sweeter than Wine!' and there was yet another section, simply labelled 'Müller' and this is what it said;

'Saw Müller by sheer chance in Bath. He was another of that Brice crew. I had great pleasure in knifing him after I told him who I was.

'Any last words?' I asked him. 'Do you have any regrets?'

'Nein.' he replied, 'I deserve to die. All my life I have wondered how I might atone for my part as a member of the SS in the war. It must have been possible to refuse orders or even to desert from the army but I did neither. God forgive me and thank you for your mercy.'

I stuck him like a pig and then bagged him up and dropped him way down in the river. I still don't know how Ward and his undercover operations with Brice got information about my HQ in Kariba, but maybe they wish they hadn't now. As for Ian Smith, and his dreams of UDI, well he's gone, but the struggle goes on until we achieve our aims and our partners join us on our day of victory.

As for me I've arranged with Colonel Burton to work on Operation Trust elsewhere in Europe for the time being. Despite my failure in Africa he has complemented me on the work I have done there. He says that I have the 'killer' instinct that he admires in those leaders of the past who seized power through guile and diplomacy, as well as ruthless determination. He said that I will have an important role to play with our 'partners' (code G)

Kiwi was worried by these last comments. They confirmed her worst fears that Matlock and others in the shadowy Cerberus would actively promote violence and unrest until they prevailed just as Duke had said those many weeks ago, and Code G obviously referred to the mysterious planet Gonda that Jim Lucas had referred to.

Could Matlock still be looking for others associated with the murder of his wife and family as well? For now she was feeling rather sorry for Frau Müller.

She looked at Jean and said, 'Poor Müller. You know I felt quite sorry for him. He was thinking about Auschwitz wasn't he? Was he a victim or, having chosen his path, was he then ultimately responsible for his war crimes, even under orders?'

She paused, 'and do you think that free will always means a free choice? Perhaps it's like a cat with nine lives. We all get chances too but don't we sometimes ignore them for convenience or maybe pride. And then suddenly our number's up and it's too late to turn the clock back. His was.'

She was also thinking about Don Washington who had also been in the wrong place at the wrong time. Duke had been so moved at the events at Matlock's home that she wondered if he would ever get over it. There would be an enquiry of course, but they had been assured that no action was likely.

Jean sat quietly listening and then said,

'Maybe some of us get a better deck of cards than others but it's up to everyone how they play them isn't it? I'll just finish reading the file. Just wait a moment.' Then when she had finished she just said, 'Well, well, well. This is excellent. I only hope we can make it stick. He'll deny it all you know. He'll say you made all this up and fabricated the copies. I do hope you know what you are up against.'

Kiwi smiled confidently and, speaking very quietly, she said, 'Look again Jean. Those aren't copies. They're all originals and they're all in his handwriting.'

Jean did look, and so did the Superintendent, and so did Internal Affairs. A warrant was issued for Matlock but a search in Portsmouth revealed that he and his family had taken the ferry across the Channel.

Kiwi remembered that St Malo had been mentioned so France could be involved, and she was sure that Operation Scorpion would track him down there eventually.

Now the full extent of their mission was about to be revealed as Franks and Tucker outlined the implications of what the pair had discovered so far.

'You've done well,' said Franks, 'but you've only scratched the surface and we'd like you to do a lot more. You already have some leads and you work well together so what do you think?'

Kiwi looked at Duke and he looked at her before saying, 'Excuse me for saying so but we are hardly professionals in the espionage business are we?'

At this point Hilary Tucker spoke up 'It's a bit different for Jo I agree, but actually you are a trained CIA operator are you not? It's precisely because you both have a touch of the amateur sleuth about you that makes you perfect for this task' she said. 'Perhaps I should tell you that we have at least another dozen teams doing the same job in different parts of the world but they are mostly full time professionals and some are probably known to Cerberus already. It's your anonymity that makes you so suitable as well. We are closer now than we have been before, but also more concerned. We thought that Cerberus was not working alone and now we know it for sure, but DCU efforts to find a peace formula with Gonda have come to nothing and Operation Scorpion will have failed unless we keep up the pressure now.'

Now Franks took up the conversation.

'I can't pretend that this won't be dangerous work and you know that already, but I'm going to tell you something that only a few Ministers and High Officials know. We have reason to believe that Cerberus will have finalised their plans for what we have heard referred to as a 'pincer' movement, within six months, maybe less. We don't know what form the 'pincer' will take either. We may find many blind alleys along the way but our main aim is to locate Alpha and stop Operation Trust in its tracks. You'll observe that we have no idea who Alpha is, or where their main base is. We think that General Dallas and Chemico might be involved but we can't be sure. And now we have that other dimension to contend with, namely the Gondians, and we need to know how far their own collaboration with Cerberus has gone So this is how you can continue to help. Identify Alpha, locate the base and expose their plans. That should neutralize any threat that might come from them, but we also need to know if the Gondians are here in strength yet, possibly hidden away in deep water locations. If so you must find them, and then we can negotiate.

'In that respect we already have a lead for you and that's Colonel Burton, whose name has come up quite a few times as you know. In a few days he is attending some 'management games' at an old castle and we want you to attend and see what he's up to. Take a day off work and then go to the Castle Capulet. You might even enjoy yourselves'

Kiwi felt like saying. 'Is that all Sir?' but as she looked at Duke he nodded, so she nodded too.

'Do you think that we might get a break after that sir?' she said, but Franks was already leaving the room.

The case had seemed to be over but it was far from over.

2

EUROPA

Matlock had fled it is true but although the double murder in Bristol remained an open case, it seemed that there wasn't much that Kiwi could do about it. However it had become plain to the local police as well as to the DCU that he had contacts in the UK as part of Cerberus and that they were bent on damage to the State through 'Operation Trust' and maybe beyond. He had admitted as much in his diary stating that the murders of Ward and Müller had been almost peripheral, though of great importance to him. His main victim Ward had operated in the DCU (Deep Cover Unit) under the aegis of 'Operation Scorpion' dedicated to exposing this particular group, and this still existed. As indicated in Chapter 1, and being familiar with some aspects of Cerberus, Kiwi and Duke had been invited to participate in Operation Scorpion to locate the Cerberus HQ and track down their elusive leader Alpha. Now, given the possibility of dealing with aliens from a planet thought to be called Gonda their mission was likely to become even more hazardous.

❖ ❖ ❖

One of the names mentioned by Ward and Matlock had been a Colonel Andrew Burton DSO who was known to have links with para-military groups in the UK as well as mercenary activities overseas. Kiwi and Duke were now asked to find out as much as they could about his current activities and future plans by taking part in a weekend of corporate entertainment at a Castle that he would be attending with his team that was called 'Space Travel.'

The DCU had arranged for one of his team to have a 'slight accident' and for Kiwi to be the replacement. Similarly a ruse had been found to enlist Duke in another team. This meant that they had to be given new identities in the names of Sara Smith and Dirk Bond, together with a different address for him. They had also been given a profile on the Colonel which included links to Chemico in South Africa and historic connections with the RDF (Rhodesian Defence Force).

Profile Colonel Andrew Burton DSO

Director Chemico Inc and other quoted companies.
His 'Legacy Developers' subsidiary modernises historic sites
Honorary Colonel of 'Far Sight Rangers' with RDF links
Married to Annette (ex- Olympic medallist)
3 children at Oxford University
Military service in Africa (RDF) and the Middle East
He had been an officer in the 'Erin Rifles' in Irish Civil Rights
He is founder member of 'Vanguard' a political pressure group
He is chairman of the Maidenhead Masonic Lodge.
He is a member of SETI

Now it was up to them to expose the links between Matlock and Burton if any, and to uncover more about Cerberus and their allies. To do this they had to integrate inconspicuously into their teams.

The owners made a great fuss about the heritage of 'Castle Capulet' but much of this was contrived to attract the 'business market' and those interested in the intrigue that surrounded the likely resting place of the 'Holy Grail' (later publicised by 'The Da Vinci code.') Some claimed that there was much truth in oral and other records that pointed to a very significant past.

For now the pair had received their invitations and they were also given coloured badges and a team to join. Duke was excited when he came round to her flat before setting off for their assignment.

'Look at this activity programme.' he said,' just look Kiwi, there's Quad Bikes and 'Paint Ball shooting' and....'

She stopped him short here, 'This isn't a fun weekend,' she said, 'we've got to find out about Burton and it could be dangerous. Mind you,' she added, 'I'm rather looking forward to the 'Courtly Love Ball. See I'm to be in Burton's team and that could be dodgy for a number of reasons. You seem to have struck lucky, I see that you are in the 'Workers team,' and may the best man or woman win! Let's make love before we fight!'

There was no argument about that as a little role play then ensued, 'What chastity belt?'

The next day they arrived at the Castle and settled in. Other competitors had also arrived to be entertained by a small steel band on the patio. Champagne was served and a light buffet was available. Some played a friendly game of croquet to warm up for a competition that would take place later. Unfortunately two guests were taken ill during the evening, one was a Miss Bea Brunt and the other was Colonel Burton himself. Everyone was concerned especially Kiwi and Duke who were interested in his welfare for different reasons. A doctor had been called but put it down to food poisoning. However he also told everyone that he had taken blood samples and he hoped that this would reassure them, and that everyone would be told if there were any complications. Otherwise hygiene was to be the order of the day.

After the social get together on the Friday it was down to some serious business on Saturday from the word 'Go' because first up was to the Quad Bike race. Riders had choices of mounts and Kiwi chose the smallest. This was a Yamaha ATV50 but Duke chose the more powerful Comanche RLX450. This was not necessarily an advantage because the track was very slippery that day with a two mile course over fields, sand dunes and mud. Nothing had been left to chance with many professionals on hand to advise, guide and help the contestants but then it was up to the riders.

Engines revved and smoke billowed as the official raised his flag and they were off with a mad dash for the first bend. The ensuing muddle brought a number of bikes down including Duke. However the unexpected could always be expected and as the Quad Bikes had got underway there were soon reports that an Astronaut had crashed and now lay belly up in a pool of croaking frogs and toads. If it had been dawn it would have been their version of the Dawn Chorus, but it wasn't; in fact it was just getting dusk. The spaceman seemed almost to be one of them, as he lay with his legs and arms splayed out, his helmet and goggles at one extremity and his boots and gloves at the others. He lay just as he had fallen to earth. He was winded and it was some time before he had the strength to call for help.

'Help me! Somebody please help me. I'm stuck. I can't move! Help me!'

But no one came and other machines now whirled around him as dusk began to fall, their lights now glistening on the pool that was his prison. He continued to lie there surrounded by the many curious amphibians that seemed to give him their vocal support in his hour of need.

'Help me!' 'Croak, croak' 'Help' 'Croak, croak' 'Help!' 'Croak, croak.'

Still no one came until eventually one of the other machines stopped and a voice called out.

'Is that you sir?'

'Yes, thank God, who's that? Get me out of here whoever you are. I'm stuck fast.' he replied, gasping for breath.

'It's Mike here Sir. I'll have you out in a jiffy,' came the reply and he soon found himself being lifted out of the mud to the sound of much squelching and, it seemed, many objections from his new found friends.

And then he was out and on the bank, much relieved and feeling a bit silly.

'Thanks Mike, I'll buy you a drink when we get back to the Mother Ship!' he said with a laugh,

'Beam me up then Scotty!' Mike laughed, 'Right you are Captain Kirk, just hop in and we'll have you back in no time.' Mike's 4X4 eventually re started with a splutter leaving the crashed bike of 'Astronaut' Colonel Andrew Burton DSO in the pond.

They were soon on their way back to the hotel, and as they arrived he looked a forlorn figure as he walked into the hotel bar.

'Get me a drink for God's sake,' he called out to the assembled company, 'Can't you see I'm desperate?'

They were all there, all the teams, and not all were sympathetic. Some were curious but many, even his team- mates, were amused.

'What's it like up I space? Tell us about Deep Space Nine. What happened to your rocket boosters?'

Titters of laughter filled the room as more jokes continued until eventually someone placed a drink in his hand.

He smiled and raised the glass in a toast, 'Just you wait until tomorrow' he said, 'some of you buggers will be lucky to survive! You're not going to get me so easily next time. Now let's all raise our glasses to our new team member Sara (this was Kiwi's nom de plume) who finished a fantastic third.

This brought a round of applause and more drinks until it was time to change for the 'Courtly Love Ball' that was scheduled for later. Kiwi and Duke had joined their teams for the evening. Now they both had to go into the fitting room for an appropriate costume. She was to be Margaret Plantagenet and this was an important role. He was to be Long John Layabout, a dilettante and a rascal. She had to laugh, but on the serious side and being a resourceful young woman, she decided to use the Courtly Ball lady's changing room to her advantage. It seemed to be a likely place for gossip and maybe some useful tittle tattle about Burton.

Duke had the same idea and chose more mundane but potentially fruitful territory After all wasn't he Tom Cruise by any other name? His targets were the waitresses, and especially the room cleaning staff. 'Who knows what goes on behind closed doors at a Medieval Castle?' he thought, 'it brings new meaning to 'Upstairs Downstairs'.

From hustle to 'bustle' the changing room was chaotic with many questions about ties and drapes and drawers not to mention the CB referred to before. The most frequent question was 'Where does this go?' This suited Kiwi as she found herself ministering to ladies from all the teams, striking up friendly and quite intimate relations with them.

She soon established that her team mates Anne and Deidre were both PA's to the Colonel and not at all shy about what that entailed. Apparently they used him just as he used them. He gave them both the same job to do and then 'rewarded' the one who did it best. Nothing was ever said about these arrangements. Anne drove an Audi R8 V10 with a lovely cottage in the Cotswolds. Deidre owned a lovely 'gites' and a luxury cruiser on the French coast. They did not seem to be jealous of each other and chose not to portray themselves as rivals at all. Kiwi wasn't so sure.

They reminded her of the old song called 'Sisters' with these lyrics, 'God help the mister that comes between me and my sister and God help the sister that comes between me and my man.' However Deidre put it like this.

'He gets what he wants and we get what we want.'

Anne then made things a little clearer... 'we are also' very good friends' if you see what I mean, and it's us that share him, not the other way round.' she said.

Kiwi got the idea all right and smiled.

'Lucky you' she said, 'but tell me what's it really like working for him? I mean he seems to be very important and I suppose he's made enemies as well as friends along the way. Don't you get worried sometimes?' Anne and Deidre both laughed saying that their duties didn't include any 'business stuff' at all. They only had 'social' duties and they both laughed again.

'Why don't you join us for a nude Jacuzzi later Sara,' asked Deidre 'you've got a nice body I can see; and touch,' she added, placing a feathery fingerprint on Kiwi's near naked breast. She was of course halfway between costumes at this stage but she was careful not to back away too far. She might need them both later, but not for their agenda. It transpired that the Colonel's ADC was Tom Spooner, also in the team and she decided to use her wiles on him later.

Before their assignment Kiwi and Duke had also been given a briefing document that set out details of the scenario that they would find. It provided full details of the background to Burton's team as well as the others. Intelligence reports had suggested that he was about create an 'incident' that would undermine a new UN organisation aptly entitled IWS (International World Security) that was about to be announced. This group had a mandate to investigate unusual phenomena in the political, social and economic sphere but unusually it also included a brief to cover non terrestrial activity as well, basically meaning UFO's and the like. Such approval had been given in the past it is true, but investigations such as 'The assessment' in 1963 or 'Project Bluebook' in 1969 gave no definitive guidance, either because they had found out too little, or maybe too much to be divulged to a sceptical public who might be easily panicked. Others thought that the idea that Government sources would bother to investigate made the concept even more real and frightening. A panic had to be avoided, but even more importantly the secrets of the US military in a nuclear age had to be protected, and this had been the case ever since Roswell in 1947.

It had not been easy to get close to Cerberus in other ways so a social business weekend seemed to be a good opportunity for Kiwi and Duke to make some progress, especially as they already had some inside knowledge. Here is the document that they were given.

Team A

Space travel 'Chemicio Inc. Director Colonel Burton'. Team members Anne Lomax, Tom Spooner, Deidre Spencer and Louise Taggart (NB Kiwi/Sara took Louise's place in the team)

Profile. This American company has many interests in finance and petro chemicals as well as property development and has a controlling share in the development plans at Castle Capulet.
The MD of Chemico General Arthur Dallas (also an honorary member of the Far Sight Rangers) is named as unofficial 'advisor.'

Team B

Royalty 'Historic Association' Leader Simon Stewart Team members Sheila Stewart, Lance Albany, Teresa Albany

Profile The organisation is dedicated to protecting Medieval culture and has connections with the repositories of the Holy Grail.

Team C

Erin 'National Irish Association' Leader Sean Paisley Team members. Marie Mac Donnell, Tam Collins, Bea Brunt.

Profile The group support a United Ireland and are suspected of involvement in revenge killings following outrages in N. Ireland.

Team D

Workers 'Trade Unions United' Leader Fred Martin Team members Jan Mill, Liz Dodd and guest Dirk Bond (Duke)

Profile They are a Trotskyite group opposed to any form of Fascist tendency in Society and willing to oppose it by any means.

Meanwhile Duke had made considerable progress with the girl who came to tidy his room. Actually he came in to see her leaning over to fold back the covers and being 'The Duke' that he was, he was momentarily distracted from his objective.

He quickly turned away muttering. 'I'm sorry to trouble you Miss. Have you nearly finished in here?'

She smiled a very sweet smile over her shoulder. 'Un moment s'il vous plait,' she replied bending down and then back up again in one graceful movement. He tried to concentrate,

'Merci,' he said, 'So you are French are you. Do you like working here?'

'Mais Oui,' she replied, 'but I don't work here all the time. Madame Spencer, Deidre you know, she brings me when she goes to conferences like this and then I'm given a job to do and, as you say, keep my eyes and ears open'

He couldn't believe his luck. He had found a 'cuckoo in the nest' but could he make her talk? He began by placing a £5 note in her hand saying that this was just a sign of gratitude for looking after the room. She responded by placing a very brief kiss on his cheek adding that he must ask for her, Francoise, if he needed anything else. At first he was inclined to say nothing more but as she was leaving he said,

'How do you know Mme Spencer then. I thought that she lived here in the UK?'

'Perhaps you do not know Monsieur,' she said, 'but she has a place of her own at St Malo. That's where I live and I look after the house and the boat, and her,' she added with an enigmatic smile 'There is only a small staff, Madame Colbert is the administrator and Mr Joe Rome is head of security, I like them both very much. The Colonel has many private meetings there especially with General Dallas so we have to have tight security in the warehouse and especially in the boatyard, but it doesn't bother me. Now please, I must go. You are keeping me from my work' she said and left the room.

Just down the corridor was the Jacuzzi suite and enjoying an early dip were Anne and Deidre, taking it in turns to add a liquid ointment to their already slippery bodies.

'Here let me do that.' said Anne as Deidre lay holding the side bars like an outstretched swimmer. Anne began to massage her back only to hear a whisper in her ear. It was the Colonel.

'Shush.' he said and began to stroke Deidre's shoulders, down and down until the water flowed over her rounded cheeks. Only then did she turn and with a gasp and cried out.

'I might have known. I should recognise your touch by now.' but she didn't ask him to stop. And he didn't want to stop either as he invited the girls to help him with his costume for the night. He had arranged to be Henry VIII and soon he was as dashing and daring as his namesake; first with Anne and then with Deidre.

'I think we've broken the rules of courtly love.' he said.

He was indeed a very stately man, well over 6 feet tall with rather spindly arm and legs but fortunately with a big belly so he fitted the costume to a T. He only objected when the girls tried to fix a ruffle around his neck,

'Must leave room for manoeuvres,' he joked as he turned his head from side to side and almost to the rear while the rest of his body remained still.

'Trick I learnt in the army.' he said, 'very useful in love as well, would anyone care to try it?' but the girls were already making their escape.

There were others who didn't want to take the rules of courtly love seriously as well and Duke was one of them, but when he knocked on Kiwi's door and entered, he was in for a shock. She was not only in costume but fully in character as well. Seated demurely in a small chair, she held a breviary in one hand and a rosary in the other and now she looked up in horror at this vagrant who had disturbed her daily offices of prayer.

'What would you, varlet?' she exclaimed, 'Get ye hence before I call my attendant Sir John Thomas.'

He laughed. 'I can be your John Thomas if you wish my lady.' he said, stooping at her feet and offering a garter for her ankle.

The next thing he felt was a bang on the head with the rather substantial prayer book as she invoked the Latin phrase 'Dominus Vobiscum.' and turned back to her prayers.

Now he had no option but to leave muttering, 'Et cum spiritu tuo.' in the spirit of the thing.

He knew that his Catholic upbringing would come in useful one day.

So what is courtly love? The practice was believed to have begun in the princely courts of Aquitaine and Provence in the 11th century. Ladies were deemed to be pure and virtuous and sex had no part. Men were constrained by a series of rules namely. To attract by the eyes only, worship from afar, declare passionate devotion, accept virtuous rejection and undertake heroic deeds of valour.

There were stewards organised by the management to see that these rules were strictly adhered to in public but what about in private? This was Kiwi's chance to lure Tom Spooner (the Colonel's ADC), into some impropriety perhaps, and thereby gain some inside information. Tom had metamorphosed into Pope Clement but she knew a trick or two to 'ruffle his robes.' This would not be easy because we must remember that ladies were supposed to do nothing in the courting game except to flutter their eyelids. However, she added a refinement that she thought might be unobtrusive, but might just work. This was to tap her toes when she thought that Tom was looking at her and desist the moment that he did. His response of course was to bow rather nonchalantly but then to move a little closer. Yes, he had taken the bait and he was hooked. Now how would she land this poor fish?

She decided that a stroll to the orangery might provide the necessary fragrance to her plan so she made her way across the lawn and sat, with toes (yes those toes) twinkling in the fountain until she heard a sound behind her. She feigned horror of course begging him not to come closer but he did. It seems that he knew some of the rules too but also knew how to circumvent them. He did however stay his distance whilst moaning in that lovesick way that was expected. Now she had him.

'Stop all that medieval crap.' she said, 'Just come over here and kiss me.' (Well anything for the cause). However it was only a turned cheek that he was offered and a comforting pat on the back (Good Boy). Now she began her strategy which was to find out as much as she could about Burton and the organisations to which he belonged. She said that she was very pleased to have been co-opted into the team and wondered what the chances were of a permanent job of some sort like Anne and Deidre.

Tom laughed, 'I don't think there's much hope there,' he said, 'those two wouldn't want any permanent competition if you see what I mean.' He paused and then continued rather meaningfully,' But I can help if you'd like me to.' he said.

'Would you? Could you?' she said gushingly,' Just tell me a bit about what he does, you know, in business and in politics, even socially. I make a great Martini. And how do you fit in? People tell me that you are his right hand man so is there any chance I could get a job?

Questions put, flattery added; now wait for the recipe to boil.

Suffice to say that after about an hour she had enough to write a long report when she got back to her room. She had also decided that Tom was very close to his master but she couldn't decide if this was a matter of gender attraction or something else. Maybe Tom was the result of a much earlier fling with a much earlier Anne or Deidre she thought. She made these detailed notes for her file.

WPC Grant report on Tom Spooner ADC to Colonel Burton

I spoke to Tom Spooner for some time to elucidate some facts about Burton and his organisations and plans. He told me that his own background was in chemical research and computers and that he was now proud to be ADC to the Colonel. He told me that the Colonel was buying another property in St Malo and was thinking about moving there, maybe with Deidre. 'But don't tell Ann. She'd kill him.' he had said. He confirmed that a base existed in St Malo. Meetings were held there and it was also used for storage but he didn't say what was stored there. He called it Base2 but added that there were other important bases in every corner of the globe and that there would soon be more 'to protect our interests' he said.

I had to make him believe that I was just interested in him and his work for Burton's company, so to allay any suspicions that he might have, I made sympathetic noises about the 'state of the world' and how things are always better with firm leadership. I told him that I had friends in both Burton's 'Vanguard' and in the Territorial Army who were also members of the 'Far Sight Rangers.' He seemed pleased with this and gradually he began to tell me more about his plans. I told him that 'your secrets are safe with me.' and pressed him a little further about what ambitions the Colonel had. He alluded to 'Operation Trust' that was ready to go after months of planning and said that everyone would know about it very soon.

It'll be headline news and I'm the one who planned it he had said proudly. I tried to get more details but all he said was 'Credibility.' That's what keeps governments in power and if it's lost people look around for a reliable leader and we have one. Take Egypt for example. They get rid of a military dictatorship, don't like what they get instead and then bring it back. You might remember that once Hitler was in power he introduced the 'Enabling Act' giving him carte blanche from then on.

There's something to be said for that if you're in power but brown shirt bully tactics and Mosley's black shirt marches won't do today in this far more subtle world, so it's the democratic route for us, and then we'll see. The Colonel already has at least 300 MP's in his pocket and he hasn't used them up to now, but if there was an expose of Government ministers and their finances what then? You'd be surprised what clever computing can do and we have the very thing at our base, ready to go. I may be only a small peg 'Delta' in Cerberus' he said.' but the Colonel's a 'Gamma' and that's as big as you can get apart from 'Beta' who visits sometimes, and of course our beloved leader 'Alpha.' No one is exactly sure who he is or where he is. Mind you I'm not sure that even he's top of the tree when it comes to our allies. They seem to call the shots as far as I can see. He confirmed that the Colonel had enemies even in some of the teams here at the Castle and yes, he 'sometimes' had to strike first if there was an immediate threat, hinting that someone at the castle had to be warned off at least. He added that it didn't do to mess with the Colonel. 'It's as if he's got eyes in the back of his head,' he said, 'and sometimes I think that he really has.' he said. He'd also heard of Matlock but did not know if he was at the St Malo base. I sounded very suitably impressed and of course I'd seen the name of Cerberus before in Matlock's files but I didn't let on. And he'd made a comment about partners that I didn't understand yet. I also noted his comment about Burton's extreme vigilance, and wondered if this was a hallmark of the Cerberus organisation. In other words both Matlock and Burton had shown signs of a kind of paranoia and persecution, perhaps a little like the hunted rather than the hunters. This was another puzzle but I decided to leave it for now. I told Tom that it must all be very exciting and I'd love to get involved.

He seemed to get the wrong idea and asked me to kiss him, but I said that I had herpes. To my relief he soon backed off.

I have sent this report to Franks and Tucker marked Top Secret.

❖ ❖ ❖

Despite the tragedy to Bea Brunt the organisers decided to go ahead with the croquet competition the next day. Teams were given handicaps (bisques) and more costume was encouraged, this time in the Regency style of Beau Brummel or Jane Austen. This accorded with the era in which the game was introduced to England as 'paille maille' after the famous Pall Mall in London where street games were played by the King.

This time the Colonel's team 'Space Travel' were the winners but were disqualified after a steward's enquiry found them guilty of unfair tactics in their use of 'roquet' with 'undue aggression.' This incensed Burton who claimed that he had evidence that others had deployed illegal methods in the Quad Bike Race. To make his case he produced an engineer's report stating that the fuel in his tank contained sugar, and this naturally has stalled the engine and led to his crash. The organisers were taken aback by this so they re-instated 'Space Travel' as winners of the Croquet. Burton accepted this compromise with a warning.

'Just make sure you don't mess with me at Paint Ball tomorrow.' he said.

This last remark turned out to be a prophetic one because, after a day in the woods with teams splattering one another in the coloured paint of their own team, everyone gathered back at the command post to make a tally of winners and losers, but someone was missing. Just then, and as the teams were checking for any absent comrades, a small group of stretcher bearers came slowly into sight. A body lay on the stretcher with one arm outstretched and dragging along the ground.

'Stand back.' an official called out, 'It's Colonel Burton. He's been shot and he's dead I'm afraid. We're going to take him back to the castle and call the police. Has someone got a coat to cover him up?'

It was General Dallas, the observer from Burton's team who stepped forward with his coat and bent to cover the body, but as he did so he stopped and looked up at the crowd.

'He's been shot by one of us.' he exclaimed,' His chest is covered in red and it's not all blood. He's been hit by a red paint ball and that's the colour for 'Space Travel'

There were many gasps from the onlookers of course but stronger sentiments from Tom, Anne and Deidre who now all turned to their new team mate.

'You crafty bastard Sara,' said Tom, 'I made friends with you but you only wanted information. You got it and now you've killed him.'

He was crying and had to be held back by others in the crowd until Deidre spoke up

'I suggest that we hand the little tart over to the police when they arrive. They can deal with her.' she said.

Kiwi looked despairingly over at Duke but he had rather wisely turned away at this point so she just said,

'I'll talk to the police and I'll talk to anyone but all this has nothing to do with me.'

She stood back and eventually the body was taken back to the castle and onward to hospital for further examination.

At the police station she was put under caution by a local Detective Inspector unknown to her and the questions began. She was worried for a number of reasons; firstly could she and should she maintain her cover identity and secondly, if she didn't shoot the Colonel, which of his team mates did? Might it have been General Dallas himself? She and Duke had been instructed not to divulge the existence of 'Operation Scorpion' that Ward had been involved in because Franks and Tucker thought that they had some chance of 'beheading Cerberus' as they put it, if absolute secrecy was maintained. 'Trust no one, not even your local police' they had been told, but now Kiwi was in their hands and she was taken to the police station and detained. However she was not the only one in a sense, because all competitors were instructed to stay at the castle for at least a week or until charges were brought.

This left Duke to pursue the enquiries that he had in mind, but meanwhile he sat miserably in his room and tried to make sense of the whole affair. He was ruffled by a sense of injustice that Kiwi had been arrested. He knew only too well that 'persons in power', be they police or otherwise, always held the trump hand. He had seen this so many times in Mississippi during the Civil Rights movement and before, a time when police were KKK and the KKK were the police in some areas. Could it be the same here in the UK? He prayed that it wasn't so (yes he still prayed in extremis) and then he took a pencil and scribbled some notes on the back of an envelope. 'What had happened to Bea Brunt? Was it simply food poisoning and if so, why wasn't the Colonel more seriously affected? Tom Spooner had told Kiwi that Burton had enemies at the castle and a particular person had to be dealt with. Who were his enemies and why? Check up on each group and each individual. Was there any truth in Burton's assertion that his Quad Bike was 'spiked' and if so, who was to blame? What went on in St Malo and what was stored there? Was it also the refuge of Inspector Matlock and what were his plans for the future?'

The first of these was soon answered by news that a post mortem report on Bea Brunt revealed massive doses of arsenic whereas a similar one carried out on Burton revealed only trace elements. Duke drew the conclusion that this was probably the work of Tom Spooner who had told Kiwi that he was a research chemist. The difference between a fatal dose and a benign one could be extremely marginal, so a special kind of skill would be called for if different quantities were to be administered, one fatal and the other harmless. Spooner had it and he had opportunity as well, even though his doses were bound to lead to suspicions if questions were asked. However he obviously did not allow for the Colonel's death and post mortem as well as Bea Brunt's. But what was the motive?

Obviously Tom was acting under orders from Burton so why was Bea killed, and were others in danger as well even now? He decided to ingratiate himself with Team Erin to find out.

Meanwhile Kiwi had been placed in a cell at the local police station to await the arrival of Divisional Detective Inspector Margaret Power. Kiwi did not know her and she prayed that Power did not know her either and would not recognize her from meetings that they may have attended together. She knew that she would have to come clean eventually but, after her bad experience with Matlock she was not prepared to trust anyone on face value. Moreover she was aware that Burton's organisation reached into the highest echelons in society so why not the police?

Eventually she was brought from her cell into a rather comfortable room in which there was a rather comforting log fire, but that was the only comfort that she received there as Power began a long harangue at her expense. She said that Sara had been shown to be an opportunistic, immoral and jealous tart. Kiwi recognised the term used by Deidre at the castle so she knew that the Inspector had been well briefed by Burton's subordinates. She therefore extrapolated that Anne and Deidre had probably said more about the changing room and that Tom had mentioned the Orangery. Details no doubt were of their own making, but being forewarned helps in being forearmed she thought, and she could modify their versions to her own advantage.

'Now please don't waste my time Miss Smith. May I take it that Smith is your real name? Perhaps it's actually that common surname used for what are euphemistically called 'dirty weekends.' Well this was certainly one of those, one way or another wasn't it? Well for now I'll call you Sara, taking it that that is your real name but I suggest that you tell us exactly what happened in the wood and why you killed Colonel Burton. Maybe it was an accident and if so you'd better tell me now or it will be much worse for you later.'

At this point Kiwi decided to say nothing further and, if she was not to be charged at once she demanded to be released, stating that it was her intention to stay on at the Castle for the time being. Although it might be a serious charge there was no record of any previous charges so she was released 'on her own cognizance' for the time being.

'But don't even think about leaving.' muttered the Inspector as she departed.

❋ ❋ ❋

It was 6pm and back at the Castle she quickly arranged for Duke to come to her room, making sure that he was not seen. She was in his arms as soon as he walked in and they stayed that way until dawn. She seemed to have forgotten that he had been a worthless varlet just a few days ago, but he remembered that she'd been a haughty mistress, and he rather liked the idea as he bent her to his will. At least that was his perception, but in reality it was the opposite.

It might be true to say that she had anticipated his every move.

The next day he said that he was surprised that she seemed to be taking it so well but she just smiled.

'Look at it like a game of chess,' she said, 'It's stalemate at present and the King may have tucked himself away with the help of his castle but two pawns can smoke him out if they're smart enough,'

He smiled and gave her a kiss.

'I'm sure that's true, but you don't act much like a pawn do you?' he said with a grin, 'so let's get on with the evidence then.'

Now she purred appreciatively.

It was good to have him on her side as she remembered Frau Müller's words about her husband, 'I just loved him you see' she had said.

Now, was she herself falling in love after all? But then another thought about love and loyalty that worried her flashed into her mind.

'The Burtons were married with 3 children,' she said, 'do you think that she had a clue about her husband's affairs?'

He thought for a moment then replied, 'Probably not, or maybe she just didn't want to know.'

❄❄❄

Due to her present circumstances Kiwi obviously could not do much about questioning the members of each team. She was not exactly confined to her room but there were many whispers when she left it, so for now she immersed herself in the internet to see what it might reveal. Duke had decided to start with the Irish 'Erin' team who were still in mourning of course 'and no one mourns better than the Irish especially with a drop of whisky' he thought, 'I think a malt or two might help to loosen tongues quite a bit.'

He knew that he was a 'cool dude' with a broad southern accent but this didn't go down well with everyone. On balance he thought it might be more appropriate to be less obvious in order to gain the attention of Miss Marie MacDonnell of the Erin team. He therefore took a seat in a quiet corner in the lounge and began to read a travel magazine. She was seated just a few chairs away and was wistfully looking out of the window. Her colleagues were already at the bar, it being just after breakfast, and they were talking quite loudly to the members of the Royalty team so he decided that tea and sympathy might do the trick with Marie. He therefore abandoned Plan A and moved over to her table.

'I'm sorry to trouble you Miss MacDonnell, I'm Dirk Bond' he said, 'I wonder if you would like to share a pot of tea on the balcony. It's getting quite noisy in here don't you think?'

She was quick to agree and they were soon seated outside in the sunshine. She was about forty and a very attractive woman in jeans and a modest fleece because it was a little chilly.

'That's better,' he said, 'I suppose your team mates have to let off steam somehow'

She made a disapproving sound saying, 'The poor dear girl's not yet in her grave and look at them.'

He sympathised adding that it couldn't be easy for her either. 'I warned her,' she said, 'Just because you recognised him you didn't need to let him know that you did, I told her. I'm positive that Burton and his gang got her killed and I wish I could prove it.'

Duke was pleased with this information as far as it went but he knew that he'd have to be careful about being too inquisitive, so he said no more except to suggest a stroll maybe before afternoon tea. Miss Marie MacDonnell was pleased to accept his invitation to meet him at 4.30.

Meanwhile Kiwi was lying comfortably in bed propped up against the pillows with her laptop (on her lap) and a note pad to hand. Her first target was Bea Brunt's group which had been given the name 'Erin' for the activities at the castle. The organiser's handbook did give some further details such as the names of the team members as well as an 'official entry title' and an address.

In this case it was 'The National Irish Association' based in de Valera Street Dublin. She 'googled' all of these and established that the group claimed to be a 'social outlet' for those caught up in or harmed by 'The Troubles.' regardless of their religious affiliations. She noted this clever use of words, because although the terms of reference seemed benign, there were two obvious omissions, namely 'political and national' that some would say were even more significant. Various sites on the web revealed some activity here and there but nothing to gain her attention. It was the same story when she researched the members of the team. There were some suspicions of IRA activity but nothing seemed to be substantiated. She therefore turned to Burton's activities on the Island and came across a few disturbing incidents involving his 'Erin Rifles' brigade. They seemed to operate much in the style of the 'Black and Tans' of an earlier era but, although much was said, nothing was proven and there was no enthusiasm on the part of the UK Government or Stormont to reign them in. Maybe that was a link to Bea Brunt.

She was dozing off in her room when there was a familiar tap at the door. Somehow she sensed that it was Duke even through a large wooden door with no glass. She wondered what that kind of sixth sense meant. Could it be another sign of love? She quickly chastised herself for such 'daft' thoughts but nonetheless threw her arms around him. A little later on she relayed her findings from the internet and he promised to probe these further with Bea Brunt.

'I'm also going to have a look round the sheds and garages to see if I can pick up a clue about Burton's 'sugar-petrol notion.' I think that there might be evidence out the back somewhere' he said.

'Take care darling.' she responded, and then wondered if that was the first time she had ever (ever) said it and really meant it.

True to his word he found his way to the sheds, stables and garages that were at the back of the castle and he was soon rummaging about in all the material of diverse character. There seemed to be two specific areas to do with a new 'Development programme,' the first was a pile of dusty gargoyles and the like probably destined for a garden centre and thence to an upwardly mobile family's moated garden perhaps. The second were new building materials ready to go when the order was given. These piles of bricks and stone were protected by a large fence with hoardings that stated 'LEGACY DEVELOPERS' Underneath the sign it gave a projected stating date of July that year. It now being June he made a mental note to ask members of the 'Royalty' team with whom he'd had some conversations, if planning permission had actually been granted. Everyone knew of their opposition to developments of this kind. They had a website and even eminent lawyers to represent their views, and they also lobbied widely.

A third kind of heap (or heaps) existed, and this was the ephemera from the many corporate events that had been held throughout the year including this one. There had been Horse Shows, Antique fairs, Battles such as 'Bosworth' or 'Naseby' (never mind the historical detail), Car and Motor Exhibitions and many others, so there was much to look at.

He nearly found himself diverted by all this interesting material and had to bring himself back to his objective, namely Burton's sugar-petrol. There were the usual group of staff and visitor's cars including (it must be) Burton's Rolls Royce, number plate AB 123 of course. Unfortunately there was little to go on here except for a group of small petrol cans in the back of a Toyota pick-up with the HA logo of the Historical Association on the door. This may not have been suspicious in itself but the cans were numbered 1-6, as if they contained different octanes or mixes of bio fuels or diesel, OR, he wondered, sugar-petrol. He had not come prepared to take samples so he decided to come back after dark and take some. On his return he reported what he had found to Kiwi and asked her to do background checks on the HA as she had done before. She was feeling fed up and asked him to stay but he said that he couldn't.

'Got a date with Miss MacDonnell' he said just managing to avoid the book that she threw across the room.

'Men!' she exclaimed in mock fury, 'You're all the same.'

As he made his way to his assignation with Marie he stopped at the bar for an aperitif, noting that Stewart and Albany from the Royalty team were there as usual. He soon led the conversation around to the proposed 'modernisation' of the castle asking if it would be started soon.

'Over my dead body.' responded Stewart.

'But as it happens,' added Albany, 'it'll be over his. But we don't think that it will go ahead at all now. He was the driving force you know so we're well rid.'

Duke smiled and said that he was glad as well.

'We Yanks just love all that old history stuff you know, the Bloody Tower and all that.'

He noted with a smile that this did not amuse Stewart and Albany at all. They looked deadly serious.

The meeting with Marie MacDonnell started well enough but it was a bit like an internet date in which a certain amount of sparring was going on behind the scenes. She was wondering why he wanted to meet her and he was trying not to tell her so it was small talk for most of the time as she told him about her family who still lived near Strabane, and that he should visit sometime. However she said that after a degree in Social Sciences at Belfast University she stayed in the City to work in education.

'A pity,' she said, 'but I felt that I could make more of a contribution to the cause from there.'

Duke knew what she meant about 'the cause' being that of Irish nationalism of course, but he asked just the same to enhance his status as just another parochial American. In fact he was very sympathetic to the Irish Republican cause, and like many Americans there was Irish blood in his family on his mother's side. Her mother had come from Cork and on marrying a British soldier during the early 'troubles' of the 1920's she had been forced to leave Ireland for ever. Soon afterwards they had taken a Blue Star Liner to the States (not the Titanic!) carrying with them a deep sense of injustice that had pervaded the family from then on. Together with his father's experiences in World War Two, it was hardly surprising that Duke wore his heart on his sleeve.

For now Marie was happy to fill in some background, but he detected a sudden defence mechanism kicking in when he asked a question about Bea.

'You were good friends with her I suppose,' he said, 'and you said that she had 'recognised Burton.' Do you know what she meant exactly?'

She looked at him quizzically.

'I think I've said too much already,' she replied, 'but it was all in the papers at the time. Just look up 'Ballybofey' in the Herald and you'll find out'.

She had changed. The warm Marie was now the strict school teacher and she stood up to leave.

'Thank you for the tea,' she said, 'it's getting late now so I'm afraid that I have to go. Good night.'

It was only 6pm and he had blown it. However he did have one crumb of comfort that he would ask Kiwi to investigate later, and he could do with some comfort himself he thought after the mock book throwing incident. On returning to their room he told her about Marie's comments and Kiwi duly looked up the area mentioned on the internet. It revealed a chilling story in which a brigade of irregular British forces alleged to be the Erin Rifles attacked the small hamlet of Ballybofey.

A young girl had been raped but no charges were ever brought.

'I reckon that poor girl was Bea Brunt,' said Kiwi, 'you told me that she lived in Strabane which is only a few miles from there. She'd never forget a face that did that to her. She'd probably never seen him since and couldn't resist telling him what she remembered. She had also probably said that she would tell the world so she had to be killed to protect his reputation'.

Duke agreed adding that, although this made perfect sense it didn't go very far to explain who killed HIM. Maybe one of her team mates in revenge, but he agreed that there were many other possibilities.

Now he was ready to go out in the dark. He had 6 empty Tonic bottles in his bag as he headed for the stables planning to take his samples. Unfortunately the security lights came on as he approached the buildings so he was forced to stay in the shadows before he eventually reached the pick-up. He stepped carefully to the tailgate and, opening his first tonic bottle he peered inside in the semi darkness. The bottles were gone! He looked around. Had he gone to the right vehicle? Yes he had, no doubt about it, and then the penny dropped. He had foolishly spoken to Stewart and Albany in the bar about the development and they had smelt a rat. He was disappointed, but this very fact seemed to prove that the Royalty team were implicated in the sugar-petrol fiasco and if that, why not the shooting of Burton in the woods?

He couldn't answer this so he decided to ask Kiwi to find out more about the Historic Association, and after some research it turned out to be more of a masonic association than an historical one in the broadest sense.

In Masonry one is allowed to have one's own Lodge and this is called the appendant tradition and the Stewart/Albany Lodge was indeed Capulet Castle. Even more important than their links to other so called lodges, they were also part of the ancient Merovingian tradition who jointly claimed to possess the Holy Grail. This was said to be in the form of natural wealth secreted away by the Knights Templar, but for some it was a much more valuable Holy Grail in the existence of documents that proved that a family line existed from Jesus Christ to a living relative today.

The 'Guardians of Knowledge' such as Stewart and Albany would do anything to protect their inner sanctums. These had been especially important in Bristol since 1137 AD when land grants by King Stephen/Queen Matilda began many centuries of influence until 1307 AD when the order was suppressed in France and beyond. 'The Templars have something to do with everything.' said Umberto Eco in his book 'Foucault's Pendulum.' It is not surprising therefore that the Templars would not give up their heritage easily. Indeed they would use every legal means to avoid change, but their commitment to their oaths as guardians meant that other methods might also be necessary. The Colonel was known to be a mason as well, so any hostility to him on their part would probably be because of the threat to their own particular lodge at Capulet Castle. He was the driving force in the development of their cherished sanctuary for profit. But could that be reason enough for murder?

It was fortunate that Kiwi had completed her research on the HA because the next morning she was told to come to the police station and to 'bring an overnight bag.'

Naturally she was upset and pleaded with Duke to double his efforts to find out who murdered Burton.

'If we don't find out soon our cover will be blown and we'll never find out about the Colonel's death or what Cerberus is up to. We'll never find out about St Malo either or whether Matlock is there. And I forgot to remind you that I'm just about to be charged with murder.' she pleaded.

He understood all right and took her arm, 'Don't worry darling,' he said, 'I'll have you out of there in no time and I'll find the killer before the weekend and that's a promise.'

She did feel a little reassured but had she heard right? Had he called her darling? Well that was a start, and definitely worth going to prison for she thought.

And so the questioning began. Inspector Power now had a man with her, one of those men Kiwi recognised as a 'plain clothes detective' of one type or another, and she knew it would not be long before her identity was revealed whether she liked it or not. Power began,

'Let me tell you straight Sara that we think you killed Burton. As I said before you might not have meant to, but you were jealous of the other girls and Burton had turned you down.'

Kiwi couldn't help smiling to herself. The idea of Burton turning down sexual advances seemed amusing, but she said nothing.

The man now spoke up,

'Put it another way Miss. You may know that the Paint Ball competition only allowed for two competitors from each team at a time. Yours was the last group to compete consisting of you and the Colonel, Lance and Teresa Albany, Sean Paisley and Tam Collins and lastly Liz Dodd and,' here he paused and looked at her closely, 'your very good friend Dirk Bond. You'll note that we've done our homework. Let's say a little bird called Francoise gave us quite a story.'

The Inspector now took up the questioning again and re-iterated her earlier point about an accident or maybe Bond was involved.

'He didn't like you flirting with the Colonel so you exchanged paint guns and he did the shooting. Is that how it went?'

Kiwi now decided it was time to go on the offensive. If they knew about Duke it wouldn't be long before both their cover stories were exposed.

'All right you've got me there, but that's what these 'junkets' are all about isn't it? I bet you have some fun at police conferences. Anyway, what was to stop anyone sneaking into the woods, even though they were not in that team? It could be someone who lives in the neighbourhood. It could be anybody really couldn't it?' The moment she said all this she wished that she hadn't.

'And how would you know about that?' asked the Inspector quietly. 'It sounds like you know all about the police force, how we behave and how to solve a crime.'

Kiwi now back- tracked,

'Just common sense I suppose.' she muttered, 'how would I know?'

She was relieved when they moved on to other matters and even more so when they said that she would not be detained 'for now' but once more 'stay at the castle, we will want to speak to you again'

'Phew,' she thought, 'I hope Duke is making progress, we may not have much time left.'

❀❀❀

He had indeed been getting on with it. There was only one team that he and Kiwi had not looked at and that was his own 'Trade Unions.' Actually he'd been getting on with them well before the incident in the woods, he liked them and they liked him so there weren't any real suspicions on either side. They thought that he was a cowboy all right, but more Bob Hope than Dirty Harry. Naturally he encouraged this persona and made a mental note to try it out with Kiwi at a later date when the case was over. He had concluded that the group were more idealist than activist as they chatted to him about issues such as Cuba and the Pentagon Papers for example. Moreover Jan was pregnant with Fred's baby and Liz was still at college. Most unlikely conspirators he decided.

By now Kiwi was back and looking forward to some stress relief with Duke. She took her time in the shower and re-appeared with fair hair. She added a white basque and accessories as well as heels and then lay on her back, contented yet expectant.

He was pleasantly surprised to see 'that beautiful blonde' on the bed again and decided to leave his cowboy image out of it for now. This morsel was definitely deserving of the 'tender touch' and lonesome cattle ranchers aren't especially good at that. But was she secretly playing the part of Francoise to keep him up to the mark he wondered?

Once more she knew how to please him physically whilst always leaving a question in his mind. This time he wondered if she suspected a liaison with Francoise, but he didn't want to spoil the moment(s) by asking. After all nothing HAD happened so why did he have a guilty conscience? Actually he knew that it had been a close run thing, so guilt was in order after all.

Hours went by and energies were renewed time and again, but their contentment was eventually broken when a note was pushed through the door with a very loud clonk. It was addressed to 'All members of the MM '(Management Motivation) group and they were to meet in the courtyard after breakfast with a view to a joint visit to the woods where Burton was killed. Police Inspector Power had requested this in the hope that the scene might jog someone's memory or even 'cause them to confess.' the note said. Kiwi had a good idea about who she was referring to in that respect, but she also welcomed an opportunity to visit the scene of the crime which had been staked out and guarded closely for days.

The teams met as arranged. It seemed fitting that rain was falling and that it was drizzling off the noses of the horrifying gargoyles that supervised each and every corner of the castle as if they all had colds. Duke thought that they resembled many Hindu gods and goddesses but the gargoyles seemed to have no redeeming features at all. They were not only ugly and gruesome but also threatening and frightening. He reflected that this was the 'other side of the coin' in the eleventh century to the courtly love espoused in those days but then again, maybe it was fear that drove piety. Not so far different from today he was tempted to reflect when religious, political or other groups will always use an element of fear to attract followers. Sometimes this fear is identified with a danger to a set of values or norms, but it may also be harnessed to upset those very same values as in the case of Cerberus. He knew that they seemed to be bent on a new world order that would exist after the overthrow of the old, and then that a new social and racial purity would be ushered in by force if necessary. He knew all this, but now began to wonder whether he and Kiwi had made any progress at all on their primary mission to identify Alpha and find Hades itself. No they hadn't and they hadn't made any progress on Gonda either.

So Burton was dead but that only seemed to make closer scrutiny less likely. Fortunately, he reassured himself, there was Tom Spooner's information about St Malo to go on and that could still lead somewhere, and Francoise had also said that it was important. He resolved to follow up on these as soon as possible, but with Kiwi under suspicion for murder there was little to be done at present.

He fantasised that Cerberus seemed to have the gargoyles on their side as well, and how do you fight a gargoyle he wondered, waving an imaginary sword at a large leering head with clawed hands for ears.

'Whatever are you doing?' asked Kiwi, somewhat amused but also concerned that he was 'losing it.'

He just smiled and said,

'I'm just practising at being St George.' he said, 'come let's catch up with the others.'

'Yes, let's do that,' she said, 'I see that the 'Inspector Power Dragon' is leading the way. I bet you don't fancy taking her on. She's fiery all right and she's a bit like a gargoyle.'

He smiled,

'So you didn't exactly hit it off down at the station then.' he said.

She shook her head. 'You could say that but watch out,' she replied, 'she may be a dragon but she's not a daft dragon.'

The small group soon arrived at the woods and the Inspector gave them precise instructions on how to behave, especially to keep to the paths and not to disturb anything.

'My officers have gathered any relevant material already,' she said, 'and when we get back you will see two tables set out in the billiard room, one with Burton's effects and the other with any items we've found in the vicinity that probably don't mean very much. Now follow me.'

The group obediently followed her lead until they reached a small clearing where she stopped.

'This is where he was shot,' she said standing before a tree, 'shot in the chest, close up as if he knew his killer. Evidence from ballistics estimated the gun at not more than 2 feet away. It was a .22 Smith and Wesson, not a usual gun at all, more a collector's item I'd say. Actually we didn't need them to tell us the make because the gun was found dropped at his feet, but with no fingerprints so we can't absolutely rule out suicide.'

Now the crowd began to buzz with all kinds of comments and possibilities but the Inspector stopped them.

'If you haven't got anything useful to say,' she said, 'just keep your opinions to yourself. You may have been told that a stranger, a man in a dark hat and coat was spotted in the wood, but it is all open countryside, so he really might just have been a local man walking a dog, although a dog wasn't seen. Anyway we're looking into it. We'll go back now and look at the evidence then maybe I'll allow a little speculation.'

Most team members gathered around 'Burton's' table so Kiwi and Duke wandered over to the other one with two or three others. There were crisp packets and condoms (fortunately sealed in plastic bags) as well as betting slips and a bus ticket, cigarette stubs and packets, not forgetting one pair of 'ladies' briefs.

'Not much to go on here,' he joked 'just a normal day at the office.'

Not everyone thought that this was funny in the circumstances but she couldn't help smiling. Soon the other table cleared and they went over to see what was there. Burton had been a meticulous man so his effects were what one might expect in the way of a mobile phone, a diary and a wallet but there was also a small plain folder that Kiwi thought worth investigating.

You could say that it was a hunch but with Kiwi it was always more likely to be a dead cert. This was not a 'skill' as such, nor was it based on experience although these attributes might be contributory. No, her flair was pure intuition and where that came from no one seemed to know. She called Duke over and asked him to 'divert' the Inspector while she removed the folder.

'I'm going to take it to the 'Ladies' she said, 'check it out and then put it back. It's up to you to see that no one notices.'

He could think of only one thing and that was to faint. As he lay on the floor he thought it was a pity that people didn't care for each other like this all the time. It nearly always took a crisis for someone to show that they cared. Not so much cared, as simply noticed, he conjectured. How many times do we pass others without even saying hello?' he thought. Then as hands lifted him gently and tried to put water to his lips he wondered if he was dying and how pleasant it was.

'Brandy,' he croaked and soon this libation was added to the rather bland water that was being administered. Could he keep his attendants busy for a little longer? With this in mind he got to his feet rather unsteadily only to fall again into the rather unwelcoming arms of 'the dragon.' She seemed to be the exception to the Good Samaritan syndrome as she brushed him away in such distaste that he fell to the ground again. The process of recovery began once more, but soon between gasps and groans and half shut eyelids he saw Kiwi placing the folder back.

'Funny,' he said to his well- wishers, 'I'm feeling much better now.'

She soon moved to his side and took up ministering duties whilst whispering.

'I've got some details. There's a delivery note to a place called St Servan/copy to the City, and a booking for the cross channel ferry to St Malo for two and reservations for a Mr and Mrs Bellamy at the 'Grand Hotel des Thermes' on the 'Grand Plage de Sillon' next week. There's also a brochure that gives more details about 'this resplendent venue known for its Spa facilities and 'Aquatonic' pool'. I rather fancy it myself. That should put the cat amongst Burton's little chickens don't you think? Let's talk later.'

He nodded, but as they were looking through some of the other items on the two tables, suddenly she seemed to freeze on the spot. He was right by her side and put his arm around her,

'What is it?' he said, 'you look as if you've seen a ghost or a gargoyle.'

She was staring at the bus ticket that had been found among all the other general rubbish. She now picked it up carefully and showed it to him.

'What do you see?' she said. He took the ticket and studied it for a moment and then said,

'It's a National Bus Company ticket for a few days ago. It's from Windsor to Bristol and it must be Burton's ticket. See it's got his name on it.'

She smiled her best 'knowing' smile.

'Whose name?' she asked,

'Burtons,' he replied. 'Look it says 'Passenger A. Burton'. It's his all right.'

Now she was triumphant.

'So who does the Rolls Royce in the garage belong to then? Is it yours?' she added cheekily.

He was speechless. He literally couldn't speak for a few moments. He felt like escaping in a faint once more but said.

'So what does it all mean then? Just what are you getting at?' he said.

She was glad to put him out of his misery.

'It says 'Passenger - A. Burton' but I bet it's not Andrew but Annette Burton, his wife. She's travelled down in secret, then dressed as a man in the woods and killed him. Do you remember that she was an Olympic medallist? Well my guess is that she was in the Bisley shooting team. We can check it out later or the Inspector can. Now Mrs B is probably at home having tea and scones with friends. She must have finally had enough of his philandering and maybe she got to know of his latest plan with a certain Mrs Bellamy, That sounds like Deidre to me and maybe it was Anne who told Mrs Burton out of jealousy.'

He was listening thoughtfully and replied.

'You're in enough trouble with the dragon already and if you are seen to be on the ball in this she'll be even more suspicious. If we want to continue our work for Operation Scorpion you'd better let me report it and then I can take the credit as well.' he added with a smile.

'Good idea,' she replied, 'she's over there. Good luck. I'm going for a shower and a lie down. Maybe you'd care to join me later if she hasn't burnt you to a frazzle. I like it hot but not that hot.'

Duke immediately found the Inspector and pointed out the details and significance of the bus ticket and she had to agree (rather grudgingly) that it was very suspicious to say the least.

She admitted that 'his' theory about someone else using the ticket was quite plausible in the circumstances, and confirmed that the police would investigate all aspects in detail. She said that he would find out what the outcome was in due course.

Actually it only took a few days for the papers to print that a Mrs Burton had pleaded guilty to the murder of her husband Colonel Andrew Burton DSO, and that a trial date had been set.

❊❊❊

There was little time for Kiwi and Duke to celebrate their success before they were soon called to the makeshift offices of the CIA in the Estate Agents aptly named 'Land of Home and Glory.'

In a back room Hilary Tucker from the CIA was there as well as an assortment of officials including Tom Franks from MI5 and a Chief Inspector Waterhouse from Scotland Yard. Hilary made brief personal introductions and then moved on to what she called 'the business in hand.'

She said that they had worked hard but nothing much had yet been achieved. Kiwi thought that this was very unfair but said nothing.

'The point is this,' said Hilary, 'Matlock got one of us and now we, that is Mrs Burton, has got one of them. It's a draw but we need to be ahead and fast. If what Spooner told Jo is true there might still be hell to pay in a very short while. We need to find out more about these power stations as well as the significance of water in their calculations. Perhaps most important of all are the references to 'allies.' Just who are they referring to? I've therefore asked Tom Franks here and Scotland Yard to authorise her to go undercover to St Malo. Naturally we in the CIA would like Duke to go as well but there is a problem. Either of you might be recognised by Burton's four accomplices over here, so we're going to arrest them and keep them incommunicado on suspicion of terrorist offences. We may be able to hold them for a couple of weeks but perhaps not much more, so you'll have to get results damn quick Any questions?'

Kiwi and Duke looked at each other and then spoke in unison, not by design but because the same thought had crossed their minds,

'Four?' they both exclaimed.

Then Kiwi continued,

'Why four?' she said. 'there was Tom and Anne and Deidre but who else?'

Franks now intervened and said.

'Perhaps Duke will remember a girl called Francoise, maybe not an important figure but she'd be bound to recognise him and she worked at the St Malo complex.'

Kiwi remembered that he had told her about the role that Francoise played there. And it's just as well he did she thought.

Now another complication came into her mind and that was Inspector Matlock. If he was there he would recognise her at once. He'd even got used to her frequent changes of appearance so new looks wouldn't really work, certainly not with him. She knew that this might mean that she could not go on the mission and she was disappointed that Duke would, and that she would be left behind.

However there was nothing for it but to tell Franks and Tucker of her concerns but when she did Hilary Tucker said,

'Yes we've thought of that, The fact is that we don't know if Matlock is there at all, even if he was ever there so I suggest that Duke goes over first and you join him if there's no sign of Matlock. Does that sound OK to you?'

Kiwi was pleased. She had somehow got very used to him by her side at work (and at play) and she knew that she only operated on half speed or thereabouts when he wasn't there and one day, maybe one day she'd tell him how essential he'd become. But when would she ever feel so sure to say, 'I love you, I want you and I need you?' She hoped that he was wondering the same thing.

'Thanks,' she said, 'that sounds like a good idea.'

It transpired that the joint teams at 'Land of Home and Glory' had made provisional plans for this incursion into the Cerberus base at St Malo but they had not located it and therefore needed Duke to find out exactly where it might be.

Indeed until Tom Spooner's conversation with Kiwi, they were unaware of any specific plan or indeed any resources that were there. With this in mind he would be given new papers in the name of a Cambridge academic with cutting edge skills in computers.

'You'll need to age yourself a bit,' said Franks.

The ploy was to replace Spooner. Edwin Black already operated under deep cover for the secret service at Cambridge. His usual tasks in that regard were to be aware of and report suspicious activity from International agents known to be working there. However he had been persuaded to take a holiday in Fiji with his family, new passports in the name of Stanley.

Duke therefore only had to make his presence known around the 'Base' with a few comments about the way that his ground breaking work was being ignored, and wait to be approached if he was lucky.

Kiwi (if Matlock wasn't there) would pose as a housekeeper with fabulous credentials. (Miss Louise Bellamy) This ploy was to replace Francoise. Duke thought that this was a fitting role reversal of the parts that they had played at the Courtly Love Ball. The next day a certain Professor Edwin Black boarded the Brittany Ferries ship the 'Bretagne' out of Portsmouth to St Malo. He was booked into a rather less magnificent hotel than the Colonel had been, namely 'La Madeleine' a budget Ibis hotel on the Avenue de General de Gaulle in the district of 'Impasse de la Peupleaire.' It was comfy and roomy and each room was a double. What a pity he thought.

As for meeting Cerberus contacts, he remembered that Burton had a delivery note for St Servan and this was worth an enquiry. He soon found out that this district was only a few miles away and had been the centre of major piracy in earlier times. He decided to make a reconnoitre of a local hotel, the eighteenth century Malouiniere named 'La Valmarin,' and couldn't believe his luck as he arrived in the middle of a computer conference. He read through his profile notes before going in, but then a terrible reality dawned on him. He was Professor Edwin Black of Cambridge University an esteemed and renowned academic. What chance was there that he would not be recognised in a room full of computer 'nerds' attending a conference entitled COMPUTERS IN THE BRAIN. Most unlikely he decided, so an urgent email was sent to Tucker back at HQ. It read,

Black ID suspect here. Please send new papers.

A package arrived by courier the very next day. And he was now Edwin White from Bosham Polytechnic Suffolk. A note from Tucker was attached, 'Obscure enough for you?' it said.

It was good to think that she had a sense of humour he thought, and of course now he could go back and book into 'La Valmarin' not forgetting to cancel Professor Black's room at La Madeleine.

Actually he was quite pleased at the way that his instincts had come to his aid. There might have been a really awkward moment and he might even have been arrested for impersonation. He remembered that Kiwi had spent a night in a cell recently and he didn't want to do the same. He made his way up to his room having registered (apologies for being late) for the conference. He was tired and lay down fully dressed and was soon asleep, only to be woken with a start as Kiwi appeared from behind the billowing net curtains. She was naked and smiling, but as he reached out she disappeared.

***

The next day he joined the conference after breakfast. He was given a lapel badge and a designated place at one of six tables in the room. There were five persons at each table and he soon discovered that all of his table-mates were Chinese students studying at London University. He thought it unlikely that any of them would be helpful to him in locating the Cerberus base or be informed about any persons working there, and he suddenly realised that he had put the cart before the horse. He reassured himself that this wasn't entirely his fault as he had rather stumbled on the conference by accident. Nevertheless he knew that his primary aim must be to locate the base itself and, as of now he didn't know if it had another name. His mind wandered as the Chinese continued to speak in Mandarin, 'I can't just wander about asking questions,' he thought 'I've got to get myself noticed, preferably without getting arrested.'

With this in mind he waited until the lunch break and then made sure that everyone noticed that he was getting drunk.

'Too many bloody foreigners,' he said, 'what happened to the good old days when you could have a civilised conversation. It's not like this in the good old 'Deep South' in the States. A normal white guy could get a job easy but now I'm virtually unemployable despite all my top qualifications.'

Naturally this behaviour caused the organisers to ask him not to attend the next session. This suited him very well as he continued to prop up the bar until the tea interval at which point he joined the others, noticeably avoiding his place which had been laid at a table full of Nigerian businessmen.

'I'm not sitting there,' he grumbled, 'find me a decent table or I'll ask for a refund.'

By this time his nominal team leader Mrs Delia Churchill (late of ICI) had had enough and called him to one side.

'This won't do at all Mr White. We have our reputation as a world- wide study group to adopt a multi- racial approach but I'm personally not unsympathetic to some of your views. I can put you in touch with Henry Madison who runs 'Clever Computing' not far from here if you like, but please don't join the group again. I've known him to be outspoken on things like this and you might even get a job. The offices are by the hydro dam, you know the 'Barage de la Rance' and meantime I'll put in a word for you'.

Then after a few moments thought, she added, 'Naturally we will refund your fee.'

This seemed to have worked out very well for Duke so far. He had an entrée into 'Clever Computing' but was there a link to Cerberus?

He was about to be given an opportunity to find out.

❈ ❈ ❈

Henry Madison was a Canadian from a small town called Yellow Knife on the Great Slave Lake in the North West Region. He proudly stated that it was the deepest lake in North America and that it was in his charge there as well.

'You may have heard of Operation Morning Light' he said, 'you know, when the Kosmos crashed and left part of the nuclear reactor behind (On 24/1/1978). Well, we, that is my organisation, got our hands on it before the army arrived. It's going to come in very useful one of these days. And another thing you may not know about,' he added, 'is that that place is crawling with diamonds. There's the Ektaki mine for a start, and then the Diavik Kimberlites of course.

Did you know that Canada is the third largest diamond producer in the world? It all stems from the 'Slave Craton' of course. There's diamonds down there no one has a hope of reaching, not yet anyhow.'

Duke pricked up his ears because this description reminded him of the 'Zimbabwe Craton' in the previous chapter, and how diamonds and the Kariba Lake had been the centre of enquiries there, following Ward's disappearance.

Madison looked and sounded like one of the famous red coated Mounties of the Royal Canadian Mounted Police. As many Canadians are he was warm and friendly from the start, gripping Duke's hand in a vice like grip as if he was wrestling a Grizzly.

Duke immediately noticed his warm countenance, so unlike others in Cerberus such as Matlock and Burton who seemed to have that suspicious and controlling air about them.

'How are you Edwin?' he said, 'Delia told me all about you. I can tell you that you made quite an impression down there.'

This remark caused them both to smile, then to giggle and then to begin to laugh so loud that the papers fluttered on Madison's desk. Almost immediately a kind of bond was established between them, although Duke knew that his part was deceptive.

'Can't say I know much about Bosham Polytechnic in Suffolk, good old England,' said Madison, 'you being a Yank and all but she said that you know your stuff all right, and it does so happen that I'm looking for experienced staff. The thing is though that most of our work is highly confidential to say the least, so I'm sure you won't mind if I do some background checks will you?.'

Duke nodded and said that that was what he had expected, adding that he'd be happy to start work when Madison gave the all clear. At the same time he was praying that Franks and Tucker back at the 'Land of Home and Glory,' had done a thorough job, especially as they had made that quick change. Hurried alterations could often be a problem he thought, and that is when something simple might be overlooked and prove disastrous. One thing came to mind and that was that his original 'Black' identity was predicated on the age of the Professor, say about 55, and he'd added some grey hair to avoid questions as Franks had asked him to. However with his new 'White' identity he had already removed the grey but hadn't thought to ask or tell Franks. Unless Franks was on the same wavelength, his new papers might well be for a 55 year old male in a 35 year old body. He had a clammy feeling that he'd blown his new identity already and couldn't wait to hurry back and tell Franks before it was too late.

'Thanks Henry,' he said, 'I'll wait to hear from you then. Goodbye and thanks again.'

He hoped that his new found friend did not find his hurried departure at all suspicious but he was in a hurry to get to Franks before Madison checked his new identity. He did not underestimate Henry Madison. He couldn't be sure that he was a Cerberus operative, but if he was Duke knew that he would check every detail. Back at his hotel he therefore put through a call to the untraceable number that he had been given. (The telephone record for this number was cleverly set to record that a call had been made to the relevant bank account for each operative. It might have been easier to make it 'Tesco' but a diligent agent might ask why such a call was made.)

Hilary Tucker answered the call,

'Hello Hilary its Edwin White here' he said rather nervously. Thanks for the package but did you alter my DOB for my new identity? I'm just about to be vetted and I wanted to make sure that we had our ducks in a row.'

There was a moment's silence before she spoke.

'It's OK.' she said, 'we know how vain you are so we assumed you'd revert to your own age as soon as you could. If you check now you'll see that we did it already, but you really shouldn't make such assumptions.'

He was very relieved, said thanks, and put the phone down. He suddenly felt weak and reached for a decanter. He wished that Kiwi was there but he knew that she would be in danger if Inspector Matlock had any part to play in St Malo. He'd have to wait for his own identity clearance, and then begin to make himself indispensable and trusted before he could even begin to make enquiries of that nature. It could be some time.

※※※

Duke didn't know it of course, but Kiwi had been given a change of plan, and she was no longer to go to St Malo.

Franks gave her the usual reason for confidentiality,

'It's on a need to know basis,' he said, 'There's no point in worrying Duke unduly and what's more, if he doesn't know he can't let things slip can he?'

Actually Franks had Duke's latest potential error in mind but he didn't say so. Instead he reminded Kiwi of her report from Ward's office in which names and places had been listed and he pointed out that most of them had begun to form part of the picture already.

'We know about Matlock, Burton and Spooner and Rome and Colbert (and Green who died at the farm) and St Malo of course. However we haven't found out much about 'Anya Stein,' or 'Bridgewater'. We know that there is a Somerset historian by that name working at the Sedgemoor Museum near Bridgewater and we know that the Hinkley Point Power Station is situated on Bridgewater Bay. As you know its good practice to look for connections in police work and we have a feeling that Cerberus seem to favour power stations of one kind or another as their bases. We don't know why but we've already had Kariba and now there's St Malo. Could Hinkley Point be another? Maybe it's a coincidence but we'd like you to follow it up. Go down there, nose around and get back to us. What do you think?'

Kiwi had so many mixed emotions on hearing this that she didn't know where to start, so she just said,

'Thank you Sir, I'll be glad to do what I can.'

Franks stated that details would follow and she was soon on her way home, her mind buzzing. She was scared, she was flattered and she missed Duke, oh how she missed him. He would know what to do, he would know what to say and he would know how to make her feel confident. So what would he do first in this situation she wondered when she finally arrived home? Actually she wasn't far out. However it wasn't a decanter that she reached for but an unopened bottle of St Emilion and a glass, as she settled down in front of the TV to watch Dr No and dream of her own 007.

In the morning she became sensible Sandra Newton, Post-Graduate Mature student with closely cropped dark hair, a white blouse and black skirt/trousers to suit. (All as per instructions from Franks)

Flat heels and a smart briefcase completed the picture.

The next day she arrived at the Sedgemoor Hotel in Bridgewater and leafed through the various advertising leaflets for local scenery and events until one from the local museum caught her eye.

It listed a number of dates when Professor Anya Stein would be holding seminars on the Monmouth rebellion in 1685. She hurriedly made a phone call and booked a ticket for the event in two days. She planned to use that time to read up on the rebellion so that she might ask questions, but above all so that she could meet the Professor. Kiwi was quite good at modern police work, but she wasn't sure how she would get on in the seventeenth century. It wasn't hard to find many reference books in the hotel library so after dinner the following day she sat in a formidable leather arm chair, fortified herself with another bottle, and began to read.

The Battle of Sedgemoor 1685

Just outside Bridgewater in Somerset the army of King James the Second met and defeated those of his illegitimate nephew the Duke of Monmouth. James had alienated many of his erstwhile followers by seeming to follow 'Catholic' practices but matters came to a head when he had a son, thereby threatening the settlements of the previous monarchs. Monmouth was seen by many as a more acceptable choice but he failed and was executed. The battle and its aftermath are remembered for the 'Bloody Assizes' that took place afterwards under the supervision of 'the 'Hanging Judge' Jefferies in which more than 300 were hanged in different towns and others were transported. However 3 years later James' niece Mary and her husband William of Orange took the throne as James fled.

The article was written by Stein and below there was a profile.

Anya Stein was born in Tallin in Estonia. She is thought to be related to Edith Stein who, after conversion to Catholicism in 1933 became St Benedicta of the Cross, the Virgin Martyr of Europe. She was gassed in Auschwitz in 1942. Anya is a respected author of books on European and as British History. Her first published work was Self Determination for the Baltic States' but recently she took a wider world view with her seminal work 'Not Born to Rule' which explores how quite ordinary citizens might seize power and become leaders for the good of all. She makes a plea for a revival and renewal of long lost values in society but admits that, as in the past, vested interests will always resist change.

Kiwi was pleased on two counts, firstly that she could now discuss Monmouth without looking stupid, but secondly because Stein's profile sounded tailor made for the Cerberus enterprise, and could easily have been written for Matlock himself or even for Burton.

She decided that Stein was going to be worth getting to know and she soon got her chance at the meeting. It was full of the 'usual suspects' of retired academics and rather keen young students and the Professor was certainly an excellent speaker, so much so that Kiwi's prepared questions were soon rendered irrelevant, She was determined to make her mark but she had to wait for a few other questions from the floor such as, 'Who were the main supporters of Monmouth, why did they fail and if they were all executed, how is it that William and Mary were greeted so warmly by them only three years later?'

At this point a rather buff gentleman in a tweed coat called out from the back,

'Perhaps they had all been resurrected from the dead in the name of Protestantism' he said.

Everyone looked around and then at the Professor to see if she was smiling and she was. This seemed to give approval to the remark which otherwise might have been offensive to some. Stein took her cue and introduced a note of levity into her reply as well.

'Don't forget to say your prayers then.' she said. With some relief in the air Kiwi now posed her question with a flattering introduction.

'I'm Sandra Newton and I've read your books Professor,' she said, 'and I generally agree with your thesis but why did this not play out in 1685 or 1688 for that matter?'

Her reply was that change is usually a concatenation of events not a singular one, which it was in this case, adding that she would be free to discuss the matter further and sign her books after the meeting. There was polite applause and then they all moved into another lounge.

Kiwi prided herself on a kind of innate ability to 'read' people' as she had done with Tom Spooner, and in this case she had got the impression that the Professor wanted to talk to her as much, if not more than she did. With this in mind, as she observed a queue beginning to form, she put on her coat and very obviously left the meeting by the main entrance. A few moments later she looked into a side window and felt quite sure that Anya continued to look up at the exit to see if she had returned. But no, Kiwi was making her wait. She couldn't be sure if it was her interest in Anya's lecture or in the wider aspects of her writing that intrigued the Professor, or maybe it was that familiar figure from Lesbos that she had met before. 'Let's put the poor woman out of her misery,' she thought as she walked back in.

Was there indeed a sigh of relief from the Professor as she saw Kiwi advancing slowly and very smoothly to her desk?

'I'm so glad that you returned.' she said rather huskily.

Kiwi had felt that Anya was interested in her for one reason or another, but she also suspected that she was dealing with a very clever and seemingly ruthless woman given her historical heroes.

Nonetheless they got on famously, firstly with Monmouth and the tragic Jacobite dynasties that followed, and then on to more mundane matters such as romance. She told Anya about the Courtly Love Ball where she had bewitched the Cardinal, but when Anya laughed and asked where it had been held, warning bells rang. It just could be that Stein knew about the death of Colonel Burton at Castle Capulet and that would have been disastrous so she improvised, saying that it was a part of the annual celebrations for Shakespeare's birthday in Stratford on Avon and prayed that Anya would not enquire further.

'Stupid Cow,' she chastised herself under her breath,

'The first rule of policing. Never volunteer information.'

Fortunately the rest of the evening passed by very pleasantly and Kiwi felt herself drawn to this somewhat mysterious woman in her early fifties whose eyes sparkled and whose laughter tinkled like musical bells.

They decided to meet the next day to spend at the Cheddar Gorge which is not far away, and the following day they agreed to visit the mysterious town of Glastonbury.

By now Kiwi was getting those conflicting feelings of duty and dishonesty that Duke had experienced with Henry Madison, but she had a job to do and she was going to do it. However Anya stopped any hopes of further progress when she announced that she had to go back to her 'real job' and couldn't see her for a while. To Anya's delight Kiwi appeared suitably crestfallen, which she was; but not for the reasons that Anya inferred. Isn't it strange how mere dishonesty can turn so quickly to deceit?

'Oh I shall miss you so much,' she said, 'when can I see you again?'

Anya reassured her at once,

'It's my shift you see, three days on and three days off. The museum business is only voluntary now.'

'So what happens on the seventh day?' Kiwi asked.

'Well Sandra that'll be our playtime.' she said mischievously.

The next three days passed by uneventfully until Kiwi received an invitation to meet Stein at the local 'Smugglers Inn' for lunch. They greeted each other warmly if rather cautiously as young lovers do. 'That' wasn't on the menu as far as Kiwi was concerned but she knew that she hadn't much time before Anya realised that her 'prey' was not 'gay.'

For the time being they chatted about this and that until she manoeuvred the conversation around to Stein's private life.

'It's a pity that you can't work full time at the museum,' she said, 'and I hope that you are still writing.'

Anya replied that she did write, but only 'tracts' for what she termed 'influential media.' She didn't elaborate but then she gave Kiwi a real surprise with her next statement.

'I haven't told you about my job yet,' she said, 'it's not secret if you see what I mean, but it does need a security clearance. You see I'm a tourist guide and administrator at Hinkley Point.'

Kiwi could hardly disguise her surprise. A connection between the Professor and the Power Station had dropped right into her lap. Quite how significant it might be, she had yet to find out so once more she fawned over her new friend.

'That must be wonderful,' she said, 'you have so many skills and talents. I just wish I could go there.'

Anya smiled and just said,

'I don't see why not. I can put your name down for the next visit if you like. I think that it's the local WI so you'll be amongst the fair sex. But don't get any ideas because I saw you first.'

With this she smiled, her eyes sparkled and her laughter tinkled gently as she reached out and took her hand.

'She certainly is captivating', thought Kiwi, 'this is going to be a question of mind over matter.'

❖❖❖

As promised she was able to join the Wells WI on their day out, and was soon chatting to a Christine, an Eleanor and a Flossie, all of whom were in their seventies. She didn't wish to arouse Anya's suspicions so she avoided conversation with a rather younger Swedish woman named Ingrid in the group, but noticed that Stein was actually paying that young lady more than her fair share of attention. She thought to intervene but then remembered that her mission was to please Anya in order to find out more. She therefore dutifully followed her around asking a question or two to demonstrate her interest. Others did the same as Anya guided them through the control boards that monitored nuclear power delivered to the Grid. She was keen to point out that the public only had access to a limited part of the whole power plant. There were other parts she explained, where sensitive data and dangerous materials had to be protected.

'I'm sorry that I can't authorise anyone else to view there.' she said and no one objected although Kiwi was desperate to get a look but decided to say nothing.

Later they went for a drink and Kiwi told her how much she had enjoyed the day.

'It's such a pity I couldn't see the most interesting part, the reactor and all,' she said. Anya looked at her in that way that she had, and bit her lip.

'I probably could manage it if you give me a little kiss.' she said, then added, 'I'm only joking. Don't worry. I'll see if I can get you a pass anyway.'

Kiwi gushed gratefully once more.

'That will be wonderful but you really don't have to you know.' she said, she was feeling relieved that Anya had not put her to the test but then, as it does sometimes, a thought that she had been keeping at bay crept into her mind.

'What harm could there possibly be in a little kiss?' she wondered.

'It won't be disloyal to Duke if it's only with a woman will it?' she now reasoned. What's more, back then she had really wanted to, as Anya had bit her lip just those few moments ago. Regrettably the moment had passed, but somehow she thought that there would be another one, and she was quite looking forward to it. That night she decided that a change of 'look' might move things on a bit. Time to recreate the 'stunning redhead look' she decided, but as she applied the lather and looked at herself in the mirror, she began to have grave misgivings.

'You're a proper Machiavellian Mata Hari,' she said to her reflection, but it just smiled back. 'Is that really me?' she wondered, and then it dawned on her that her ploy might be more about the prospect of a kiss than a device to find out more about Cerberus. This should have been an uncomfortable realisation, but it wasn't. It was far from it and she couldn't wait to see Anya again.

Stein arranged a pass and a visit for the next day and they met in the Hinkley Point car park as she had arranged.

'You look lovely today Sandra,' she said and Kiwi was left wondering why Duke didn't seem to notice when she had made a special effort, unless it was in bed of course. Anya then took her arm (Oh so gently) and led her to the entrance.

They walked in together showing their passes as they did so.

'Good morning Bill,' she said to the man at reception. 'This is a colleague of mine Miss Sandra Newton, please give her a 'Privileged Visitor' badge and then she'll sign in. By the way how is Mrs Young?' she asked.

Frank replied that his wife was somewhat better but many residents living near to the 'Point' still felt that it was responsible for some unexplained ailments.

'Make sure you get her checked by the medical team here as well as your own doctor.' insisted Anya adding that she wished to be kept up to date.

She then led the way into a bewildering array of inner passages that finally ended up at a vast control room with flashing lights on all sides. Strangely though there were only four officials in white coats who seemed to have responsibility for monitoring the whole lot. She seemed to know everyone.

'Hello Suzie, I've brought a friend for you to meet.' she said, 'Tom and Alex, come over here and meet Sandra.'

It was a very convivial start on the whole but she only nodded at the fourth engineer who was doing her best to ignore us as well.

'Good morning Miss Stein.' the woman said briefly and rather tersely before returning to her work at the control tower.

'That's Tania,' she whispered, 'a bit of a strange bird. She's also from Tallin. We used to be friends in the Estonian PF (Popular Front) for years. You see that she still wears her PF necklace, but for some reason she has ignored me since you arrived and I don't know why.' she added with that enigmatic smile.

Kiwi knew why all right and so did Tania it seemed, for the chemistry between Anya and Kiwi was palpable. However, as she looked at her 'rival' Kiwi noticed that Tania seemed to be on edge, looking this way and that, like a bird, in much the same way that Matlock and Burton had done. She seemed tense, Almost like a bow, already strung and ready to fire an arrow 'probably straight into my heart.' Kiwi thought. Could Tania be a Cerberus agent too, and if so what was that 'hunted' look all about?

As they moved on and crossed over the many small bridges that led to the reactor she was convinced that the lights flashed on and off at Anya's bidding as if she personally controlled them by sheer magnetism. Anya then guided her as if in a dream to the 'Holy of Holies,' the viewing platform for the advanced gas cooled reactor.

'Unlimited power at the push of a lever, but don't press the wrong buttons!' she said; and once more her tinkling laughter echoed through the cavernous chamber in honour of her double-entendre.

Kiwi gave in. On that platform, with the power of the Almighty at her fingertips she kissed a woman for the first time, and it felt good. They thought that they were alone, but unknown to them the viewing platform itself was also being viewed from the control tower.

'Nice one Anya,' said Tom, but Tania wasn't smiling.

It was odd that nothing followed from that brief encounter. It was as if all that was desired had been achieved and that went for both of them though they never discussed it. If Kiwi had been asked she might have said that it was a beautiful moment, complete and fulfilling, and not in need of repeating. It had been perfection.

The pair moved silently to the Power Station library, both deep in their own thoughts until Anya broke their silence.

'Quite an experience one way or another,' she said, and once more that tinkling laughter rang out.

'You can say that again.' responded Kiwi, 'I could feel the forces of nature.'

This brought more mirth as they dispensed coffee from the vending machine. They were alone in a very substantial room with large windows and comfy chairs and tables all around.

'I've really enjoyed today' said Kiwi, 'but perhaps you could tell me a bit more about your role here and how you got involved. Is it just a job or does it fit in with your work as an historian or maybe with your writings in one way or another?'

This was a successful ploy because it enabled Anya to share those things that she held dear, namely history in general but specifically history as it has evolved to the advantage of those 'Not born to rule' as in the title of her book, namely those outsiders who took control by any means. Now she was prepared to say a bit more.

'I've always tried to make a difference in life. I do have skills and I do have contacts and I'm also in the right place but I'm only one of many in our organisation. I can't go into details now but I'll just lay out a hypothetical scenario for you to consider if you think about joining. I used to think that nations could be autonomous and make the right choices, but now I realise I was wrong. With chaos in the world it is now time for a determined group such as ours to impose a sense of order on society. I found out about all this the hard way as despite being involved in the Popular Front (PF) in Estonia and the Baltic Independence movements for many years but it was not a happy time. What was needed was firm direction and leadership, but once more progress was bedevilled by foreign finance.

'Put it like this. The world is in a mess but it's controlled by the few vested interests that have always run things as we've seen before. To achieve lasting change you must control the 'commanding heights' of society be they financial or economic and those who have the means and the methods can control both in due course. The way to achieve this is through destabilisation and that's where Hinkley comes in as well as Sizewell, Oldbury, Dungeness and others in Europe and elsewhere. As you could tell from my chat with Bill back there in reception, people are yet to be convinced that EDF and other companies are to be trusted. There are just too many risks such as disposal of waste, fallout and pollution not to mention terrorism. From the power stations we can also nullify the 'Grid' and cause 'outage' wherever it might do the most harm, such as at Airports. The economic side of things could be handled in the same way but that will be all about trust and credibility and the way that the internet can be used to sow seeds of doubt and mistrust and Operation Trust is nearing completion. You may know that my home country Estonia has probably the most advanced digital democracy and e-governance in the world at present. We are currently using that as a basis for future action and we've sent one of our best agents there recently. On the political front, in the UK we still have 'Vanguard', despite the loss of Colonel Burton recently and we have others throughout the world such as General Dallas and the Chemico group in the States ready for action when the time comes. They have worldwide bases and will be a major player when the time comes.

'You may as well know it now, but our group is called Cerberus, after the guard dog to Hades you know. Appropriate don't you think? We have some local autonomy but we are also under close scrutiny from region and in turn by Alpha our leader On top of all that we are in very close co-operation with another group that I'll tell you about in the strictest confidence. It might seem strange to you but we have formed an association with a hybrid race from a planet called Gonda that is suffering from global warming.

They need a new home but all you need to know is that we plan to help them to find sanctuary here in deep freshwater lakes, and to provide their energy needs through normal sources and in their case, crushed diamonds or gold.'

Kiwi thought that this all sounded very much like Fascism and she remembered that Matlock had also said 'We'll decide when the time comes,' so she just said,

'I'll definitely think about it. I agree that the world is going to pot as it is, and I'd really love my grandchildren to grow up in a really secure environment with the right values.'

She now had another positive statement about Cerberus, and it was beginning to dawn on her just exactly what the 'pincer' movement that Franks had spoken of was. Firstly there was to be disruption to power supplies, then an attack on political 'trust' by subverting internet securities, and thirdly the use of formal fringe populist political groupings. There might be others but this will do for now.

The scenario reminded her of the Shakespearian quotation that she had learned at school, a bit like 'When the bough breaks' but more apt. It was 'Detune that string and hark what happens.' In other words Cerberus did not believe in brute force, but in their ability to render societies to become 'out of tune' through pressure on economic and civic institutions, leading them to seek harmony and certainty once more, and this is what Cerberus would offer. However she recognised that any transition might be far from peaceful especially if it involved aliens that she knew very little about despite some clues from Franks and Tucker some time back and what she had learnt from the Ward case back in Bristol.

It had been an exciting few days and Kiwi had got what she had come for, and now she couldn't wait to tell Duke that she was free to join him in St Malo as originally planned. It was difficult to say goodbye as she had grown genuinely fond of Anya, who had made a private and very personal dream come true. Anya's kiss had seemed like a fleeting fantasy, but now she was beginning to wonder if it was actually a reality, and if her feelings for him might change.

✳✳✳

Meanwhile Duke had got himself a job with CC (Clever Computing). His identity papers had all been checked and Madison offered him a position as a senior 'logistics co-ordinator.'

He was shown a large web drawing on a wall, well actually it was also a bit like the map of the London Underground, the point being how stations, or in this case 'trusts' or companies, were shown to be linked to each other, sometimes in ones and twos and sometimes in dozens. This was not a social linkage but a financial one, and from the web/map and computer backup it was possible to track a route for the flow of money from one financial house to another. On another wall was a long alphabetical list of the main share and stockholders in these companies. His job was to identify 'Persons of influence in Government' with this web of financial activity. It was especially important that ruses to avoid tax or to bribe foreign governments or persons should be identified. The purpose was not to report such misdemeanours but to collect them as evidence for any legal action.

Madison said that he couldn't tell his new employee all the detail but he implied that 'CC' belonged to a world- wide organisation that would soon change the world. He said that Duke had begun to make his mark and that he was going to extend his remit.

'We recently had an 'import' from the UK, a highflyer by the name of Matlock who was going to take over from me here but they sent him to the Baltic for some reason, so now there's only me and you. We all have to be versatile in this kind of work and I'm expecting to go to 'Hetch Hetchy' quite soon.'

Duke made a mental note of this obscure name but he was thinking of the message he had received from Kiwi, and that he'd soon he'd have her in his arms again.

Madison explained that his 'extended remit' was to further co-ordinate computer logistics within the organisation, but this time at the 'Barage de la Rance' itself.

This great dam reminded Duke of the Ruhr Valley Dams of 'Dam Buster' fame. It appeared both impressive and impregnable. Madison told him that the 'Organisation' had identified crucial economic sites and the Barage was one of them.

'In this case', he said, 'we are a contractor to 'Dynamo' who run the plant, but that puts us in a perfect position to control the generation of power in a crisis and we will decide when that moment comes.'

It was arranged that he would visit the Barage after the weekend to take up his new duties, and this suited him fine as he had another case to attend to. He needed to obtain official clearance for Kiwi to join him and to be his eyes and ears at St Malo.

This was agreed but, given her exposure to possible Cerberus links at Hinkley, Franks had decided that she needed yet another new identity in the name of Sally Monroe, and in keeping with her new surname Kiwi now became a blonde bombshell with heels and a prominent cleavage.

'Goodbye Miss Prim and Proper Sandra Newton, hello Monroe!' she said as she looked in the mirror.

The next day she booked on the ferry and was soon at Duke's hotel.

She couldn't wait to see him again and, although a little apprehensive, she felt quietly confident that things would be as before, especially with her new 'Monroe' look. Indeed he was suitably impressed and for a while there was not much talk about business.

'Kiss me,' she said and he was happy to oblige. 'Now kiss me again, but gently this time.' she repeated, 'I want to feel you breathe in me.'

Moments went by and then she spoke again.

'I've been thinking,' she said as they lay happily side by side.

'Please don't,' he pleaded placing his hand over her mouth, 'Let Franks do all the thinking, I'm only interested in you.'

'But that's what I've been thinking about,' she replied, 'Us, I mean.'

He wasn't the most romantic of men but he thought he knew where this was going, and he thought that he knew how to respond.

'You know that I love you,' he said, 'and haven't we been sharing love together just now?'

Of course this was his second big mistake, to equate their urgent love making with love; the first being that he had thought that he knew what she meant in the first place.

She looked at him with despair. She was thinking about Anya and that loving kiss, hesitant at first as Anya's warm lips had touched hers so gently. It was as if time had stood still. Then Anya's eyes had looked deep into hers and entered her soul causing her to shiver uncontrollably. That's what love is surely she thought. How could she even broach the subject with him again? But just then a change came over him as he took her in his arms.

'Sorry, I didn't mean that,' he said,' I just want you to know that you are the most precious thing in the world to me and I've missed you so much.'

She smiled and clung to him tightly, wrapping her arms and her legs around him, then, weeping joyful tears she turned her head and whispered,

'Kiss me. Kiss me.'

They were together again it is true but as there did not seem to be an opportunity for her to join him at the River Dam, they decided that she should stay at the hotel and organise her report on Hinkley as a template to compare to the Barage after he had studied it at some length.

He hoped to find a similar scenario and then they might have something substantial to report together. As they anticipated there were many similarities, but the main thing in common was the crucial strategic position of both. It followed that any major disruption 'at a time of our choosing' to either would cause havoc and panic, and a major breakdown of energy supplies.

This was fine as far as it went but Duke also had an unexpected ace up his sleeve that he had discovered.

'You remember that big wall chart that we spoke of before?' he said, 'Well they have an even bigger one at the Barage and guess what. It plots a number of Power Stations throughout the world including the UK and Europe the USA, Japan and Australasia. It's my notion that they act as regional HQ and maybe 'sleepers' until a date is set for them to be activated by Cerberus 'when the time is right'. One of them must be the Headquarters, but which one I wonder?'

The next day began as usual and he was about to go to the Barage for his duties on the roster, when a confidential email from Franks appeared on Kiwi's lap top. It read 'Urgent and Confidential.'

Code X (Top Priority) return soonest. Duke stays.

Considering that she had only been there for a little more than a week this message upset her greatly, and she looked over at him for help but he just said,

'They told us this might happen darling and you probably won't be gone for long anyway.'

She was far from reassured, but she also knew that there would be no point in asking Franks to change his mind. She'd have to pack and that was that. It was a shame they didn't even have time for a cuddle.

❖❖❖

There were three persons waiting in Frank's office when she arrived. Franks was there of course as well as Hilary Tucker, and they were seated at the desk. The third was a woman who had her back turned and was looking out of the window. Kiwi thought that she looked strangely familiar even from that angle, but before she could say anything, Franks greeted her in a somewhat terse fashion.

'Thanks for coming back,' he said, 'but all this might not have been necessary at all if you had kept your mind on your job.'

She was shocked and wondered what had upset him so much but then it all became clear when the woman turned around. It was Divisional Detective Inspector Margaret Power who she had tangled with at Castle Capulet during the Colonel Burton affair.

'Hello Miss Smith,' she said sarcastically,' or is it Sandra Newton perhaps. But no, I'm told by Mr Franks that you are actually WPC Jo Grant. He says that you are good at your job but it seems that you are really not up to this kind of work.'

Once more Kiwi was speechless but before she could protest Hilary Tucker intervened.

'We haven't got time to go over the past,' she said, 'Margaret, why don't you tell her exactly what has happened. I don't know how you found out that she is an agent working for us but I'm very glad that you did. We'll look into any lapse of security on our part later, but this is too important to worry about such details. Just tell her why she is here and what you know about the case so far.'

'The Professor is dead,' Power began dramatically, 'Suicide maybe but murder probably. She died from a drug overdose but whether this was self- administered or done by another is not clear at this moment in time and we are hoping that you can help us.'

Now Kiwi was shocked in a totally different way. A few weeks ago she had not only respected Anya as a professional in her field, but she had also admired her positive and dynamic character. And, yes there was more than that. She had loved her, if only for that brief moment she had loved her and now she was dead. Power could see her discomfort but she continued nonetheless.

'There was a note in her room you see' she said.' It was an extract from a dictionary defining 'traitor,' as 'one who betrays a friend, a country a cause or trust,.

We have the handwriting experts on it at the moment because we don't know if she wrote it before taking the tablets, or if someone else did. In either case a point was being made.' She paused here and looked closely at Kiwi before continuing, 'But what point was being made I ask myself and we are hoping that you can tell us.'

Kiwi felt cornered. She didn't like Power but she had recognised that she was a very shrewd detective. Now she had to decide how much to tell or not to tell, but once more the Inspector pre-empted her reply.

'I can see that you are wondering how much of your dark little secrets we know already, well I'll tell you. You were seen kissing Anya Stein by at least two of the staff at Hinkley. We have also been told by one of them that before you arrived she and Tania were lovers, and that Tania swore to 'get' you as soon as she could but you left, so only Stein remained to pay for being a traitor to their love. Now Tania has left the area and we don't know where she is but we suspect that she has travelled back to Tallin on a false passport. That will need checking with our friend Danton from Interpol.' Once more she paused in her devastating statement but fortunately Hilary came to the rescue.

'To be fair,' she said, 'this is all conjecture to an extent, so what do you have to say Jo?'

Now Kiwi had no escape.

'It was only a kiss.' she began and then burst into tears. She could not be comforted, but when Hilary asked if they should send for Duke, she cried uncontrollably even more. The meeting had to be adjourned and she was asked to write a statement of her involvement by the next day. Her head was spinning with so many mixed emotions, so much so that she kept falling asleep and then making coffee to wake up, and then falling asleep again. Eventually she finished her report by 3 am and slept again for a further nine hours. Here is her resignation statement.

> Please accept this statement as notice of my decision to resign from the force. I realise that my actions may have caused concern but I cannot say that I regret them entirely, only the context in which they occurred. I will explain this point later, but first I will lay out the entire scenario at Hinkley as I found it. You will recall that we had reason to believe that this power plant was involved with Cerberus in some way

and that the name of Anya Stein also appeared in the Bridgewater area. I was sent to investigate the nature of their interest in the plant and Stein's involvement if any. As I submitted in my reports there was much evidence to link the two, albeit in a roundabout way via her work at the local museum. According to their notes she had been active in the struggle for Baltic self- determination but had become disenchanted as confirmed by her quite recent book. This was entitled 'Not born to rule' which almost defines Cerberus in terms of tradition and tactics.

Given this background I submit that there are at least two different reasons for the reference to 'traitor' in the note. Firstly that she had become a traitor to Estonia and the other Baltic States through her recent writing, but also it might have been assumed by another Cerberus agent (Tania?) that she had been a traitor to them by openly exchanging confidences with me, and I don't mean the kiss. We had visited Cheddar and Glastonbury as well.

I return now to the kiss. I don't say that we were in love but it was a very loving kiss. If you've ever had one you'll know what I mean. I can't and don't want to explain it otherwise, so please accept my decision to resign. I will have to deal with my private life now. WPC Jo Grant.

Later, when Franks, Tucker and Power had the document in front of them, it might be true to say that they viewed it with mixed emotions. Franks was irritated, Tucker was sympathetic but Power was unforgiving.

'Of course she must go,' she said, 'she might have caused Stein's death in one way or another, and what's more it seems that she's a security risk who can't control herself.'

Franks tended to agree with the point about security and didn't pretend to know why Kiwi had behaved as she did. However he knew that any simple lapse of security in his business could be damaging to an individual, but more importantly fatal to others. Hilary Tucker didn't disagree with much of this but she wanted to voice a different and altogether more useful perspective.

'It's no good crying over spilt milk,' she said, 'let's try to get something positive out of this. I think that Jo has a point about motive for the murder if it was murder. We have already done some investigation on Tania Harju and indeed it seems quite possible that she was involved for one reason or another. I think that we should bring her in with Interpol help of course, but I would add something more. If she is in Tallin under a different name we shall need someone who can identify her and I have someone in mind, namely Jo herself. We should therefore ask her to work with us on this and postpone her resignation.'

Franks agreed but Power disagreed.

Kiwi was soon told about this surprising majority decision and Franks had yet another surprise for her.

'Tell us what you think about this,' he said, 'Duke has reported that Matlock has been sent to 'The Baltic' so we suggest that you go together but with different missions. Yours is to find Harju, and his is to visit the only major power station in Estonia on the Baltic Sea, namely the 'Narva' power plant up on the border near Leningrad. Estonia has plans to go nuclear in the near future but at present Narva is run by shale gas. We think that Cerberus needs data on that kind of operation. You can't venture up there in case Matlock is actually there but we can't be sure. As for Tania, we do know that she is an accomplished silversmith by trade so you might find her in the jewellery quarter.'

Kiwi agreed taking it that they would brief Duke about his new mission, only adding the proviso that SHE would tell him about THAT kiss when, if ever, the time was right.

❖❖❖

On being recalled Duke had taken his leave of Madison and St Malo on good terms but he was also happy to be re-united with Kiwi on a new mission. They only had one night together before she had to meet with Inspector Danton from Interpol who was to give her a background briefing on Estonia in general and how she must work with the local police on any extradition procedures that might be warranted for Tania Harju. Meanwhile Tucker and Franks would brief Duke on the Power Station and any implications that this might have in the hunt for the Cerberus hideaway.

On hearing this Duke decided to book a hotel suite for the night to give their reunion that special flavour. A candlelit meal in the dining room, drinks on the terrace and a piano playing Georgia (not Estonia!) in the bar, set the scene for a romantic night.

Their mood was gentle and loving as she had hoped it would be, and thoughts of her moment with Anya were gradually forgotten as their bodies claimed each other with sighs of contentment. Later she decided that the time was not right to confess, and she wondered if it should always remain 'her' secret. But that was for another day and as the dawn broke Danton slipped this note under the door.

> 'Estonia is one of the three Baltic States, the others being Lithuania and Latvia. All are now independent after decades of occupation by Nazi Germany or Soviet Russia. In Estonia a celebrated milestone in their peaceful moves to independence was the phenomenon of the 'Singing Revolution,' in which public places were occupied by choirs not tanks. The Popular Front (PF) was a leading political party at this time and helped to organise 'The Baltic Way' in which thousands of Baltic citizens held hands across the three states. Independence is highly valued, but the country has looked to the West and not the East recently. This has alienated many, so divided loyalties remain. I am told that both Tania Harju and Anya Stein had been members of the PF but Stein had become disenchanted and had begun to write about different options not related to the EU or Russia.
>
> If Tania thought that Anya was working against the PF that could be a reason for killing her. My advice is to be careful and not to indicate that you are knowledgeable in any way. Good luck.'

Meanwhile Franks and Tucker had been giving Duke some data on the Narva Power Plant, namely that it is powered by shale gas at present but it could be converted to nuclear in a few years. They told him that they had information that Cerberus could be planning to study the conversion process and maybe use this as a 'soft' base in Northern Europe for their further activities. The plant is on the Estonian border near Leningrad so it is in a sensitive political area, and that could be used to their advantage. The giant Russian energy company 'Gazprom' is not far away and this could be vulnerable also. His task was to go to the area and find out what he could about these technologies. At the same time he was to see if Matlock was working there and if so, what was his function.

With their respective briefs Kiwi and Duke now made plans to go to Estonia. She asked Franks if they might travel on by sea on the 'Empress of the Baltic' the flagship of the Swan Hellenic Line but the answer was a resounding NO!

Franks pointed out that time was of the essence in her case if she was to stand any chance of finding Tania Harju. Duke thought that, as he had more time, he might enjoy a cruise to the Baltic but he had to run for his life when he mentioned it to her.

'Just joking,' he said but she had no mercy.

'There'll be no cruise for you,' she said as she cornered him in the bedroom, 'But here's a bruise for you instead,' and with that she thumped him hard, pushed him on to the bed and began to pummel his chest.

'Stop it, I like it,' he cried out before she closed her arms around him with a sigh.

'Make the most of it,' she said, 'We're going on a diet again when we get there so I think we can have seconds.'

The next day they flew to Tallin and touched down at the 'Lennart Meri Airport' where a 'Krooni' taxi took them to their hotel 'The Majestic'. Fortunately they were able to have a few days together before he made his journey to the Narva Power Plant.

Their guide and mentor was a local Interpol agent named Yuri and he suggested a meal and a stroll around to familiarise them with their surroundings. Before setting out however he suggested that once more Kiwi took on a new 'persona' in case Tania spotted her first. He thought that a short cut blonde Swedish look might be appropriate, plus glasses and a headscarf which is quite common in the Baltic. She was quite pleased about the first part if not the last, but she agreed that it seemed like good advice.

Yuri called for them that evening and his first stop was the imposing Alexander Nevsky Cathedral with that Onion Dome so reminiscent of Russian Orthodox churches everywhere. Next it was the contentious statue of the 'Bronze Soldier,' seen by many as a pro Soviet icon.

He then indicated the artistic area that he knew she was interested in saying,

'I'll leave that to you now but if you spot her do not approach her. Call me and I'll be there with immigration and the police as soon as possible. You must then just indicate who she is and we'll do the rest. She'll probably be taken in for questioning and you'll have to come down and officially identify her later.'

Kiwi only had one more night with Duke before he had to leave. It was a bitter sweet experience. They knew that they were both in danger, but they were each more concerned about the other, and once more Kiwi's thoughts turned to love as she said goodbye.

'I shall miss you,' she said, 'I love you Duke.'

He seemed a little taken aback but responded warmly,

'Me too, my little bird,' he said.

Duke soon arrived at the 'Volga Hotel' in Narva and began to make his plans. It would not be easy but he had been given the usual (if unimaginative) cover as IT correspondent for the Boston Herald. This was actually quite appropriate because the advent of the Internet had been embraced much more in Estonia than elsewhere. He hoped that an interest in and around the power plant in this respect would not be seen as suspicious but rather the opposite. From the President down, Estonia had been lauding its success and achievements to the world and this would be another opportunity to do so.

At the Chamber of Commerce he was given the name of a PR agent from the power station and a meeting was soon arranged there. Her name was Katherine Kursk. She was a 'Russian' Estonian and as such epitomised the dichotomy that existed for many who lived in those states bordering the old Soviet Union. From the outset she made little secret of her disdain for the EU but was pleased to promote the links between Narva and Gazprom.

'We Estonians are at the cutting edge of the technological revolution,' she said, 'but what's the point if all the benefits go to Germany?'

Duke kept quiet counsel but he could see how Cerberus might benefit from this situation, namely that Estonia had 'made its bed' with the West whilst the Soviet Union had been too divided to intervene. Even now the Russian Federation was powerless but a 'third force' might suit some very well. He deduced that Narva could indeed be a useful test bed for Cerberus to cause havoc 'when the time was right.'

Katherine now offered to show him around but she steered clear of what she called 'secure' areas. He noticed that, despite the plant being powered by shale gas there were those familiar 'radioactive' signs as they passed by certain corridors. Once more he did not comment but made a mental note. He decided that, given his brief visit, he had learnt a lot and that it was best to leave it at that. Only one aspect of his brief remained, and that was to track Matlock if at all possible. This was tricky so he thought that a little charm might break the ice with Katherine and then he could find out more.

'I'd be pleased to,' she said in answer to his invitation to dinner at the Volga Hotel 'I don't get many offers.'

Later she met him as arranged and at first he did not recognise her. This was a blonde beauty in a black sequinned gown with high heels, a low front and diamond earrings. Earlier she had been 'sewn up' in a suit, and the transformation was amazing.

'Wow,' he said, 'you look lovely.'

He might have work on his mind but this was something different. Strangely this busty beauty suddenly seemed coy,

'You like?' she asked simply as her eyes looked down demurely at her cleavage.

Now he was in trouble,

'Sure I like,' he said, 'I like very much. Let's have some champagne to celebrate glasnost.'

At this they both laughed, and after a few drinks moved into the dining room. This was safer ground he thought, but not safe enough, as there was only one disconcerting view from across the table and it wasn't the candles. Suddenly she seemed like a siren, just too beautiful to be resisted, and he felt himself drawn to her sheer magnetism. 'It's as if she's a different person.' he thought. This afternoon she was all business like and now she's a vamp.' He knew that some women could be 'exotic' when they wanted to be, but this was different. She genuinely seemed to have two identities, and this put him in mind of Matlock and even Burton for that matter. It was strange but perhaps Cerberus instigated some type of corporate identity that spilled over into personality, and led to this kind of stereotype. Actually he'd seen it at the CIA but not as evident as this.

He needed information fast before he weakened, so after a few personal anecdotes he thought it safe to pose a question.

'You've told me that Narva has a close relationship with Gazprom, but do you get any advice from the West then? For example my readers might like to know if the EU or any other agencies send persons from time to time?' he asked. It was a long shot but it worked.

'A French company called 'Clever Computing' sent an IT expert named Matlock recently,' she said,' but now he's gone to the States I think. He was too big a fish for us. Why do you want to know?'

He hurriedly backtracked. He had his answer and melons were no longer on his menu. Now he played his trump card.

'I hope you'll excuse me,' he said, 'I've just got to phone my wife. I always do at this time.'

With that he got up and went into the lobby and stayed there for five minutes. When he returned she was gone but she had left a terse note.

'Never trust a Yank.' it said.

'Good,' he thought, 'I think I'll have melons after all'.

❖ ❖ ❖

Meanwhile Kiwi had taken the opportunity to wander into the old medieval corners of the City. The area that she was interested in was 'Reval' (the medieval name for Tallin) and it was a bit like Montmartre in Paris where there were artists aplenty on the streets, musicians playing and many arcades selling a miscellany of wares.

The morning passed by without incident and at lunch time she sat comfortably at a small table outside a bistro somewhat appropriately called the 'Café de Paris.' What is more, strains of music from the 'Hot Club of France' emanated from within and she began to miss Duke. She always thought of him that way when jazz was playing, and he would have been in his element here she thought.

No matter, she was soon on the street again, looking here, peering there and poking around in there. Then she spotted a small silver-smiths named 'Silver Threads.' In the window a small group of girls with headscarves were busily demonstrating their skills and as she looked a small shiver ran down her back.

A girl was seated at a table near the window and obviously concentrating hard as she leaned over, but as she did so her necklace fell away from her chest and swung loosely over her work in progress. It was a familiar brooch; it was the PF brooch that she had seen Tania wear at Hinkley. Kiwi did not suppose that there were too many 'Popular Front' girls there and although she could not see the girl's face, she immediately recognised the almost imperceptible familiar movement of the girl's head from side to side.

She called Yuri from Interpol and he was on the scene in minutes accompanied by a police officer and an immigration official. As they took her out, Kiwi watched from the shadows and was content to see that it was indeed Tania Harju.

Now she would have to go to the police station for a formal identification and also hear what Tania had to say about the tragic events at Hinkley. However Tania made it clear that she was not responsible in any way, and in rather dramatic fashion, clearly pointed the finger at someone else.

This was the statement that she made to the police.

My name is Tania Harju and I am an Estonian citizen. I came to the UK to go to UWE, the University in Bristol, where I trained as an engineer. When I qualified I got a job at the Power Station but remained close to my family and my roots in Tallin. We had all been involved in the 'Singing Revolution' as members of the Popular Front as had Anya Stein and her family. At that time I was a 'sleeper' in the Cerberus organisation and invited her to join. It was through her that I got my job and we were soon lovers. She told me that she had had doubts about the PF for some time but it did not affect our love for each other.

She also told me that she was attracted to Sandra Newton and suggested that we might make a threesome one day. I said that I was prepared to let fate take its course, but I became worried when I overheard Anya's discussion with Ingrid Borg who was one of the WI visitors to the site. They met later I know because Anya telephoned me in tears. She said that Ingrid had brought a message from Beta and it was this. They had found out that Sandra Newton was a police officer and that Anya had told her about the group. This was treachery in their eyes and she was given a choice. They would kill her and her family or she could commit suicide. She did the latter and I grieve for her every day.

I didn't kill Anya Stein. Sandra Newton did.

Kiwi was crestfallen. She had not imagined that a few discussions and of course that lingering luscious kiss could have put the blame on her. A well of remorse filled her every sinew and when she went back to her hotel she cried all night. In the morning there were no tears left. They had been replaced by an implacable sense of revenge against Matlock, Cerberus and all they stood for.

Having completed his mission Duke returned to their hotel and they compared notes before making their separate reports and arranging to go home. She requested that they be allowed to travel back on the Swan Hellenic Line to 'recharge their batteries,' and this time Franks agreed. So it was that, on a balmy night in the Mid-Atlantic that Kiwi told Duke about Anya.

He listened carefully and, when she had finished he just said,

'I had a near miss myself you know.' She laughed, but did she detect a new tenderness as if they had both been tested emotionally yet been brought closer by it?

There was not enough evidence to extradite Tania but Kiwi's mission had revealed yet another ruthless side to Cerberus. Duke's report was much more informative, containing as it did, details of Cerberus roots across the Baltic and into Russia itself. Furthermore it was beginning to be recognised how IT might play a crucial role in their future plans, and they had both supplied confirmation of the alien dimension that Franks had alluded to earlier.

On arrival back in the UK they were both summoned to the DCU to meet with Franks, Tucker, Danton and others to discuss a 'serious new development.' that would turn their lives upside down.

Tucker had decided that it was imperative that Duke return to the US to track down Matlock who had been located in California, and who had now been identified as 'Beta,' namely second in command to the whole Cerberus project. They had indications that 'Operation Trust' could not be more than a few months away and they were getting very worried at the lack of progress, as they put it, and that 'Everyone must now give their own assignments utmost priority'

Duke thought that this was rather ungrateful after all they'd been through, but it was a reminder that he and Kiwi, and probably many others, were expendable, despite what Franks and Tucker, and the DCU, might say and that wasn't a very comfortable feeling at all.

However those officers seemed to be quite oblivious to this perception and went on to say that they also had a lead on Charlie Swann (from the Ward files) working in 'securities and futures' at the 'Frisco' bank and another familiar name had cropped up, namely that of General Dallas from Chemico who was a Director at the Bank. Duke might expect some support from Madison they said, but Kiwi would have to go into deep undercover. She had been a little careless they said, and consequently been identified and maybe even betrayed at Hinkley, and they could not risk another expose. This was hurtful and she knew it to be true but, 'A kiss is still a Kiss,' she thought as the old movie 'Casablanca' came to mind.

She recalled that this had all begun with Duke's mention of the murder of Senator Joshua Prince from California, and now she would soon be on her way there. Once more she had mixed feelings of fear and anticipation, but she was nothing if not resolute; and Duke would be there to hold her hand.

The case had seemed to be over but it was far from over.

3

AMERICANA
(DUKE'S STORY)

I n some ways Duke was pleased to return to the USA even though it was to the West Coast. He had grown up in the Deep South but there were compensations, such as the beautiful beaches and girls. Naturally he had to put that latter thought aside as he would be with Kiwi for most of the time, and he was very glad of it. Franks and Tucker had selected California for three reasons. Firstly they had information that Matlock was there, but another factor was a sense that LA could be a central hub for Cerberus activity in the financial sphere, as another name from Ward's list had cropped up in the 'Frisco Bank.' Thirdly he was told that new information had come to light that NORAD, the North American Defence Agency also had an interest in the area. He knew that this was probably in response to persistent UFO sightings there in Area 51, but so far there had been no connection between these and the activities of Cerberus or any connection with the planet Gonda.

This is Duke's account of the next few months.

In some ways I was pleased to return to the good old US of A but I couldn't exactly call California home, not by a long way. There's not a lot in common between the Deep Bayou in New Orleans and the leafy suburbs of Los Angeles. Still, I thought that it would be good to show Kiwi some of the sights as it was her first visit, and I knew she'd enjoy Santa Monica.

I had been there before on business and we would be staying at the same hotel for a while, and that's the 'George' at 1415 Ocean Avenue. It was built in 1933 and became known as 'The Lady,' being a haven for gamblers and gangsters during the Prohibition era and later a convenient refuge for Hollywood stars. You can imagine Kiwi's pleasure when I told her that we had been booked into the room that had been occupied by Clark Gable and Carole Lombard. How romantic is that?

We had arrived unpacked and showered, and I didn't have to wait long for my answer when she came in from the bathroom wearing only a towelling robe. She looked at the bed and spoke in a very husky voice,

'Which side would you like Clark?' she murmured.

This was my moment, my one moment of film fame when I was able to utter those immortal words,

'Frankly my dear I don't give a damn,' and before more could be said, she was in my arms and kissing me so passionately that the censors would have definitely given the scene an X certificate!

Unfortunately we only had that day at 'The Lady' together before we had to move to a more permanent address in LA, a rather modest block of flats known as 'The Waterfront' although it was nowhere near. Maybe it was a Brando legacy I thought, and maybe a little more role play may be on the cards later on. There was not much time for that however because once there we were called to a top secret meeting with our new controllers.

They only wanted to be known as Marks and Spencer and we were to meet them in the Hollywood Warner Brothers Museum by the Batman and other exhibits. We would be approached by Marks who would just say 'Stoobeedoo' and we were to respond, 'Where are you?'

He would then lead us to a small room behind the Harry Potter exhibition. I thought that the whole thing sounded like a scene from the Marx Brothers, and when I told Kiwi this we nearly laughed ourselves silly. However, the meeting was in deadly earnest and we were reminded that any lapse of security could cost us our lives.

Franks had already told them about my good relations with Madison as 'Edwin White' in St Malo, so I was told to keep this identity and make myself known to him again. They had information that he had indeed been transferred to 'Hetch Hetchy' as he had indicated that he might be. This strange name turned out to be that of a major reservoir and power complex in the Yosemite National Park near Los Angeles. It would be my job to study its role in any Cerberus/Gonda plan as well as seeing if Matlock was actually there. Kiwi would also retain her identity as Sally Monroe and in addition to that she was 'given' impressive formal qualifications as a 'Financial Futures' specialist and instructed to seek a position at the Frisco Bank. Once there she was told to make contact with 'Charlie Swann' who was known to be working there as well.

He had been mentioned in Ward's papers, and had since been identified by Operation Scorpion as a key figure in the Cerberus financial networks in America and maybe in the world. I had my cover story ready for Madison, namely that I had relatives in San Diego (which I did have) and that I'd been invited to spend a long vacation there. A gloss on this tale was that I had been dismissed from my post on the Boston Herald for my unwelcome, not to say unpatriotic views about the State of the Nation. Naturally this story was supported in every way by disinformation put about by my controllers, because it was expected that it would be checked for authenticity. It also explained why I needed a job, and that gave me a good reason to contact Henry Madison again.

'Well look what the wind has blown in.' he said after agreeing to meet me at Ruby's Diner at Belmont and Wilshire in Pasadena. 'Am I glad to see you.' he continued, 'things haven't been going so well here recently. There's been a big stir about security and we've had the big chief here to check us out after that debacle at Hinkley. I'm pretty sure that he was behind the decision to dispose of Stein and I wouldn't put it past him to do the same here'

I made sympathetic noises and relayed my story in more detail to allay any suspicions that he might have had on that score. Strangely though he seemed to have none and I think that he genuinely liked me, and I certainly liked him. True he was an imposing figure, somewhat like a Mountie without a horse and a red coat, but his bonhomie was infectious and soon we were chatting like old buddies.

'So who did they send to check up on you then?' I asked all innocently.

'You won't believe it,' he responded at once,' it was that guy Matlock again but fortunately he's gone now. They say he's being groomed for the top job.' Well that was a stroke of luck I thought, so I began to ask a little more about the operation at Hetch Hetchy.

He seemed pleased to have someone to talk to, not only about his immediate responsibilities but also about the 'organisation' itself. He was still a little nervous about discussing specifics and once, when he stopped himself in the middle of a sentence, I asked him if he was worried about something.

'Wouldn't you be?' he replied, 'after what happened to Anya. I'm divorced but I've got two little girls and I wouldn't want them to grow up without a father. We spend a lot of time fishing up at Lake Tahoe in our weekend log cabin, and a move would ruin our life. It's also a major centre for skiing and the girls are just starting to learn. Matlock said that I could end up in Fukushima or even Australasia if I didn't get things right here, and that really would be the end of the world as far as I am concerned.'

He seemed hesitant and I began to sense that Henry Madison might be a weak link in the Cerberus chain one day. He did not have that ruthless streak so easily adopted by Matlock, and I reasoned that this might be useful later on. I sensed that he was keen to tell me more so I just let him go on.

'Now I'm being blamed for what they say is 'increased flyover' activity over the lake' he said. 'Well it's quite true and I'm the one that reported it, but of course they could just be weather or climate monitor operations.'

I sympathised but wondered if these were all part of the NORAD surveillance that I had been told about.

Over the next few days he took me on a considerable guided tour of the immediate locality, explaining how the reservoir fitted into 'the system' that supplied water and power supplies throughout California.

'The reservoir is the guarantor of sustained life here,' he said, 'water and power, those are the essentials and I can control them. If they go, chaos reigns. My job is to accomplish that at the touch of a button when the time comes and if I have to.'

I noted that familiar phrase again and asked what he meant by the 'system'.

'You'll get to know it soon enough,' he replied and went on to explain that generators at the O'Shaughnessy Dam delivered 1.6 billion kw hours of electricity all along the California coast, making it a vital strategic target. Furthermore it was somewhat in the wilds and therefore easier to occupy with minimum force. Here he mentioned the US Far Sight Rangers under General Dallas (also the MD of the giant Chemico multi- national conglomerate) as the likely occupying force, and naturally that rang a bell with me as I recalled his involvement before. He added that his own remit included oversight of the Fukushima Nuclear Plant in Japan where Cerberus agents there reported to him as Pacific Controller. His explanation then took on a rather apologetic tone as he concluded,

'I hope you'll agree that none of this would be necessary if world governments started to act reasonably; but we must be prepared.'

I nodded my assent and eventually we ended up in a Tapas bar in San Jose. It had been a fruitful week and I couldn't wait to send off a report and tell Kiwi, especially the absence of Matlock.

Meanwhile she had enrolled at the local Job Centre and been taken on by another bank as a counter clerk. It wasn't what she was looking for but it was a start. She said that she hoped to make contacts with other bank staff over the next few weeks and hopefully land a job at the Frisco Bank in due course. Naturally she was pleased that Matlock was no longer there, because it meant that she could walk about freely without the fear of bumping into him. She hadn't realised that he was probably the man who decided Anya's fate, but when I told her she was not surprised.

'That man is very dangerous.' she said, 'I'm hoping that we catch up with him soon, but don't let me get my hands on him.'

I had not detected this side to Kiwi before. I knew that she could be relentless in the way that she assembled evidence until her target had nowhere to turn, but this seemed different. It had become personal for her and I was reminded again about her undoubted affection for Anya, but it was even more than that. I would class her attitude as one of grim determination and I didn't like it. Was there a side to her character that I had failed to spot over these many months? Perhaps we are all two persons in one after all, I thought as I recalled what Herr Müller had said about his role in the concentration camps. At the time I remember thinking that 'There, but for the grace of God go I' but now I could see that Kiwi also had a ruthless streak, so did I as well? I loved Kiwi and I suppose that I put her on a pedestal, but it was unnerving just the same.

At the weekend I took her sightseeing in Santa Monica especially along the Pier where parrots and musicians entertained the public, and then along to the world famous 'Big Dean's Ocean Front Café' for lunch.

We strolled around the Bay-side district and sat in the shade of palm trees in Palisades Park before eventually walking arm in arm back to 'The Lady' along Pico and Colorado. That night there was a full moon and we made love in the grey twilight; and again at dawn. We had become one, and as the sun rose over the blue Santa Monica Bay I told her that I loved her.

She said 'I love you too. I thought that I did before but now I know it. It's as if a sort of spiritual feeling has come over me since we've been here.'

I joked that maybe the local Shaman had something to do with it but she persisted.

'No.' she said, 'I think it's because I feel vulnerable in every way here except when you are close to me, and I didn't feel that way before. I have a sense of dread as if something terrible will happen and only you can save me.'

I sensed that reminders about Matlock had really spooked her this time and I hastened to allay her fears.

'Matlock's gone you know,' I said, 'Far away, maybe even to Japan or Australia as far as I know. Madison mentioned the Fukushima Nuclear Plant earlier so that wouldn't surprise me.'

She seemed reassured and said, 'Hold me' and I did.

The next day I got a surprise request from Madison.'

I'm in trouble and I need some help,' he said,

'Matlock has sent a report in which he makes criticisms of my financial operation here. The logistics side is fine he says but he wants me to send a trusted computer expert to work in the Frisco Bank with our agent there. I immediately thought of you. Will you do it?'

Of course I said that I would, not only to please him but because it gave me an entrée into the Frisco Bank. Kiwi might not be pleased, but I thought that once I had my feet under the table, then I might to able to get her a job as well. Things were looking up.

An interview at the bank was nodded through on the recommendation of Madison but before I took up post he wanted to talk again 'Man to Man' he said.

We arranged to meet at 'Tara's Bar' (in honour of Clark Gable) off the Boulevard at 222 Joplin and he soon arrived in his big bustling style and sat next to me at the bar.

'I like you Edwin,' he said, 'and I want you to know that I trust you so I'll give you the lowdown and then you can decide whether to join our organisation or not. At the moment you've been working for us, one might say as a hired hand on our version of the' Ponderosa.' Here he paused and laughed that big belly laugh of his before continuing in a much more serious tone.

'I'm not sure if you know all this already but the organisation that I've spoken of is called Cerberus and we not only believe in a different kind of world but we have actual plans to achieve our aims. These are being developed throughout the world as we speak and should be ready within the year.'

This was going faster than I could ever have dreamed of and I wondered what would come next so I just said,

'I'm flattered by what you say and I appreciate your confidence. I'm ready to join right now. You already know my track record and I'll do anything that I can to help the cause.'

He reached over and gave me a Big Bear Hug.

'That's great.' he said 'but there's one thing that I forgot to mention and that's the Initiation ceremony. Everyone has to go through it. OK?'

I felt like saying 'No Not OK No Way.' but I just said, 'Fine. Set it up.'

He then told me to make contact with Charlie Swann at the Bank where I was to begin work on a series of interconnected global deals. It turned out that 'Charlie' was a 'dame' or should I say woman perhaps? Yes, I should I know, but I couldn't forget that I was in the shadow of Hollywood and after all, Kiwi had called me Clark.

As it turned out she was delightful in every way, not only smart and intelligent but dark haired and rather languorous. I kept thinking about Carole Lombard but she went straight into business mode from the start at our meeting

'The world revolves around money,' she began, 'it's not just desirable, it's essential. If the money runs out, the show closes down and that's where we come in. We need to control the 'futures' markets in every respect so that world institutions come to a halt when we decide. Naturally we have to be discreet and operate clandestinely at every level and that's the reason we are here and not in New York, London, Paris or Hong Kong. In addition we have to be cleverer than them in order to disrupt their systems. We will use well tried tactics such as the 'Game -Over Zeus Botnet' and 'Crypto Locker' but we have a few surprises up our sleeve also. Our aim is to upset stability in the markets and choke off the financial resources available to major enterprises such as Power Stations and infrastructures.

'We are very fortunate in that respect to have the Chemico conglomerate on our side. They are a major player in the markets and can make the investments that we need at the time that we need them, to have the biggest impact.'

She paused for a moment to see if I was paying attention to her words and not her legs, but the jury was out on that one! Actually she didn't take her eyes off me for a moment. She watched me like a hawk and I couldn't help thinking about Matlock's nickname as 'Bald Eagle,' but she seemed more like a vulture waiting to see if I made a mistake.

'The key is in the 'futures' market, so if the money ran out world trade would come to a halt and that goes for most major industrial enterprises where we also have agents. Government money is a different matter but I can assure you that we've thought of that as well. If Treasury Bonds and the like are compromised then the whole deck of cards falls down. No military, no social services, no hospitals and no schools. In addition we can immobilise strategic energy supplies and then bring in our partners who are waiting patiently. I'll say more on that later if I can trust you.

'If Matlock is a fanatic' I thought,' surely here's another one.'

❊❊❊

These developments led me to reconsider the plans laid out for Kiwi and me. After all, I was now in the position that Franks had laid out for her at the bank and I thought that I could make progress there instead.

She agreed and put forward a plan of her own, namely that she would befriend Madison and his girls in order to find out more about the secret side of Cerberus. We had found out quite a lot about their intentions, even the scope of operations such as 'Operation Trust' but we still didn't know who 'Alpha' was, or where he (or she) was either. Kiwi's notion was that we would both invite the Madison family for days out together (We would love to see the countryside around here) and hope that we would eventually get an invitation to their log cabin retreat. When we had become firm family friends she would then offer to 'take care' of the girls when he was too busy. In this way she hoped that he might begin to share any doubts that he had might have with Cerberus, maybe with her or even with me. Eventually we might be able to offer some kind of amnesty if he would agree to turn State's Witness.

We put this plan to M&S as well as to Franks and Tucker and, although they thought it was a long shot, they agreed that it could yield dividends. I'd also told them about my forthcoming initiation ceremony and here they were less enthusiastic, primarily for my own safety.

Tucker put it like this,

'We at the CIA always try to protect our agents when they come into harm's way' she wrote, 'but we also value initiative, and if the agent fully comprehends the dangers in any given situation, we will back them up. However please be aware that it's most unlikely that we could mount a rescue if you get into difficulties. Frankly this could be a break-through as we have never had someone on the inside before, so we will approve your plan, but please be careful.'

I must admit that I was apprehensive, but Henry Madison was to be my sponsor and he was his normal ebullient, confident and comforting self.

'We need people like you,' he said, 'there's too many hard liners here and sometimes you get better results through compromise in my opinion. But don't say I said so' he added with a grin.

I liked him, and with sentiments like that I felt that he might be 'turned' eventually, but for now he was definitely 'one of them,' and as my sponsor, an important figure at the ceremony. So, on the day in question it was he who took me on a short drive to the venue.

To my surprise it turned out to be the Paul Getty Museum just off the Highway, but as we got inside the gates he stopped and said,

'Sorry chum but you've got to be blindfolded from here.'

I nodded and he fitted a loose bandana around my forehead, making sure that I could not see but also that it was not too tight.

'Comfy are we?' he asked, and I immediately thought of him tucking his two girls into their beds at night. Yes, this man had feelings unlike Matlock and Swann, and this also confirmed my view that he might be an ally one day.

He now drove on for about ten minutes on a route that I suspected was to the back of the estate before he stopped and ushered me out. Only then did he remove my blindfold and I found myself standing in front of a very small chapel that seemed to be abandoned. He ushered me towards the door and as I approached I could not help noticing that, instead of the expected Christian symbolism the sign on the door was that of a Square and Compasses, the familiar sign of the Masons. Henry saw my glance and remarked,

'Take no notice, this place has been derelict for years.'

However, as we entered the chapel I noticed that it seemed far from derelict and that some of the walls had other masonic symbols also. I didn't know what to make of it, but before I could conjecture further I was led to the altar rail where a figure stood in a white gown and conical masked hat. My heart jumped. I had seen this figure many times before, in the woods around Baton Rouge when I was a boy. The figure began an incantation in a low monotone but I was thinking of Billie Holiday's 'Strange Fruit,' that song that evoked memories of the many Ku Klux Klan hangings from trees in remote areas, and all too often outside deserted chapels like this one. At this point Henry took my arm and motioned me to go forward. As he did so, two shadowy figures emerged, each wearing a different mask. I was reminded of the gargoyles at Capulet Castle, so horrifying was the effect. The first of these was tall but the other was at least a foot taller and that seemed to make him even more menacing as he seemed to drag himself with difficulty rather than pace easily. They both wore blood red cloaks against which hung a dagger in a mock simulation of a crucifix but it was too late to run away, and in any case I was rooted to the spot in fear, so I clung tightly to Madison's hand (just as his girls might), and knelt at the altar as commanded. Now the three persons held hands and began a musical chant not unlike a psalm, as their leader spoke these words over and over again.

'This land is ours. It is not theirs. This land is ours. It is not theirs'

He stopped, and then the mantra was taken up by each of the others in turn as suddenly a smoky mist appeared from within the chapel, making the whole scene more mysterious and scary than ever. Now it was my turn as they motioned Henry and I forward to utter the oath. I was then guided back to a bench and encouraged to kneel while the master of ceremonies gave a short homily about loyalty on fear of death, at which point the others drew their knives with menace. The blades were clearly pointed at me and then thrust forward in a menacing motion. I thought I saw that the taller figure had six fingers on each hand but I could have been mistaken. The leader then signalled to me to go, and that was the best bit of news that I had heard all day.

Author's note - In 1970 the President of Grenada (Gairy) reported that he had seen a 7 foot 'space creature' with six fingers. Soon afterwards he was ousted from office by US government special forces.

We were then allowed to leave but I was a quivering wreck as Henry guided me to the car after he had spoken to the hooded group.

'Not so bad was it?' he chuckled, but offered me a flask of bourbon just the same.

'Well I wouldn't want to go through it again.' I replied, 'Just pass the rest of that Jack Daniels.'

I had bonded with Henry Madison and we had shared a blood oath and now I must betray him. Yes I felt a twinge of conscience, but I had probably already convinced myself that necessity must prevail over nicety. I was on the inside and now I had a job to do at the bank, but in addition I'd been wondering what significance the Masonic symbolism might have. I recalled that both Matlock and the Colonel had been Masons, so was there a connection? I'd put that in my report and ask for advice. I just hoped that Henry and his family would not be hurt in the process.

At this point he stopped and said, 'Do you realise who that was?'

I was feeling light headed so I replied, 'The Devil himself I wouldn't wonder.'

Henry laughed,

'Close,' he said, 'that was Matlock on his way to Fukushima. He looked in to see you and I think that he was quite impressed. I've also now been told that the other two were Alpha himself and the leader of our associates, known to me only as Omega.'

I didn't know whether to feel flattered or just frightened, but I was glad to get back to the hotel for another and yet another drink. I was also feeling uneasy about the oath that I had given. In my book a man's word was his bond and I felt a twinge of conscience that I had been so deceitful. All in the line of duty it may be but I still felt kind of dirty. Of course I couldn't sleep, and when I did it was only for a few seconds before I awoke in a sweat, conjuring up images of the tall man and his knife standing over me as I lay spread-eagled in the shape of a cross. As dawn broke I was even more determined to pursue Alpha to his hiding place, but now I had a bigger incentive. The man had nearly frightened me to death and I wouldn't let him get away with it. Who the heck was Omega and what was his 'organisation,' and how did it tie in with Cerberus? Could he possibly be from Gonda? I very nearly forgot that I didn't really believe all the stuff about aliens, because he was the most alien of humans that I'd ever seen. Then I realised that I had made the assumption that he was male. What if he was female or even something in between I wondered. Now I felt really sleepy and slept for 10 hours.

Now it would be up to Kiwi to add her special gifts to the situation by giving the girls some of the love and attention that they probably lacked without a mum. I was absolutely sure that Henry was a great dad, but these were girls after all, and fishing isn't the only pleasure in life.

To fit in with this proposed domestic scene Kiwi decided that she'd adopt a short brown haired look instead of her Monroe blonde. 'It's to make the girls feel more at ease.' she said when I complained.

Molly and Mary Madison were 12 and 9 respectively. Molly was rather tall, dark and elegant (rather like her mother according to Henry) whilst Mary was short, blonde and rather like a tomboy. Henry had been pleased to take up our suggestion of a day out and naturally it had to be Hollywood and the Warner Brothers studios. The girls had not been before so they were absolutely thrilled, especially at the Harry Potter exhibitions that seemed to dominate the showrooms. Of course Kiwi and I had been there to meet our local 'controllers M&S' but we didn't let on and of course that made it all the more exciting for everyone.

The girls were a bit nervous with me at first but they took to Kiwi right away and she to them. Soon they were chatting away like old friends, sharing ice creams and goggling at young male actors who strolled around in tight pants. Henry and I talked about baseball nearly all day. It was good to get a break from work and I'm sure that he felt the same.

All good things come to a halt and soon it was time to head for home.

'Can we go out again soon? Please, please Daddy.' chorused the girls.

'Sure thing honey lambs,' he responded, 'that's if Edwin and Sally don't mind.'

Well we agreed like a shot and another day was soon arranged, this time at 'Sea-World' a fantastical complex of undersea experiences as well as 'Pirates of the Caribbean.' The girls were enthralled once more, and as Henry dropped us off at the hotel he said what we'd been waiting to hear.

'Say you guys, we're off to the cabin next weekend. Why don't you come along? There's plenty of room and Ed (He'd shortened it now, another good sign) and I can catch some trout while you girls do girlie things.'

We accepted straight away, although Kiwi later confided that she didn't really know what girls enjoyed doing these days.

'Don't worry,' she said 'I'll work it out.'

I now had a week at the bank to see if I could make some headway with Cerberus's plans in the financial sphere. I must say that Charlie was very helpful and friendly in every way especially since I had (by virtue of my initiation) become a 'Delta' in the ranking order. I surmised that she was probably a Gamma or even a potential Beta. We had been told that she was highly regarded in the organisation so I set out to make myself useful, hoping to pick up a trail along the way. I didn't know what it would be, but I was looking out for any financial links between those activities, businesses and governments that Cerberus identified as targets. The starting point was a very large manual that Charlie showed me

'They trust you and I've been instructed to trust you,' she said, 'but there's only one of these in each region and it's locked in my safe. You are the only other person, apart from Beta Matlock to see it, so if there's a security lapse we'll know who to come to, and I wouldn't be in your shoes if we do. I can assure you I'll be watching your every move.'

I've just said that Charlie was helpful and friendly but she also seemed to have that dual personality that Kiwi had mentioned about Matlock. 'One minute a doting husband and father and the next a cold blooded killer.' she had said. I had heard that there was a Mr Swann and children, and I had no doubt that she also fitted Matlock's model in that both respects. I reassured her that I would be careful, but I noticed that she held on to the binder very firmly as if still reluctant to let it go before she handed it over to me.

'I'll look after it.' I said, 'and I'll hand it back personally to you and only to you when I'm done. OK?'

She grudgingly agreed and I was allowed to take the file into a small room to study it. Of course I wanted to use my mini-mini-camera to record some salient features but the old axiom came to mind that 'discretion is the better part of valour.' I was already aware that Charlie was observing me from across the office and I had also detected surveillance cameras hidden in the room. I was pleased with myself and wondered if some other poor dope hadn't been so careful in the past, and paid the price with his life. I shivered as I remembered the blood red cloaks and daggers at my initiation. Perhaps these would be the judges, the jury and executioners at my hearing if I slipped up. I felt very cold.

As it turned out the book revealed much of what I expected, as it listed places and areas of commercial or industrial interest across the globe, delineating each in terms of location and priority. However what was more significant was that the financial centres of the world, such as New York, London and others were all given a 'shadow.' In the case of New York it was right here at the Frisco Bank in Los Angeles and I soon discovered that every transaction at the NYSE was recorded here and action taken or deferred as appropriate. As we know the Cerberus long term objective is to undermine the stability of society, but this obviously has to be undertaken in complete secrecy and no action approved that might alert the markets. This is why they had given much attention to the long term futures markets in which a stranglehold might be placed on commodities before traders become fully aware. I had been told that a sophisticated IT programme existed but needed some refinement, so I set about analysing and cross referencing the data so that I could make a recommendation to Charlie. My work had to be genuine and it had to be useful if I was to appear credible, but I did have an idea. This was that I would acquaint Tucker and Franks of any decisions that followed my ideas. They could then neutralize them through their own back channels without compromising me. It would be fatal if I was rumbled before Operation Trust or any other Cerberus programme was ready for implementation. Unfortunately Franks thought that this might not happen for six months so he told me to play cat and mouse in the meantime. Consequently he advised me to be useful, 'but not that useful.' I hoped he realised that he could be signing my death warrant by following that advice. If they suspected that I was not genuine I'd be a dead man, but I said that I'd do my best, and pray.

Actually it was easier than I thought as I played around with future grain stocks in the Ukraine, copper deposits in Zambia and oil reserves in the Gulf and many more. I carefully positioned each of these so that one careful deposit or withdrawal would spook the market, handing control in that sector to Cerberus who would have funds available either way. I recommended the use of 'spread betting (IG style), and also established useful contacts with the other 'shadow' banks in different parts of the world. I even got on first name terms with other Cerberus personnel there. For example in the UK it was the 'Utility Bank' at the retirement capital Torquay in Devon. Once more this was a discrete operation and somewhat remote. The manual had revealed that a Geraldine Lewis was our 'man' (woman) there and she was very receptive to exchanging data, under secure conditions of course.

I told Swann of my progress but emphasised that, timing would be critical and nothing should be done at present 'until the time was right.' I could see that she was impressed by my inside knowledge and my initiative, as well as the use of that familiar phrase so now I could feel more at ease And maybe look forward to the weekend.

※※※

Henry had told me that his cabin was at Lake Tahoe which is not so far from San Francisco on the border of California and Nevada. It only took us an hour travelling through the Sacramento Valley, but it seemed like another world. As we approached along the base of the Sierra Nevada, the hills, so popular with skiers, rose majestically on either side leading us inexorably to the Lake itself. I was reminded of an old cowboy song about 'Pure Clear Water' as the waters shone and reflected the blue sky above. We soon reached the log cabin which was near a small township called 'Sparks' between Carson City and Reno. A small stream ran behind a substantial plot of land that was mostly birch trees and brush, with paths running down to the water. Henry said that the Humboldt River was not far away and that was the best place to fish in his opinion. It had also been a good place to pan for gold during the Gold Rush of the 1840's and Henry had told me that he hoped to find more. Actually he confessed that it was a good ploy to interest the girls if they got bored with fishing, which they often did he said ruefully.

Now I could see that he was keen to get started, but Kiwi suggested a barbecue so that she and I could get to know the girls better. Fortunately the vote was 4 to 1 in her favour with Henry accepting defeat graciously, and so began our first day at Lake Tahoe.

The barbecue was a sort of success as Kiwi prepared burgers and Molly prepared the salad, looking at Henry nervously to see if she was doing it right. Meanwhile Mary swung on a rope ladder.

'Come on Mare,' Molly called out, 'Aren't you going to help?'

There was no reply because Mary was obviously reliving the Pirates of the Caribbean up there in the tree (I mean crow's nest), and doing her best to impress her Dad as well.

'Look at me. Look at me' she called out.

'Never mind shipmates,' Kiwi said with a smile, 'she just won't get any victuals that's all.'

Now Molly was triumphant, running to the tree and calling out, 'No food for you! No food for you!'

This soon brought Mary back to the table where she graciously accepted a bowl of crisps to put on the table. Mini crisis over I thought but I made a mental note not to set sister against sister if I was ever in a position to do so in the future.

Later, as we lay snuggled up in bed Kiwi told me about the Colonel's 'entourage' back at Castle Capulet. His secretaries were friends, even lovers, but also rivals in love. She started to hum the song and I joined in, 'God help the mister who comes between me and my sister, but God help the sister who comes between me and my man'. The song had a subtle rhythm to it, and this was soon transferred to our warm bodies as we began to move.

'Shush' she said, 'you'll wake the children!'

The next day we did go fishing (to please Dad it seemed), and, with a lot of help I managed to land my first trout. The girls had gone off with Kiwi down river 'panning for gold' she said later. That evening we sat around a camp fire and cooked the trout. Henry had caught five to my one, so we were very well fed with beans and rice as well. He then took out an old guitar and started to play the blues. He wasn't half bad either and soon we were all playing something. I chose the teaspoons and Kiwi played the kettle while the two girls tootled on their recorders as they had probably done many times before.

We finished our 'jam session' appropriately with the St Louis Blues as the sun went down. Fishing was on the agenda for the following day also, but Kiwi had managed to persuade Henry to allow her to go skiing with the girls at the nearby slopes, leaving me with him on the banks of the River Humboldt. I felt that this might be a good time to add to my rather sketchy details of his operation and also maybe to see where his real loyalties lay, but I had to be careful. Fortunately I landed a big fat trout almost at once and showed my appreciation by placing it in his bag.

'That's to thank you for everything.' I said.' I just wish I could be more helpful, but I'm not sure that I can do any more once I've sorted out the bank. What do Cerberus agents do after a job is finished then?' I asked.

He laughed that big belly laugh of his, and it seemed to echo along the stream and up into the hills almost like thunder. No, it WAS thunder and we were soon sheltering under some trees but barely keeping dry.

I imagined that Matlock was in charge of the heavens too, and was just giving us a warning.

'We move on.' he said, picking up my earlier question, 'sometimes to bigger and better things and sometimes we're put out to grass, or worse if we've failed.'

Now was my chance to persuade him to share his thoughts about Anya and other fatalities that he might have known about so I put it to him straight.

'This seems like the right kind of job for me, being single and all, but it must be very worrying for a man with kids like you. Don't you sometimes wish that you could leave? You've done your bit and now you can leave it to us.'

He seemed a bit taken aback by this sentiment and replied in a sort of jokey way,

'Seems like you want my job old boy,' he said, 'well you're right, you'd be welcome to it if I could get out without a fuss. But I should tell you that it's never been done. The oath is for ever, 'on pain of death,' and I'm not ready to die yet. It's a bit like the Catholic Church or the Masons. Once you're in, you're in it for life or in this case death. I'm an optimist though. Once 'Operation Trust' and others are implemented it's possible that I might be allowed to fish every day, all day. What bliss. Still, I'll have to be patient and see what happens.'

I had my answer. He was trapped for now, but if and when he could see a Cerberus funeral pyre I thought he'd be ready to co-operate. In addition I wondered whether his reference to Catholics and Masons had been relevant to Cerberus at all, or perhaps it was just that he was both.

I decided to leave that conundrum for another day so I just said,

'Well let's just enjoy my fat fish when we get back.

'Right on.' he replied.

We returned to the cabin and Kiwi already had a fire going with jacket potatoes hungrily waiting for a nice juicy trout and I was happy to oblige. We were soon all seated around the 'old camp fire' and singing cowboy songs, such as 'Home on the Range' again. However, when the topic turned to the skiing, sisterly rivalry broke out once more with Mary taking the lead.

'Molly fell flat on her face.' she crowed.

'Oh no I didn't.' protested Molly, 'you slipped on your bum.'

I laughed although maybe I shouldn't have as I asked Kiwi, 'Did you stay upright then?'

'Well, most of the time,' she replied with a grin, 'you see I haven't skied for ages. It's very exhilarating you know, why don't you try it?'

At this point Henry interrupted proceedings saying that he planned to take me fishing out on the lake. Now I was in a fix. What was my fate to be? Neither choice appealed to me, but fortunately our weekend was over for now and perhaps I might feign an injury next time.

Back in 'civilisation' Kiwi arranged an outing for the girls as it was their half term from school, and to show his appreciation Henry invited us to a meal out at the famous 'Lighthouse' on Hermosa Beach some way between Santa Monica and Long Beach near Los Angeles. Henry hadn't told me that he was a jazz fan but for me it was a wonderful surprise as I remembered it as being the 'Mecca' of West Coast Jazz in the sixties.

'They all played here,' he said, 'Howard Rumsey and the Lighthouse All Stars of course, Art Pepper, Shorty Rogers and the Giants and so many more.'

I didn't like to tell him that those names had been emblazoned on my heart over many decades because he was like a boy let out of school.

'Sounds fantastic,' I said, 'tell me more.' He needed no encouragement, but as he rambled on I could sense Kiwi giving me 'that' look. I took the hint immediately,

'Care to dance?' I asked and took her arm as a small trio played 'Tenderly', leaving Henry somewhat in the lurch, and probably in the middle of a notable Stan Getz solo in his mind.

She held me tightly, so tight I could hardly breathe but I didn't mind.

'Thank you.' she said, 'thank you so much'.

I asked her what for but she just hugged me tighter as if to say 'that's what for.'

I suddenly felt very happy and just said, 'I love you Kiwi.' She sighed a very deep sigh and clung on even tighter,

We returned to the table where Henry greeted us with a bottle of champagne, raising his glass in a toast.

'Cheers to you two,' he said, 'I've grown very fond of you and wish you many years of happiness but' and here he paused as he was wont to do when he had something important to say, 'but I'm afraid I've received some very tragic news and it's going to spoil the party for a while.' here he stopped again. 'The fact is that last night a Tsunami hit the coast off Fukushima and hundreds are dead or missing'. Now there was an even longer pause before he continued, 'And Matlock is one of them.' he said grimly.

I didn't know whether to laugh or cry. The tragedy was beyond comprehension but if Matlock was dead, well that was a bonus and I could see that Kiwi thought so too. However she was an experienced operator in such circumstances and she disguised her true feelings by simply saying,

'What a tragedy. I hope that they find him and the others soon. Just think of their families and all the other children.'

My job was slightly more delicate, as Henry knew that I had taken a dislike to Matlock in his KKK uniform, but at the same time he was an authority figure in the Cerberus set-up.

'I'm sorry to hear it too,' I said, 'he was probably a good guy under that hood.'

I was a good liar as well.

Unfortunately there was more to come as Henry held his hand up to gain our attention once more.

'The place is wrecked,' he said, 'and someone has got to go out there to pick up the pieces.' Here he stopped and looked searchingly at me. 'I'm sorry Ed,' he continued, 'I'm afraid it's got to be you. I want you to go as my deputy because I can't leave here at present.'

I knew that he meant it as a compliment, but quite frankly I didn't want to accept, not only because of my own safety but because it would mean leaving Kiwi again, but I knew that I must.

It was actually a golden opportunity to get deep inside the Cerberus network, and who knows where it might lead, maybe even to Alpha or to the mysterious Omega who had been at my initiation. Perhaps even more important was the prospect of finding out more about Gonda. Kiwi had been told about the legend of the Gondian homelands, and I'd also picked up bits and pieces myself and Franks and Tucker had alluded to an involvement with Cerberus of some sort, so to put it mildly I had my hands full.

Kiwi played her part well given the circumstances,

'Why can't you send someone else?' she asked, 'surely there must be others just as suitable.'

Henry smiled and replied. 'Don't take this badly and, to answer your question, no, there is no one I would rather send. It's not just because Ed is well suited in the technical and economic and IT spheres, no, it's because I trust him, and trust is a rare commodity in my business.'

He placed his arm around me and I suddenly felt very shallow. It might be true to say that I had not been really tested up to now. You see I was fairly sure when a matter was right or wrong in my eyes, but I didn't cope very well with all the stages in between and this was one of them. Betrayal and deception did not fit into my self-image at all.

'Duke is as straight as a die.' my friends and colleagues would say, and now here I was on the other side of the tracks. My only excuse was that old standby 'orders', and where had I heard that before?

A little later we bid goodnight and made our way back to our room. Once inside Kiwi clung to me as if I was going to leave her there and then.

'Don't go darling,' she said, 'I've got a feeling that I shall never see you again. It's like a premonition. I have them sometimes, in fact our family were well known for it back in Queenstown. My Nan was known as 'Granny Grant' to everyone, and people came to her for her readings of the runes or the stars. I don't think that I have her gift but I am blessed with very sensitive antennae, and usually know when trouble is ahead. The problem is that I don't always know how to deal with it. Now in this case you know very well that there are dangers of all kinds. On the practical side there is the Tsunami legacy of floods, disease and radiation of course. Then there are Cerberus agents whom you don't know, aliens that you don't believe in and all this coupled with the fact that Matlock might turn up at any moment. How can you be sure that you'll survive and come back to me?'

She started to cry and I tried to console her, but I knew that she was right.

'Kiss me.' she said, and with such feeling that I thought it really would be the last time.

We gradually merged together with such ease and such passion that it seemed that we had truly become one at last.

> *This latest Tsunami off the coast of Tokyo followed other serious ones in the past and safety measures had been taken. However they had been proven to be largely ineffective and fears of latent radiation still remained.*

On arrival in Tokyo I was met by my host, a young engineer called Tom Takagi. Like most Japanese he was courteous in the extreme and took me immediately to the Holiday Inn where I would be staying. As we went to reception to get my keys he bowed two or three times and said,

'I hope you will be comfortable here 'White San.' Please let me know if you need anything and I'll call for you tomorrow and take you to Fukushima.'

It had been a long flight so I was pleased to go to my room and relax, knowing full well that there would not be much relaxation at all in the next few days.

And so it turned out, for as we approached the power station there was devastation on all sides.

'How can people survive amongst all this?' I asked him. He shrugged and just said,

'Not many did. My sister and my brother are still missing but I still pray that they will be found.'

I found myself lost for words so I just mumbled, 'I am so sorry. There is always hope.' But I knew that there wasn't really.

He stopped the car and asked me to get out, leading me to a large area of the ruins.

'That was Yokotaki, our base, and as you can see it is just a few metres from the main buildings. As far as we know no one who was there that day has survived' he said resignedly. He stopped and bowed toward the rubble and tears appeared in his eyes. 'Forgive me.' he wailed, 'I know that I should have been on duty so I should be dead as well.'

I tried to comfort him but he was busy building a miniature Shinto Shrine with pieces from the wreckage, and nothing would disturb him until it was done. There was no sign of life, and just a few pieces of paper fluttered in the breeze amongst the debris of broken desks, chairs and computers.

I knew that it was insensitive but I just had to ask an all important question.

'Was Sam Matlock on duty that day?' I muttered. He said nothing but picked up a black briefcase, covered in dust and blood and handed it to me. The initials were SM and no more was said, but on the way back to Tokyo he confided his private thoughts to me.

'We much in distress White San but we know that the spirits of the dead do not want us to grieve too much, so tonight we will be happy. You know that our partnership with Gonda is nearing completion. It is their ancestors and ours who will soon be joined in a glorious future and mankind will be redeemed once more. I will show you more tomorrow when we visit Lake Inawashiro and I'll explain why the lakes are important to us. Meanwhile be watchful and you will be given a sign, maybe sooner than you know. The next day you must meet members of the board and take charge.'

Me? Take charge? I thought. That's a joke but I knew that's exactly why Henry had sent me, and I was now in for a penny or a yen. At the same time a shiver ran down my neck as this polite young man spoke with such certitude about a future with Aliens.

❈ ❈ ❈

As I said Tom Takagi was a very attentive host and with his wife Susi, they made sure that I would enjoy Japan.

'Konnichiwaa (hello) White San.' were Susi's first words as she greeted me, backing away and motioning me forward into their living room. By western standards this seemed to be sparsely furnished but in Japan it would have been the norm. A large round table was in the centre of the room but it was only two foot high, meaning that persons hoping to sit could not do so as there were no seats. Instead comfortable cushions were provided and one had to squat rather than sit. Tom motioned me to my seat (sorry, my squat) and very soon Susi brought a tray carrying a teapot with cups and laid it on the table.

'Honoured guest,' she said, 'I like to show you ancient Japanese tea ceremony. There only being three of us, this is called Chakai. There are different words for larger groups and sometimes Saki is served as well.'

I looked around hoping to see some, but Tom shook his head while Susi continued.

'Each ceremony means 'the way of the tea' she said,' and it is always green tea, or 'sado' in Japanese. The small water bowls that you see are to wash your hands for purification. Now shall I be mother?'

We all laughed at this somewhat incongruous Western phrase in the midst of such a Japanese tradition.

'Kampai,' I said, but apparently that was not appropriate. The hours passed amicably until it was time to give me more Japanese 'education' in Tom's words. Susi would stay behind while he was to take me to the notorious 'Hanamachi' district.

As we drove there in a taxi Tom gave me some idea about what we were in for and what protocols should be observed.

'Edwin San,' he said, now taking on the familiar rather than formal address back at the factory or at home, 'Edwin San, I should tell you that the Hanamachi, or Kagai district is not a red light district in the Western sense, except that most things can be bought there, or more correctly, traded there, such as favours and influence rather than for money, and that may or may not include sex with Geisha.

Let me explain a little more. You may have heard of the Geisha in this context but before we enter into their world you should know a few things about tradition and protocol there.

First of all the girls are not 'The Geisha' but simply Geisha and they are strictly organised in a formal hierarchy, in some ways by age. The older Geisha are called 'Jikarta' and adopt a kind of supervisory role on the younger girls. In addition they are usually entertainers with many skills including dancing or musicians. The younger Geisha are called 'maiko' and they might be sixteen or quite a bit younger. If you approach a maiko you should look to nearby Jikarta for an approving nod, and if you don't get it I suggest you try elsewhere.'

With his advice ringing in my ears we soon arrived at what seemed to be a large theatre from the outside but was more like a ballroom inside. There was a large open wooden floor around which were grouped a number of chairs and couches and a Filipino band played quietly in the background. They were playing 'Tea for two' but there wasn't much tea around. Small tables carried bottles of Saki as well as every other spirit or beer that you might think of. We were shown to one of these tables and soon joined by a very glamorous Jikarta called Madame Nakano and a lovely maiko whose name was Lily. From time to time she got up and danced. She danced alone in a kind of dreamy way and I could swear that she didn't take her eyes off me for a moment. Perhaps it was the Saki that was confusing me but towards the end of the evening Tom took me aside to give me some very surprising news.

'You most favoured American,' he said. 'Madame Nakano says that you can go with Lily to Hilton Hotel where room is booked in name of Truman. Madame will stay in lobby until you are finished. Then she will take Lily home. There is no charge. All expenses paid for by Fukushima.'

I didn't know what to say as I looked back to Madame Nakano and Lily now seated on the couch beside our table. Madame just nodded her head and Lily fixed me in that alluring glance as she crossed her legs modestly, or was it immodestly? Yes I'd been tempted before but this was different. You might say that it was irresistible and as I looked into her eyes and took in her lovely kimono as it draped modestly over her tiny breasts, I knew that I was lost. Tom could see that I was hesitating and nudged me in the ribs.

'You must go,' he said, 'refusal is loss of face not only for them but for you, me and all Fukushima.'

He might have said the whole of Japan the way that he put it, so I bowed and went back to the couch for more Saki.

A taxi took as to the Hilton and to the reception desk where we had to sign in as Mr and Mrs Harry Truman. I realised that this name had been chosen with care, maybe the sign that Tom had spoken of, to remind me of the inhumane Atom bombs dropped on Nagasaki and Hiroshima just a few decades ago, but why? In typical Japanese fashion their reasoning was obscure but I rather think that it was not about Japan at all but a 'coded message' from Gonda through their associates Cerberus, that there was a better way to run the planet. At the Hilton that night, I was Truman and his 'Domino Theory' and I was also the Bush/Cheney 'New World Order,' as well as every other war crazy American who betrayed the human race. Like them I was an evil creature not fit to rule, but this was my chance to encourage those in power to mend their ways and co-operate with Gondian justice or face retribution. It was becoming clear that a betrayal of humanity would be the charge.

Maybe I was reading too much into it but somehow I sensed that I was right. Now I was feeling very woozy as we entered our room, and once inside Lily helped me off with my jacket and I flopped gratefully onto the bed. She did not join me but sat on the floor, arms akimbo on the duvet, and stared straight into my eyes. I stared back, she was so lovely, so tempting; and then the room began to spin around and around with Lily at the centre, but no, now she was Kiwi and then Lily, then Kiwi again. Then I fainted and when I awoke it was 4am and Lily was gone. She had left me her card, and I still have it today. It had a Lily on the front and it said.

Thank you White San no loss of face always our secret.

I was grateful, and to be honest very relieved. I'm not really one for betrayals if that's what it would have been, but I could hardly congratulate myself could I? What if I hadn't passed out?

Now it crossed my mind that I was going crazy if I believed that it was a betrayal of humanity that drove Gondian interest in our planet. That just didn't make sense unless, yes, unless the Gondians are in some senses human as well, maybe from a very distant time. Now that theory is not so far- fetched as it may seem because there are many theories out there about UFO's RETURNING to Earth rather than just visiting, and this fits in with stories of 'Ancient Aliens' recorded throughout history. Evidence is sparse and scepticism rife, but I was beginning to think there was room for doubt. I would have classed myself as 'Sceptical First Class' but now I was wavering. I remembered that it was not so long ago that Professor Hubble located 'VAR', the variable star, and this in turn led to the discovery of a vast Universe (or Universes) outside our own. Perhaps Gonda was in one of those constellations I surmised.

My thoughts now turned to Kiwi, and I wondered what she would make of it with her almost uncanny insight. I couldn't wait to see her but Tom had promised to show me Lake Inawashiro implying that it not only served a special purpose but was personal to him. And naturally I was curious to find out what it might be. Tom had started to open up to me and I wanted to encourage him.

Lake Inawashiro is the fourth largest lake in Japan. It is known as the 'Sky Mirror Lake,' some say for its clarity and the reflection of Mt Bandai that is ever present. It has hot springs and millions of Swans visit in the winter, and I wondered how this benign beauty fitted in with Cerberus plans. It was quite a drive but the view was certainly worth the journey and we sat speechless for a while in the car before Tom got out and bowed toward the Lake and the mountain beyond, and I thought it polite to do the same. He then motioned me to sit on the grass and this is what he told me.

'Here is the home of my ancestors.' he said, 'Many millions of years ago visitors from another planet arrived on earth in small cylinders and nestled in deep water lakes throughout the world, and this is one of them. At first they were also able to survive in the sea, but pollution has now made this impossible despite several experiments as in San Francisco Bay. The planet Gonda was beginning to warm up so a new home had to be found and earth was one of the possibilities. All that Gondians needed was clear fresh water and a power source if at all possible. From the depths of these many habitats and over many millennia, the Gondians emerged to mix and mate with humans, thus creating a kind of hybrid race. However, with news from Gonda that the planet had cooled sufficiently for life to resume, many returned there. Nonetheless many stayed behind and my ancestors were among them but many faced persecution due to their somewhat unusual features and practices such as communication with the Stars.

'Now Gonda is facing another heat crisis and contact has been made for their return to earth. This contact has been aided by Cerberus with its own agenda for promoting a new start on Earth, and up to now their objectives might seem to be the same, although I warn you that there is some friction over the 'race' and persecution issues as before. Many Gondians did indeed breed with non- whites, so that matter has still to be resolved. Over the last decades a new 'seeding' of the lakes has already begun in the Great Lakes, and elsewhere where there is uncontaminated fresh water. But pollution has become a problem even there due to nuclear and other activity. Some of our Gondian friends are dying in the depths and something must be done urgently to purify the lakes for them, and for the imminent arrival of others. In the meantime you and your colleagues in the 'host community' must be 'persuaded' that there is no option but to co-operate. We already have a number of multi-nationals lined up such as Chemico and there will be many more. Once we have control of finance and economics, politics will follow so resistance will be futile. Now all we have to do is to prepare and wait 'until the time is right.'

As I said, I was not convinced that any of this was more than just romantic notions about a long lost past but what if it was true? Certainly the remark about San Francisco Bay matched the sighting by Senator Joshua Prince in which he had stated that he had seen alien craft lifting OUT of the Bay, not descending into it. You may remember that it was my view at that time that he was killed because he wouldn't keep the matter quiet. The whole thing was more than I had hoped for and I couldn't wait to make my report, although to be perfectly honest I wasn't quite sure what to say, except to note his comments about 'seeding' in the Great Lakes. But first of all there was the dreaded Board Meeting to attend the next day, and it turned out to be quite a surreal experience.

There were 12 members and I was immediately guided to the chair and the head of a long table. The 12 remained standing until I bowed. Then they followed suit and we all sat down. I won't go into all the details of the meeting but naturally we discussed the disaster at some length. It was only when we got to making plans for the future that there seemed to be an impasse. Quite frankly no one seemed to know what to do. When I raised the question of appointing a contractor there was no reply so I fixed my gaze on the Chief Engineer (I had been given their titles but not their names).

'What do you recommend for the clearance?' I said, and at first I thought that he had not heard me as he remained still with his eyes shut. I repeated the question but there was still no response and just as I was about to ask again he opened his eyes and looked at me in a puzzled way.

'That is what you are here for White San.' he said and closed his eyes again. My questions and suggestions to others got the same stony response so I decided to really take charge with this pronouncement.

'Thank you honourable board members,' I said, 'today, with your approval I recommend that we close down our operations at Fukushima and concentrate our energies elsewhere.'

I waited nervously for an objection but one by one they all stood and raised their water glasses to me in a toast.

'Kampai White San.' they called out in unison. They then all bowed and filed out of the room….. I told you that it was surreal.

※※※

Not only had I pleased the board but I was pretty sure that Henry Madison would approve as well. What is more I felt certain that Franks and Tucker would like the idea that a Cerberus base had been neutralised in this way. A good result all round I would say but now I had to test out my theory on Henry when I got back.

I bade my farewells to Tom and Susi and took a JAL flight back to LA. Kiwi was there to meet me with tears in her eyes and I must admit that I was crying too. We spent a day of togetherness and tenderness and it wasn't until the next day that we made love. It was as if we both wanted to wait, almost like young lovers again; and then we melted.

Henry had arranged to see me at his 'retreat' saying that he liked to spend more time there these days, and also that it was good for the girls.

'Don't forget to bring Sally,' he said, 'the girls are so looking forward to seeing her again and we can sneak off for some fishing while you tell me your story.'

Oh no. I thought, not fishing again, but it was a small price to pay to lure this big beast to my net. So it was that on a grassy bank overlooking the river that I gave an account of events in Japan and waited to see his reaction. As I had hoped it was very positive and I felt that he was relieved to be 'relieved' of this far away responsibility, but now I had to be very careful if I was to persuade him over to our side. You might recall that I had broached the subject before but I felt that he might be more amenable after the tragedy at Fukushima.

'I think that we did the right thing in Japan,' I said, 'but I'm not sure that Matlock will see it that way and you know what he can be like. I hope that you'll be careful from now on, you remember what happened to Anya Stein and if he thinks we made the wrong decision it might go badly for you,'

I paused a moment for effect, 'and your family unfortunately.' I added.

He looked scared, 'Yes I know that you're right but what can I do?' he replied, 'I told you that there's no way out once you've sworn loyalty, just as you have.'

It was now or never. I knew that he was ripe for conversion but did he? I probed once more,

'What would you say if I told you that it doesn't have to be like this.' I said, 'What if there was a way out?'

He looked bemused,

'Such as?' he said.

Now I had him, and I played my trump card, namely security and a new life for him and his family if he would co-operate.

He appeared confused,

'So what can you do?' he said, 'I suppose you're going to tell me that you worked for the CIA all the time?'

I smiled. I told you that he was perceptive but this was a long shot even for him, so he was very surprised when I answered in the affirmative.

'Sure that's right,' I said, 'I'm sorry that I duped you and I believe in loyalty too. But to whom might I ask? In your case surely your little girls must come first, and you can still have your private thoughts about the CIA and all that's wrong with the world, but if you can work with me I'll promise you a new start and a new life where your family will be safe. The trick will be to retire from Cerberus on health grounds. Just say that you are a nervous wreck and get a doctor to certify it. That should satisfy any suspicions.'

He seemed rather disappointed in me, as I knew that he might be, but in the end he gave in.

'Well Ed I suppose I've been avoiding this for some time and now at least you've given me a way out.' he said.

I was relieved, but when it came to his inside knowledge it was a different matter. It was like pulling teeth and he would only tell me something if it could be confirmed, and therefore attributed to another source, and he wouldn't be drawn on Gonda. This would take some time but I knew that it was for the best. We shook hands on the river bank just as he landed a big trout, but I thought that I'd been the better fisherman that day.

We returned to the cabin in good humour where Kiwi had prepared a grill to receive the expected trout and it was delicious. Then we all played games around the camp fire until it was time for bed. 'Oh what a night it was it really was' was a rather raunchy song from Johnny Ray back in the fifties and Mum put it on her 'censored' list along with Lady Chatterley's lover at the time. She needn't have bothered because I was far too innocent to know what it all meant at that time, but now was different, and it was a heck of a night. Unfortunately we had to take our leave of the Madison's to return to the UK and make our reports. I also had to set up a 'debrief' and a secure future for Henry and the girls so it was a rather tearful breakfast as we made our plans to fly from LA back to the UK. The girls had grown to love Kiwi and she them, and I was very fond of Henry and I knew that he liked (and trusted) me. We now had to make our way from the 'Madison Retreat' to the Airport and this was some miles away.

Plans made, car ready, just a last minute check of my emails and 'Damn,' I said,' There's a message from Tucker.' I read it while all the others looked on, I then read it again in disbelief before I handed it to Kiwi, she handed it to Henry and this was what it said.

> Interpol say that Matlock and family alive and well took flight from Tokyo to Chicago on Lake Michigan. We believe that Cerberus have interests in the Great Lakes so Duke is to shadow and report. Jo identity is compromised with Matlock so we advise separate base at Detroit on Lake Erie with very careful coordination, Leave soonest Tucker

This seemed to fit in with Tom Takagi's remarks about the Great Lakes, but it was the last thing that I wanted to hear. However I knew that we had no choice so I looked at Kiwi and just said,

'Well let's make tonight another night to remember then.'

Her eyes sparkled as she replied,

'I'll keep you to that.'

And I did.

If what Tom had said was true and that pollution at the Great Lakes was becoming a problem for the Cerberus/Gondian alliance, it followed that this could well be the reason for Matlock's visit there. However I had become somewhat cautious as far as he was concerned so I decided to 'set up camp' on the Canadian shores of the lakes, namely at Toronto on Lake Ontario. We soon found a small cottage called 'Sunset Dreams' on the lakeside and settled in. Of course this is also the home of the Niagara Falls that supplies power throughout Canada, and any Cerberus disruption there could be disastrous for the American as well as the Canadian economy. Furthermore Toronto is the largest City in Canada and would therefore afford ample opportunity for the kind of wider industrial and political sabotage that Cerberus had in mind. If all this were true we would have our hands full, so we needed a plan.

Before we got down to details however, Kiwi and I agreed that a short sojourn in that City would not only give us some time to acclimatise to our surroundings before we locked horns with 'The Beast' (as she called him), but also maybe a little time for love as well. We expected to be split up again soon, so we were determined to make the best of things, and Toronto certainly afforded that.

We began by a stroll along Lake Shore Boulevard at sunset, taking in the twinkle of the stars reflected in Lake Ontario. I was reminded of the other lakes I'd seen in different company recently, but this one seemed more beautiful with Kiwi on my arm and I hugged her tight. Somehow she always made things seem, well, more exciting, but no, that's not quite right. I think I mean that she just made the world around her more meaningful, and she did this without saying a word. I was beginning to think that she might be a bit of a witch. Anyway she certainly had me under her spell, and I liked it. The next day we walked in the 'Sunnyside Bike Park' where many cyclists of all ages were free to cycle to and fro in the sunshine. Kiwi suggested that we might hire a tandem, but I bought her an ice cream to take her mind off the idea instead. 'Simple things' I thought, but then I began to wonder if that was what she had wanted in the first place. The trouble was that I never really knew with her. She always seemed to be one step ahead.

That evening we explored the night life exploring cosmopolitan areas such as Chinatown, Little Italy and Little Portugal as well such streets as Davenport and Dupont. Here we found night clubs of infinite variety including' Maison Mercier' and the 'Cabana Pool Club' where watery pleasures awaited. We were tired out, so that night we just held hands and drifted in and out of sleep. Somewhat to my annoyance, and to Kiwi's undisguised pleasure we had missed the 'Beaches International Jazz Festival,' so the next step on our itinerary were the Niagara Falls themselves. The Falls are actually three in one, namely, 'The Bridal Veil,' The Horseshoe' and 'The American.' In the midst of all this tumultuous power sits the 'poor' little strip of land called 'Goat Island.' I say 'poor' because I couldn't imagine a goat lasting there for more than five seconds. (Actually there were some before 1780 but they died and I'm not surprised!) The Falls straddle the Canada/USA border between the counties of Ontario on the Canadian side and New York State on the American.

Courtesy of Franks and Tucker we had booked in to the splendid 'Niagara Falls Marriott Gateway Falls,' hotel, and I don't mind telling you that we did a lot more than hold hands that night.

I can't really explain it but, as we could hear the sound of rushing water and almost smell the spray, we found ourselves transported to a sublime ecstasy that was not only physical but spiritual too. I wished that we could have stayed longer, but we had work to do and now we had to get on with it.

We agreed that Matlock's mission to the Great Lakes might be to evaluate the extent and causes of the pollution that had become so poisonous to the Gondian craft already there, not to mention the new arrivals that were expected. Tom Takagi had said that 'something must be done,' and it was our bet that it would be Matlock who would do it. It followed that he would try to make common cause with existing environmental pressure groups, maybe not Greenpeace or FOE but probably more obscure ones where he might operate undetected. It would be my job to do the same, starting here in Toronto before making the move to Chicago.

You may have noticed that I'm writing about this as if I was a total convert to the idea of alien life here on earth, but I still had my doubts. Much of it seemed like a dream, but I had gradually come to accept that things are not always as they seem to be. Take Darwin for example. It had taken me some time to rationalise his 'Tree of Life' with my Catholic faith but I had done so. My friends said that I could find loopholes in iron bars when I wanted to, so why should this be any different? However I must admit that I was less comfortable with the notion of Human/Gondian hybrids, although the idea did seem compatible with Darwin theory itself. Somehow I still felt very uncomfortable with the whole concept, and a little shiver run down my back as I woke up to the distinct possibility that I might be one myself. Not a chance I decided, but then I began to think about Kiwi. She certainly behaved strangely on occasions, especially when it came to her self- proclaimed' intuition.' She explained this as a 'family trait' and a 'Legacy from Gran,' but now I was beginning to wonder. Not for long though as I recalled her warm pliant body; and there was nothing alien about that.

So now all we had to do was to decide on our strategy. We were both known to Matlock of course, but according to Henry Madison

I had made quite an impression at my initiation, and I was confident that he might see me as an ally if I could only find him, especially if I had already made some progress with certain fellow travellers and environmental groups in Toronto. So that was to be my task.

Kiwi on the other hand had been his adversary in some senses, and we agreed that he might spot her if she was working in close proximity. We therefore decided therefore that she should concentrate on the 'other side of the coin,' namely the polluters themselves. We were fairly sure that this would include such major industrial and agro- chemical giants as ICU and TAZER, but we decided to start with the power stations around the rim of nearly all the five lakes. She would try to find out to what degree they had already dealt with pollution from the stations, nuclear or otherwise, and what extra or new precautions they were planning for the future. It might also be helpful we thought, if she could determine whether such companies were in alliance, or violently opposed to the environmental lobbyists in the pursuit of their goals. Either way this might bring her into close proximity with 'The Beast,' so it was agreed that she must have another new identity. As usual Franks and Tucker came up with all the paperwork and Kiwi became 'Professor Margaret Stone.' Stone by name, stone by nature I thought, as she appeared one morning in a lab coat with greying hair and horn rimmed spectacles. So much for romance I thought.

However, that ploy seemed to work very well as she got to grips with her assignment much quicker than I did. After a few enquiries she had managed to secure an appointment as an intern at the industrial giant 'Yukon' who ran many of the power stations. You may remember that it was General Dallas from that company who had been involved in the 'diamond debacle' so many years ago during the Ward investigation. Maybe this would lead us somewhere as well but for now Kiwi was to work for a Professor Jean Cartier who claimed to be a descendant of Jacques. According to Kiwi who almost adopted her as a new daughter confiding that his own daughter Marie had 'gone into fashion.' Apparently he had said this in such a mournful tone that he might as well have said that she was dead. I was glad that they were forming this kind of bond because the word 'intern' had revived a few unpleasant memories from the Clinton era, and I had hoped that Kiwi would not find herself compromised in any way. Actually I had met many strong and resourceful women in my life, and not least during my association with Kiwi, but I knew that powerful people could often get their own perverse way, be they men or women.

Fortunately Cartier was not one of these and he was quite prepared to spend time with her as his 'protégé.' The first thing that she learnt was that there were nearly 100 power stations around the 5 lakes, some of which were nuclear and some not. They all polluted the Lakes according to him, but, as Orwell might have put it. 'Some are more culpable than others.' For example, although he was based in Toronto he had become quite incensed over the incident at Covert near Chicago, when gallons of radioactive waste had leaked into Lake Michigan in 2013.

He told her that he had written many memos on the subject but had never received a satisfactory reply. He had then taken it upon himself to inform a local environmental group about what he knew. However, when she asked him the name of the group he said that it would not be in her interests to know saying, 'I can assure you that it's better for you not to ask about such things. To put it mildly the whole issue is very fraught here, even dangerous for some; me included, and I wouldn't want you to get mixed up in it.'

Eventually I did start to get my act together with the environmental groups themselves and after frequenting a few bars in the Red Light area, I eventually found myself in a dingy downtown basement of the Maple Leaf Bar, itself somewhat redolent of reefers. There I was introduced to Marie Giraud (code name Vixen) who told me about 'her' group called Water Watch. She said that there were many other groups around, but in her view they tended to be too diversified and therefore less effective on single issues.

'We meet daily,' she said, 'sometimes here sometimes elsewhere because we know that we are under close scrutiny by the 'heavy mob' of the power companies as well as law enforcement itself. We use social media to get in touch with our followers and to get our message across. If you want to join just give me a few details and I'll sign you up for $10.'

This seemed such a far cry from my initiation into Cerberus with the sworn oath and the hooded men, that I signed up at once. There followed a short meeting with a speaker called Axel who made much of the threat to white fish in the lakes.

He said that many were already extinct, and that the large 'Lake White Fish' (proper name 'Coregenus Clupeaformis') was also now in danger. He distributed pictures, and as I looked at the fish closely I began to understand the biodiversity of underwater life a little clearer. It seemed to me that they might not be so far removed from the Gondian life forms that shared their habitat, and that were also under threat. Axel went on to explain that it was largely man made pollution that was the killer, and he blamed the Agro-Chemical Industry more than the power stations. He used the term POPS time and time again and this was the first time that I'd heard it. Naturally I didn't want to confess that I had no idea what it meant, but then I worked it out for myself. POPS is 'Persistent Organic Pollutants.'

POPS is a generic term for all kinds of pollution such as insecticides, DDT and PCB's that can travel on the wind for miles and pollute the lakes. Without an umbrella there is no way to stop them, so the efforts must be made, he said, to stop their production, reduce their consumption and work on developing alternatives. He added that a new danger had also become a threat, namely the onset of 'fracking' in the area. Such underground fracturing could well lead to instability in the Lake region he said, and the process itself was very dependent on unpolluted fresh water. He was making a lot of sense, and then he went on to another major factor that was affecting the lakes, and this was the disposal of paper waste into the Lakes by the large conglomerates and vested interests of the logging and media industries. He finished by saying that the various government watchdogs such as COFI (Council of Forest Industries) were toothless and probably in the pay of the industrial giants. He finished his speech to polite applause and I was left thinking that Matlock would have his work cut out to have any impact at all.

There is no doubt that 'Water Watch' meant well, but it did seem to be all talk rather than direct action. However I was soon proved wrong when Vixen asked me to take part in a raid on the CPPC paper mill at Montreal on the St Laurence Seaway.

I must admit that I had not anticipated this development but it seemed like a good way to get on the inside of Water Watch and therefore increase my chances of gaining acceptance, not only in their world but also with Matlock later on.

I told Kiwi of the plan and of course she warned me not to go.

'Look Duke,' she said, 'If this was an investment you'd turn it down. The risks far outweigh the potential return and what's more it could put your life in danger. Cartier has already told me that I might be at risk and the same goes for you. Don't go. Please.'

I wished that she hadn't put it like that because I was determined to go, no matter what she had said. Deep down I knew that this was probably mere bravado on my part, hoping not only to gain Vixen's approval but also, rather perversely to impress Kiwi as well. I must have been feeling very vulnerable at this time because I actually wanted her to feel anxious as if it might strengthen her love for me. I can see that now but then, in my own eyes I was the hero, the knight in shining armour about to do battle for the fair maiden. I repeated that I couldn't back out now and in the end she just said,

'Make sure you come back to me or I'll never forgive you.'

At this we both laughed and spent that night together with that special tenderness that Kiwi had on occasions. Perhaps my tactics were working after all, I thought.

The next morning I met Vixen with three of her followers, Eddie, Susan and Sarah at a jetty on the Lake, and there we boarded the paddle steamer SS General Montcalm, I was rather amused at the thought of that French general cruising the lake in all his majesty, after all the trouble that General Wolfe had gone to in order to remove him from the heights over Quebec. There was not much time to dwell on that however before a band struck up, and we were welcomed on board to the strains of Scott Joplin's Maple Leaf Rag in true Dixie fashion The musicians were assembled on deck in neat rows and in neat uniforms looking a little like toy soldiers. They wore white jackets with red and blue stripes, white trousers, black shoes, red socks and a helmet that reminded me of the Household Cavalry at the Trooping of the Colour in London. There were two trumpets, a trombone, two saxophones/clarinets, two violins and a rhythm section of banjo, piano, bass and drums. On both sides of this assembled company, banners declared that they were 'Ruby Starr's Stars.' She had not yet put in an appearance but, as the band began to play 'All of me,' she walked on to the stage with a flamboyant wave of a large handkerchief. There was certainly a lot of 'All of Her,' and I surmised that she wasn't far short of 20 stone, but when she began to sing that was all forgotten. She reminded me of the irrepressible

Velma Middleton who spent so many successful years with Louis Armstrong, and I loved it.

Unfortunately Vixen didn't seem to share my enthusiasm and said,

'Come on Duke, we haven't got time to sit and stare. We've got work to do. We've got to agree on a plan and how to split up our 'forces' when we get there.'

I thought that this sounded a bit too much like last minute planning and it worried me a little. It was one thing to embark on a mission of sorts, but a lack of planning could lead to disaster. However it turned out that she did have a plan after all and this was to block two of the four pipelines that spewed 'poisonous muck' (her words) into the lake. There being five of us we would work in twos with one in reserve. I was to be her partner. I did ask her how it could be that organic wood pulp might be harmful to eco systems in the lake to which she responded with a look of pity.

'It's far from organic when it spews out,' she said, 'it's gone through so many poisonous chemical processes that all the technicians have to wear protective clothing and masks. They use Celcure and Creosote as well as other treatments, some of which have an arsenic base.'

I suppose I must have seemed a bit stupid at that point, so I decided not to ask any questions again but just mumbled, 'Oh, thanks.'

The 'General Montcalm' soon berthed at the lakeside and we transhipped to a small coracle like craft that was waiting for us, but no cockle-shell heroes were we. Within a few moment of launch we were shipping water, Susan and Sarah were both sick, and I wondered if we'd make it to the Paper Mill but we did.

By then it was nightfall and as it came into view it reminded me of Alcatraz, with searchlights probing the night skies, watch towers on every corner and all surrounded by barbed wire. Impregnable, I thought, but of course I didn't say anything. Somehow I knew that Vixen would find a way no matter what I said so I just had to sit and wait for my orders. We beached our small craft and she led the way up a steep incline towards a corner, seemingly hidden from the watchtowers. Someone had obviously reconnoitred and prepared this approach, because in front of us was a small lichen gate, and it was unlocked. She looked at me triumphantly.

'Let's go Duke.' She said and began to slither forward on her stomach.

I did the same and we were followed at a short distance by the other three.

Just then all hell broke loose as light were switched on all around us and a voice rang out.

'Stay where you are and do not move or you will be shot.' it said.

Eddie had no intention of following orders, and with a cry he shouted out, 'Run for it.' He charged down the slope followed by Susan and Sarah hot on his heels, but they had not got more than a few yards before they were cut down in a hail of gunfire. Vixen and I looked on in dismay and were glued to the spot.

Soon two men in combat gear approached and bid us follow them. There was little choice but to do as they said, and then we were taken inside the building. The men showed us a cell and motioned us to go in, but as they did so they bludgeoned us both with their heavy rifles. I was glad when they left and locked the door.

The next morning there was a short interrogation, but as neither of us would admit to anything, our captors sent for a senior officer.

He read the papers given to him and simply said,

'I think that they need to meet 'Old- Grizzly' don't you. Perhaps he'll get them to talk.'

The others nodded and we were soon led out and loaded into a Humvee kind of vehicle to take us 'God knows where.' I surmised that 'Old Grizzly' might be a retired intelligence officer of some sort and that he might use more strong arm tactics on us, and I wasn't looking forward to it, but we were in for a far worse fate than that.

The vehicle drove for about an hour and then pulled up in a clearing in the forest.

'This'll do.' said one of our captors, 'put him over there and put her over there.'

He motioned to the others who took hold of us and led us to two trees on either side. They tied us firmly to the trees and then climbed to get back into the truck and as they did so their leader called out,

'Have fun you two. You shouldn't have gone down to the woods tonight should you?'

With that they all laughed as they sped off into the night, leaving Vixen and me helpless. I was wondering what was in store for us, and then it dawned on me. His farewell remark was obviously a barbed reference to the Teddy Bear's picnic, and we were going to be on the menu. I struggled but could not get free. I was desperate but as I looked over at Vixen she just smiled and called out. 'Don't worry. It's all in a good cause.'

I tried to smile back but couldn't, and then I heard a rustling in the bushes.

They had arrived.

First on the scene were two (rather lovable?) cubs followed shortly by a large female and an even larger male Grizzly Bear. At first they seemed more interested in nuts and berries than us, but after a short while the cubs spotted Vixen. They approached cautiously but then, as in a game, they began to jump up and down all over her using their sharp claws for purchase. I couldn't bear to look but she didn't make a sound. What fortitude I thought. Was she a Catholic too? I had visions of Joan of Arc being burnt at the stake as she had looked to the heavens, but it was me doing the praying, not Vixen. Her head lolled from side to side as the cubs continued their assault, and I was sure that she was dead. Was I going to be spared I wondered? And then the large male approached and placed his snout firmly on mine. By this time I was hysterical and began to hum 'The Bare Necessities' as he sniffed me all over. He can't have liked what he smelt or heard because with a rather pitiful whimper (Thanks but no thanks?) he backed off and without even looking around, led his pack back into the woods.

I suppose I should have been offended at his rejection but I wasn't, far from it and he'd actually done me a favour. I had been sweating so much that my bonds had loosened, and now I could wriggle free.

I immediately ran across to where Vixen lay spread-eagled against the tree. As I said I had feared that she was dead, but now I could see that she was still breathing although unconscious. I carefully untied her and carried her across the clearing to a grassy knoll and laid her down gently. Her jeans and blouse had been torn and she was covered in blood. I looked around to see if there was a stream nearby to wash her wounds but there was not. Then I remembered that we both carried water bottles, and in addition I had a tube of disinfectant cream that I carried for insect bites. My next task was to undress her and this I did carefully as she lay on the ground. She was soon down to her bra and pants, pink as I remember, but there was nothing sexual or even sensual about my ministrations. I took care of her just as a doctor or nurse might have done and then I dressed her in a check shirt that I carried.

She looked the picture of childish innocence with her pink pants just showing under the tails of my checked shirt. On any other occasion I might have taken some interest but not today. I just sat back and waited for her to wake up.

I suppose that it might have been about an hour before she stirred and when she did she gazed at me with dark lustrous eyes that I hadn't noticed before.

'Nice shirt Duke,' she said, 'Thanks.' She then snuggled up to me and lay in my arms for another hour until it was nearly dawn.

Finally she stood up and stretched, 'I think that there's an early morning ferry back to Toronto,' she said, 'we haven't got the canoe but if we hurry we can make it.'

With that she reached out and took my hand.

'You can't go on the boat dressed like that.' I objected but she just said,

'Have you any better ideas? Maybe you'd like to give me your jeans instead. That's what a real gentleman would do.'

I laughed but didn't offer my modesty for hers, and anyway my check shirt covered most, if not all of her vital statistics. As she said we did have to hurry, but we were just in time for the departure of 'The General Montcalm,' this time without a band.

Suffice to say that when we arrived back in Toronto Vixen had already sent text messages to her group to meet at the Maple Leaf Bar the next night. As might be expected it was more of a wake than a meeting, as many tears were shed and eulogies read over the loss of Eddie, Susan and Sarah. Vixen announced that she planned to join up with a larger group in Chicago and would be leaving soon. There were cries of protest, but to be honest I think that the rest of the group were so shell shocked that they had lost the stomach for a fight. It was different for me. Vixen was the only card that I had so when the meeting broke up I asked her if I could go to Chicago with her to continue her mission. She looked a bit surprised but agreed with one proviso.

'Yes you can come,' she said, 'but don't get any silly ideas just because you've seen me in my underwear.'

She gave me an address in the 'Windy City' and said that I was to meet her there in a week's time. This suited me fine as I was desperate to see Kiwi again and to discuss our next moves at our lakeshore retreat. I took a taxi there the very next day after I had rested up for a while. She was waiting to greet me and drew me to her with a very big kiss.

'I love you,' she said and I just mumbled

'Je t'aime' in her ear. Surely I wasn't thinking of Vixen was I?

***

As agreed previously, Kiwi had already made her plan to relocate in Detroit courtesy of Professor Cartier who had arranged a transfer to the Yukon Laboratories there. Now I had an entrée into Chicago with Vixen so we were free to move on to Plan B. The trouble was that we were to be parted yet again and I could see that she didn't like the idea, but nor did I for that matter.

'It'll be such a pity to leave Sunset Dreams,' I said, 'Henry Madison would have loved the fishing here.'

She laughed, 'Maybe so,' she replied, 'but you hate fishing. What is it that you'd really miss? Could it be this?'

With that she turned her back on me, and I noticed for the first time that she was wearing one of my old check shirts. She looked over her shoulder and then, very slowly slipped the shirt off of her left shoulder, and then the right shoulder, holding it just long enough to leave me wondering. Then she allowed it to fall to the ground and I'd been right. There was not a pink bra or pink pants to be seen anywhere. This was Kiwi all right, and I forgot all about Vixen for the next two or three hours; and well into the morning.

However when dawn broke the next day it was Vixen that I had to meet up with, and my feelings about that were mixed. I did want to get on with our mission to track down Matlock, but I envisaged much danger as well as temptation along the way. It might seem strange but we Catholics always believe that there is evil lurking within us, usually disguised by the goodwill that we proclaim to others, and the 'good' that we often try to do in our lives. But be off guard and a darker side can easily appear. We try to keep that 'devil' at bay by going to Mass and receiving the sacraments regularly, but I hadn't been for ages. Perhaps I should I thought, but now it was, 'in for a penny, in for a pound' as I set off for Chicago.

I arrived at our designated meeting place that turned out to be a dingy boarding house at 2033 Michigan Avenue to be met by Vixen who had the room next to mine. It was dirty and smelly and not my idea of Chicago at all. I suppose that I had certain preconceptions about the Windy City and most of these were to do with 'the mob' and jazz. The South Side and the North Side had been the strongholds of Al Capone and Bugsy Moran respectively until that infamous St Valentine's Day in 1929. For me, as far as jazz was concerned there were still clubs such as the 'Green Mill' where the 'Bird' (Charlie Parker) had mesmerised his audiences in the 1950's. Of course he had followed in a long line of performers ever since Louis came to join King Oliver in the 1920's, and from then on the Eddie Condon 'gang' held sway with a heady blend of jazz, booze and pot as a way of life. I wouldn't have said that Vixen was a 'culture vulture,' but she had a much wider palette of interests than I did, and she was determined that I should share some of them, so the next day she took me on a short tour starting with the unique sculpture affectionately called 'The Bean.' This serves as the gateway to Millennium Park at Cloud Gate, and is a blob- like structure of blue and white steel created by the British artist Anish Kapoor. She was enthralled but I was, let's say, rather unimpressed but she didn't give up on me. She took me next to the Lincoln Memorial Park where there was a matinee of 'Waiting for Godot.' As far as I was concerned this was wasting time. I was waiting for Matlock not Godot, but fortunately I didn't have long to wait.

I phoned Kiwi that night on a new Detroit number that she had left on my answer phone. It turned out to be the Hilton Hotel at 444 Plymouth Avenue and she was in room 44. She was pleased to get my call and very excited about her accommodation which was a full suite complete with Jacuzzi and views over the park, all courtesy of Yukon. She told me that she also had an expense account and a car at her disposal. I didn't like to mention my frugal surroundings so I just said,

'I hope you're not the kind of girl who can be easily bought off by a few luxuries.'

She giggled on the other end of the line and replied,

'Temptation is such a wonderful thing. I'm not sure that I want to resist entirely. What would 'your lot' (she used this term to annoy me) think I should do? And what would you do?'

She'd beaten me at my own game again and I wish I'd never mentioned the word.

'Sorry,' I said,' you know that I love you and trust you to always do the right thing.' As I said this I felt a tap on my shoulder. No it wasn't a real one, but my own 'Mr Conscience' calling once more because I had begun to wonder how I would stand up to temptation with Vixen. Of course Kiwi made matters worse by starting to cry and blubbing out,

'I love you too Duke.'

I say 'worse' in the sense that I had enough to worry about without tears, but in a way I suppose it was 'better' as well, as it seemed to be our mutual love that protected us both from straying too far.

The next day Vixen took me to a meeting of the Chicago Water Watch at 'Al's Bronzeville Hotel' on the south side of town. This was now advertised proudly as having been one of the favourite watering holes for Al Capone and his mobsters. There were plenty of family photos of the 'Great Man' (it said) and many newspaper cuttings including one of the St Valentine's Day massacre taken, it said, 'minutes after the killings.' Tommy guns and a selection of handguns were prominent in locked cabinets, and for $10 you could dress up and have a photo taken in costume. It all seemed like a bit of fun if one managed to forget the misery and hardship that Capone and others inflicted on their communities. But there I go again, wearing my saintly wings. Maybe it's time I gave them a good clipping; but on the other hand didn't they define me as a person?

The meeting took place in a medium sizes room that was thankfully bare of Capone memorabilia and Vixen told me that we were there because Annabelle, the local organiser had managed to secure the services of an important environmental specialist from Salt Lake University named Professor Albert Townes. My ears pricked up when she also told me that he was a senior director at a company called Chemico that she believed to be in the forefront of ethical chemicals. I was suspicious immediately, having come across that name so often in the past, but she seemed captivated.

'I've heard that he's very good.' she said as she snuggled down in her seat. 'Look, here he comes.'

There seemed to some movement backstage and then Annabelle appeared leading a very tall bald headed man to the front of the mini-auditorium.

'Please welcome Professor Townes.' she said, to much applause before leaving the stage. I looked and the looked again at the man standing there and then my heart jumped. It was 'Bald Eagle' Sam Matlock himself, now apparently Professor Townes, and I suppose I must admit that with hindsight I shouldn't have been surprised at all. He began by a seemingly heartfelt and almost tearful testimony to those who had died recently 'on active service.'

He called out their names as the President might have done at Arlington cemetery.

'Edward Evans, Susan Vosper and Sarah Tong,' he intoned as in a prayer, 'Your names will forever be remembered by us and we vow that your sacrifice will not have been in vain. Our movement needs active soldiers but we would rather not have martyrs for that's what they were. Now the burden falls on us once more. These lakes are ours, they are not theirs. Please stand and repeat those words after me.'

Of course I'd heard all this before although this time he had adapted the words and he was careful not to posit it as an oath but rather as a request that could not be refused by any 'reasonable' person, given the sacrifices of the others that he had mentioned. As expected the small crowd rose as if mesmerised under his hypnotic spell and repeated his words.

'These lakes are ours. They are not theirs.

I was immediately transported back in time to that fateful day when I had taken the oath with Henry Madison, and at which Matlock had been one of hooded men who had initiated me. I had suddenly become really scared and wanted to leave but just then Vixen took my arm and said,

'There's a planning meeting later on and we are invited. It's quite a privilege don't you think?'

I didn't like to tell her what I really thought but I did want to get the low down on Matlock and his plans so I just nodded and said,

'That's good. I hope that he's got something interesting in mind.'

That proved to be a severe understatement as he came quickly to the point to a somewhat reduced audience.

'Multi nationals won't respond to pin pricks.' he said, 'If we are to clear the lakes of pollution we must be ambitious and daring. You all know that the problem is increasing year by year yet they drag their heels. I won't bore you with all the scientific details but I have to tell you that a catastrophe is imminent. The only way to get them to take action is to force them to take notice. Whilst I admire the work done by Water Watch I regret to say that despite the sacrifices made, groups like Yukon will brush off your efforts as a mere inconvenience.'

Here he stopped and took a deep breath before continuing with a sigh.

'My heart sank when I heard of your latest losses,' he said, 'I don't mind telling you that I cried when I first heard the news. But, ladies and gentlemen, let their sacrifice be not in vain. There is only one thing that these bastards will listen to and that's public opinion. I will now tell you in strictest confidence what I have in mind but before I do I ask anyone who is not with me to leave the room now and nothing more will be said.'

Of course no one moved and he continued with his speech.

'Thank you for your confidence.' he said, 'Now this is my two stage plan. Stage one will be to disable the Ferris wheel at the Navy Pier at precisely 11am next Saturday, which as you may know is the first day of the school holidays. The wheel should be full of children and some parents at that time. We will hold the wheel disabled for ten minutes while I speak to the Governor to get assurances about a moratorium on the use of the lakes for ANY Industrial purpose. I already have an assurance from Peter Dallas, who as you probably know has taken over from his father as MD of Chemico, that they will do so unilaterally but irrespective of that and regardless of the Governor's response we will reactivate the wheel after the allotted time, but with a promise that another much more strategic target will be immobilised next week if our demands are not met.

'This will be a far more serious affair and will involve the release of spores of the Ebola virus or other toxins into the water and air systems at the Gershwin Tunnel complex at the O'Hare Airport.

'You may know that next Friday is the last day of the annual conference of the Canadian Buffalo Lodges, and many will be on their way home, so disruption to flights will be at its maximum. However this time we will warn the authorities BEFORE the action, with the assurance that casualties and chaos might be averted if they follow our instructions to the letter, namely the immediate closure of all industrial and energy complexes around the lakes.'

He looked around rather smugly perhaps sensing that such actions had never been contemplated by those in the meeting.

'Well?' he asked, 'does anyone want to ask any questions?'

Once more those in the room seemed too frightened to say anything until Vixen, my brave Vixen, stood up.

'Professor,' she said 'you know that I led the failed expedition on Lake Ontario and we lost close friends there. Don't you think that someone might be hurt by mistake this time? I think that we should find another plan.'

I could tell that this intervention was not to his liking, firstly because it challenged his judgement and secondly because it had come from a girl. Kiwi had told me about his intransigence and sexism, and she'd also warned me about his sudden change of mood, but of course poor Vixen had no idea of what she was in for. A moment ago he had seemed to be the caring and considerate Professor but now he was like a cornered beast.

'How dare you,' he shouted out, 'I have given you the plan and now you must carry it out. I told you to leave if you wanted no part but now everyone here must follow orders and that goes for you too.' he said as he pointed a long finger at Vixen.

Most of those in the room were taken aback, and some looked around for a way out, and it was then that I noticed that Matlock was not alone. He had brought two aggressive men with him, and they were guarding the doors. Now he smiled as if nothing had happened.

'That's settled then,' he said, 'let's meet tomorrow to finalise details.'

He then left the room and Vixen took hold of my arm.

'I need a drink.' she said, taking the words right out of my mouth.

Over that drink I told her that I believed the Professor was a dangerous man allied to a dangerous enterprise, although I didn't go into details. I said that I didn't see any way of stopping him unless we reported the plan to the authorities, and they probably wouldn't believe us, given the WW track record. Furthermore I added, it was just possible that Stage One might work rendering Stage Two superfluous. She agreed and said that she'd advise Annabelle not to get too involved but not to scupper the plan either. Later I was told that this policy had been agreed and I was given my orders, which thankfully was only to be a look out.

***

This first Saturday of the school holidays in Chicago was bathed in sunshine and there seemed to be children everywhere enjoying their first day of freedom. As Matlock had said it would be, the Ferris wheel was a big attraction and was virtually full every time.

I positioned myself at the corner of the square and watched every little detail in case I should miss something. I knew that it was nearly 'time', so I checked my watch against the hands of 'Big Bob,' the affectionate name given to a copy of Big Ben in the square.

The hands ticked around slowly, so very slowly; and so slow that I wished that they would stop for ever and that 11 am would never come, but it did. The chimes rang out and another group of children jostled to get on board, some with their parents and some just waving goodbye to theirs as they were wafted into the air. The wheel started its first revolution, built up speed, went around twice and then, just as Matlock had said it would, it stopped.

Onlookers and pedestrians stared up into the sky silently, and then a busy chatter broke out as people tried to find out what had gone wrong.

'Don't worry,' said a bystander, 'It will start up again in a minute.'

But it didn't and some children in the sky were beginning to panic. And then the most dreadful thing of all occurred, as one little blonde girl freed herself from her mother's arms and stood up waving to the crowd, just as the wheel took a sudden lurch. It seemed that she was trying to regain her balance, but then she toppled over the side and fell all the way to the ground. There was a stunned silence and I felt sick to my stomach; and very responsible.

Maybe I could have saved that little girl I thought, and I decided there and then that I would not allow Stage Two to go ahead. The very thought of others like poor little Poppy dying in the tunnel, or maybe even worse, getting home to find that they had contracted the near incurable Ebola virus, was unthinkable and it confirmed Matlock's ruthless streak once again. He was indeed the 'Beast' that Kiwi had said he was, and I was determined to stop him this time.

The papers the next day were full of the tragedy with headlines such as 'WE LOVE YOU POPPY. YOU ARE AN ANGEL' and soon the crucifix in the centre of the square around the Ferris wheel became strewn with flowers, many of them poppies but others too. It was enough to make you cry. I met up with Vixen and told her to 'get out of town' because I was going to spill the beans. She said that she'd also been sickened to her stomach and agreed that she might go to pastures new. 'I shall miss you Duke.' she said as she kissed me. Just for a moment I wondered if Matlock might be chastened by this tragedy as well, but I doubted it. I then decided that my best plan would be to get out of town as well, and naturally I headed for Detroit and Kiwi's arms at the Hilton. She greeted me warmly and was very shocked at what I told her. I immediately suggested that we should send a message from the hotel giving all the details in code to Franks and Tucker, so that the plan to immobilise the Gershwin tunnel and Chicago airport could be forestalled at once. This we did and within minutes I was asleep.

It was only a matter of days before a new headline appeared in the press.

'SECURITY ALERT AT O'HARE.' it said, but did not go into the real details. Indeed the existence of so many 'usual suspects' from the ranks of Islamic terrorism, allowed the papers to speculate and to talk of 'credible evidence' without really having any. Pick any one from half a dozen and you could well be correct it seemed. At one time or another they were all implicated. First it was AL QUAEDA next it was ISIS, and then it was AL SHABAB and others. They all denied it of course but this seemed to make them even more culpable. This smoke screen did help the police in another way because I found out later that they had been able to round up the leaders of Water Watch in a dawn raid on the Maple Leaf Bar, I found out later that neither Vixen nor Matlock were there at the time but Annabelle and the others were taken into custody. I was pleased that Vixen had got away as I'd grown very fond (maybe too fond) of her, but I was furious that Matlock had escaped yet again.

However in a few days it all seemed to be forgotten, the airport was back to normal and any questions by the Press were stonewalled with the familiar reply that, 'investigations are ongoing.' It was all as if nothing had happened but it had, and you only had to visit the crucifix in the square to understand.

Poppies and flowers not only remained, but more were added every day as the wheel became a memorial for POPPY COLLINS. Such an ordinary name it seems, but when it became known that the family were Catholic it became an unofficial shrine, and religious ephemera such as crucifixes and rosaries were added to the many bouquets of flowers that were there. Then a local mystic called John, who had more or less become resident in the square, claimed that he had seen her flying above the wheel. At this alleged revelation, hundreds and then thousands arrived to look into the sky and pray for Poppy, and presumably a miracle for their own redemption. I was in Detroit, but I must admit that I didn't know what to make of it. Superstition surely, but why had Poppy died if not to lead others to Jesus they said. That was a bridge too far for me, but I prayed for her just the same.

I didn't go over all my anxieties and reservations with Kiwi but she could see that I had been traumatised. She didn't tell me at the time but I found out later that she had requested an immediate recall to the UK for some 'quality time' as she had put it. It seems that Franks and Tucker 'got the message' even authorising a week's stopover at the prestigious 'Madison Hotel' in New York on our way back to Heathrow. I appreciated the break but now, as I look back on it I am sure that I was pretty poor company for Kiwi as I seemed to sleep for most of the time. She was wonderful though, and on our very last night, and after a shared Jacuzzi, I told her how much I loved her and we clung together throughout the night.

Franks and Tucker had another surprise in store as we booked into the Heathrow Hilton, and that was a voucher for two for a week in Lyme Regis on the Dorset coast. By now I was becoming suspicious.

'I bet he's up to something.' I said, and I was right.

The case had seemed to be over but it was far from over.

4

GONDWANA

Gondwanaland means 'Land of the Gonds' who were a tribe that inhabited New Zealand in ancient times. It is a literal translation from Sanskrit but its origins go back 130 million years to a time when a super continent embraced virtually the whole world. This was Gondwana, but when the tectonic plates of the Northern Hemisphere (Laurasia) split from the Southern (Australis), a 'proto-New Zealand' was born, with its distinctive life forms ranging from the ubiquitous Kiwi to the prehistoric 'tuatara' lizard and others.

(Extract from George Gibbs 'Ghosts of Gondwana.' 2007)

O ur tale goes back to that Pleistocene Ice Age or an even earlier time. Observers from the planet Gonda visited these cold regions and found them suitable for migration and habitation as Gonda itself was heating up. The first 'settlers' made their homes in deep fresh water lakes and over many millennia eventually crawled out onto terra firma. From there some returned to the lakes in lizard form (the tuatara) while others made the transition to mammals as did humans much later. It was inevitable that these two species would mate over time leading to a hybrid race, and subsequent colonisation from other parts of the world diluted original forms as well. By the Holocene age it was not possible to make easy distinctions in populations, although experts might claim that original characteristics remained and of course DNA research might point to a particular group. Given the vicissitudes of earthly climate the Gondians did return to their planet from time to time, but now (in our story) another hot period is causing them to search for a new home again. This time they have made a somewhat uneasy alliance with Cerberus to achieve their aims but will it last? Would their new destination have to be earth once more, or could there be another alternative amongst Hubble's heavenly firmaments?

❖❖❖

Back in the UK after their dramatic sojourn in the USA, Kiwi and Duke had been granted a holiday at the Dorset resort of Lyme Regis popularly known as the Jurassic Coast. She knew that his last days in Chicago had been very traumatic for him, so she was determined to remind him what love was all about. Something had happened to him and he often woke up in a sweat. It would be sunshine, sea and sex, and maybe just a bit of fossil hunting if they found the time.

Now Kiwi picks up the story in her own words…

It was so good to have Duke all to myself for a short while. I'd almost forgotten his smile and loving ways and he couldn't have been more attentive, especially as I was a 'blonde vamp' for a while anyway. It was as if these moments had become more precious for him because had we faced danger together, and I felt the same way. We had room service for the first 24 hours at the Cob Hotel (famous for the 'French Lieutenant's Woman') and he played his part well, as did I very enthusiastically. Eventually we agreed to go fossil hunting and although it started off well, I must admit that a few cracks began to show. I'd noticed his rather blinkered attitude when it came to things outside his comfort zone. It's funny, because to my mind his belief in all things Catholic is no less a superstition than my attitudes to the supernatural in its widest sense.

'It's all a question of faith,' he had told me on numerous occasions. 'I don't dispute Gods of many civilisations,' he would say, 'but only Jesus offers us redemption for our sins.'

I found this a bit hard to take, but we did agree that a compromise might be found in the different cultures that had led to different spiritual experiences.

Now, after the incident at the Ferris wheel when poor Poppy had plunged to her death, he seemed even more set in his old ways.

'She didn't die in vain did she?' he said, 'Look at all those people whose faith has been renewed through her. I think that she's a Saint, and maybe old John did see her after all.'

I had thought that he had got over the shock after our holiday in Lyme Regis, but I had begun to realise that it would take a lot longer, if ever. But somehow it all seemed to draw me in, and to make me love him even more.

It followed that, when it came to extra- terrestrials and UFO's and USO's and flying saucers, he still insisted that it would only be angels who flew in the heavens, but I thought very differently. I had seen so much evidence that I knew some of it must be true, including the testimony from Senator Prince in LA that Duke had mentioned a long time ago. How did I know? Well I'm really not sure. It was a feeling, somewhat akin to Duke's faith; aspects that we just knew to be true but didn't know why. I think that I had actually inherited some of this from my Gran who seemed to be spiritually in touch with the stars all her life. I also thought that these gifts somehow made us special, as if we had a distinct role to play, but I for one had no idea what it could be.

'Look Kiwi, over here, look at this one.' he said proudly, holding up a very small fossil.

I didn't like to tell him that I had two larger ones in my bag so I just said,

'Great. They're very mysterious aren't they? Where do you think they come from?'

He didn't get my gist at first and pointed at the cliff,

'They come from up there I suppose.' he said and when I laughed he looked puzzled. 'What do you mean by 'come from' exactly?' he said.

I was amused and teased him further.

'Yes I agree,' I said. 'They come from up there,' but I was pointing at the stars that had just begun to shine in the early evening.

Now he grinned.

'It's twinkle, twinkle little star is it? Fossils come from the heavens do they?' he said.

Now I was getting annoyed. It was one thing to be sceptical but I didn't take ridicule gladly so I snapped back.

'Yes I mean it. Even you know that objects from space have fallen to earth, and it's quite possible that some of these have contained living creatures isn't it? I know that you can't think beyond the horizon, but I think that it's also possible that other life forms have also landed, and yes that includes extra- terrestrials.'

He got sulky and went off to search for more fossils and I suddenly felt cold. I needed his warmth so much. He soon returned carrying a small flower and kissed me

'I love you.' he said.

I fell into his arms and a scene from the film 'From Here to Eternity' took place there and then. Fortunately the beach was somewhat deserted, but back at the hotel there was a message from Hilary Tucker. It read;

Urgent. Action soonest.

Interpol confirm Matlock (now Dr Alec Spencer. Senior Commercial Director Chemico New York) took flight from New York to Wellington New Zealand. Please follow at earliest opportunity. Regards HT.

Duke was right. This was music to my ears and I hugged him tight and soon we were on our way. Suddenly I wanted to share everything with him and that included my family who live in Queenstown in the South Island, whereas Wellington is in the North but where there's a will there's always a way I thought, and a few days in 'windy' Wellington might be fun.

We took the next flight out from Heathrow and, with a stopover in Hong Kong I was really looking forward to a short break. I also thought that it might take Duke's mind off his traumas for a while, but this was rather hit and miss as he continued to have recurrent nightmares. We had been booked into the resplendent Hong Kong Holiday Inn just across the bridge from Kowloon and spent our waiting time with a trip to Victoria Park, viewing a very misty city below us from the heights. That night we cuddled up close, but a 6am call disturbed our reverie and we had to take a taxi back to the airport. It was a New Zealand Air Boeing 747 with really luxurious seats, so I managed to catch up on some beauty sleep before we started the approach to Wellington. It's not exactly Chicago, but it isn't known as the 'Windy City' for nothing either as our plane wobbled its way along the gusty corridor over the bay.

But Wellington isn't all breeze and bluster. It's also known for its beauty, and this poem by David Mc Wright describes it very well.

'Wellington's guardian hills encircle her pen streets. Loud with the voices of steps and trade; And in her bay the ships of east and west meet and cast anchor. Hers the pride of place In shop and mart, no languid beauty she spreading her soft limbs and dreaming of flowers, But rough and strenuous, red with rudest health, Tossing her fair hair from eager eyes that look afar, filled with the gleam of power She stands the strong city of the south.'

Extract from 'Wellington, Harbour, Harp and Hills'.

I suppose you might think 'that says it all' and to an extent it does, but perhaps it misses out a bit on the romantic nature of the bay to lovers deeply in love as Duke and I were, as we strolled around in the breezy sunshine, just happy to be together. True we stopped off at the museums, and admired the new Government building rather disparagingly called 'The Beehive,' but it was the harbour that attracted us most and there we sat hand in hand for hours.

When we eventually returned a surprise awaited us in the form of another email from Tucker. Once again this was music to my ears.

> Interpol confirm Matlock/Spencer took flight to Queenstown. Urgent you follow soonest. Intercepted messages suggest increased 'internet chat'. We expect them to make their move soon and the clock is ticking.

Naturally I couldn't wait to see my family and I think that Duke understood, although he'd had hopes of seeing something of the sailing regattas that are a feature of Wellington. However there was no time to waste and it was not long before we arrived at Queenstown to be greeted by a 'gaggle of Grants' and their neighbours. I had decided to be a modest brunette in order not to shock my Mum and it seemed to work as she threw her arms around me and said,

'Jo, my dear Jo. You haven't changed a bit.'

They had even hired that old commercial steamship the SS Earnshaw (now modernised) for a welcome party with all the bunting and razzmatazz of a State visit, with Maori musicians taking the place of jazz, and although Duke might have thought otherwise, I found it a refreshing change. They had brought out the local Press 'Local Girl Returns?' and a host of photographers as well. To be honest I was rather taken aback because the last thing I needed was publicity with Matlock around. When my mum asked me why I was avoiding the limelight when others wanted to take pictures, I just had to explain that I was camera shy. This brought its own set of problems as she didn't really believe me.

'You never used to be shy dear,' she said, 'Auntie Julie just wants to take one of us together.'

Unfortunately I was too slow to cover my face as Julie snapped and then ran away shouting out, 'Gotcha!'

I smiled, but I was worried because I knew that Julie worked for the local 'QT Herald.'

On the Richter disaster scale of 0-7 this was definitely a 6 but I still had another earthquake to endure and that was to introduce Duke formally to my Gran. She had been too ill to attend the earlier festivities, so the next day a garden party was organised to meet her. Even in the stifling heat she wore a traditional long black dress but paradoxically a Maori garland as well. She was seated on a sort of throne resplendent with flowers and comfy cushions and on her lap there was a book somewhat like a Bible. It was bound in a soft leathery substance that I thought to be crocodile or lizard skin, and I surmised that it might be a record of family history.

Duke isn't the best at assessing a situation and unfortunately his first words of greeting were not at all helpful.

'I'm very pleased to meet you Gran,' he said, 'I see that you have the family Bible there.' She looked him up and down and replied rather scathingly,

'I can't understand you young man,' she said, 'my granddaughter says that you are an American but that's no use at all here. Secondly I'm not 'your' Gran at all and not likely to be if you can't address me with respect as Mrs Grant, and what's more this is not a Bible but a far more worthwhile document and it's been in our family for centuries. We call it 'The Legacy' and not many of them remain from the old days.'

To give him credit Duke did not respond to this baiting, but it was not a good start I must say.

'I'm sorry that I made a bad impression,' he said, 'but I hope that I'll do better next time and thank you.'

Gran now seemed rather mollified and offered him her hand to kiss, as if she was Queen of all she surveyed.

'I hope so too.' she said, and I took that as a sign that she was prepared to see him again. Phew!

The next hours passed peaceably enough and her reference to her book 'The Legacy' as she had called it, intrigued me greatly but I knew that I should not involve Duke if I was to find out more. My own intuitive nature had often been explained in those terms, by those who knew me, as a 'family legacy,' in the absence of any considerable wealth that was likely to come to me.

Fortunately my Dad took Duke into the TV lounge to watch some sailing films from the Admiral's Cup and so I managed to sneak up to Gran's room as she had retired to bed early, 'to rest' she had said. However, when I tapped on her door she was sitting in an armchair wide awake and reading the book.

'I knew you'd come.' she said.

I think I knew that she would know as well. It was as if our thoughts were tied together like the 'string' theories of space research in which particles such as neutrons and photons inhabit a common string whilst still able to move freely and separately. Gran and I were like that. We lived thousands of miles apart yet our thoughts seemed to be as one (except of course when they were not, if you see what I mean) It seemed to be a generational thing because Mum and Dad did not seem to possess these insights, and Gran said that she got them from her grandparents not her parents.

She continued,

'I'm so glad that you are here Jo. I didn't know when you would come and I prayed that I'd still be alive when you got here. You may know that I have been very ill and the doctors have said that I may only have months to live, but now that you are here I can give you this,' saying which she reached down and picked up the book that nestled in her lap. It was 'The Legacy' that Duke had mistaken for a Bible.

'Take this Legacy.' she said, 'Take it and use it wisely for you are the 'Chosen One' at this most dangerous of times. The book will guide you and tell you what to do. But first you will have a test and if you pass you will be given a most dreadful responsibility and that will be the fate of the world itself.'

This all sounded very dramatic and over the top, and then as she handed the book to me our hands touched, and for the first time I noticed that not only were her hands gnarled with age, but that they were rather slippery as if she had too much hand cream on. She placed the book gently into my hands and I noticed that it too felt slippery and a little gnarled to touch, somewhat like a crocodile or lizard skin, and remarkably like the hands that had handed it over.

I loved my Gran but I shivered nonetheless. It seemed that she and the book were one, or had become one as she had aged, because as I said, I had not noticed it before. In addition the whole thing seemed vaguely religious, a bit like the communion services in the Catholic Church that Duke had introduced me to. Of course I had no aspirations in that direction and I wanted to say so, but there was no way of getting out of it so I accepted the book, and it seemed, the terrible responsibility that went with it.

I had been taken aback and tried to reassure her that she probably had years to live, but she stopped me in my tracks.

'I don't think that we will meet again in this life,' she said, 'but that doesn't matter. I have held the book for half a century and now it passes to you. Although copies have been made this is the true original from a very distant time. You will observe that it is a history of sorts, but it is also a prediction and a warning to those of us who are 'The Chosen Ones.' Every generation has had the responsibility to interpret, and to act on the specific guidance that has applied to their time. Now it is your time and you must act before it is too late.'

'Thank you for your trust Gran,' I said, 'I just hope that I can live up to it Good night Gran,' saying which I kissed her on cheek observing it to be cold and clammy like her hands, and if I wasn't holding the book in mine, I would indeed have supposed that she was very ill.

I then carried the book carefully and secretly to 'my' room, (Duke had his 'own' room too, on Gran's orders) and went downstairs to join the others. We shared a few family stories, drank Horlicks and then prepared for bed. Duke got a 'sleep tight' and a peck on the cheek. I must admit that he looked a little disgruntled.

It was not long before I got an inkling of the 'test' that Gran had mentioned when news came through of a calamitous earthquake in the region around Canterbury, some hundreds of miles north and close to the previous epicentre of 'The Ring of Fire,' around Christchurch. I knew that the family had relatives there, and that evening they met in sombre mood to discuss it. Aunt Jess had telephoned earlier to say that they were unhurt, but had had to evacuate their flat in the 'Lancaster' block in St Anselm's Square due to instability. They were currently living with hundreds of others in St Anselm's Church on the other side of the square, and were being well looked after she said. Unlike Christchurch Cathedral in 2011 it had been undamaged amongst considerable chaos all around, so she added that they felt quite safe. Nevertheless Mum offered my services right away,

'Jo will be on the next plane or bus out of here,' she said without even glancing over at me. 'Just hold on and she'll be there as soon as you can say 'Jack Robinson.'

I didn't like to say anything, but anyway before I could, my Dad spoke up.

'Ask her if she has any news of Joe (his brother) and Mary.' he said.

After a few moments of listening in, my mum passed the phone over to me.

'I can't hear what she's saying,' she said, 'it seems like the line's got very bad.'

I took the phone but all I could hear was crying on the other end of the line.

'Hello. Hello Auntie Jess. It's Jo here. Can you hear me?'

The crying seemed to reduce to a series of sobs before she replied and said,

'I don't know how to say this Jo but the Aoraki region where they live has been the worst hit this time. I've seen the pictures on the TV and they say that they are still looking for survivors.'

She started to sob again so I thought it best to close the conversation for now.

'Thank you Auntie Jess, just keep us updated please and I'll be down as soon as I can.'

With that I put down the telephone and faced the family, all of whom were waiting as one with bated breath.

'She says that there has been some damage but most of the lines are down. She's heard that emergency services are on the spot, as in her area so she tells us not to worry.'

'Well, that's a relief,' said Dad, 'I think that we should open a bottle. Grab the glasses Jo I think that we all need a drink.'

Duke and I were up early the next morning because we had found out that flights to Canterbury had been cancelled, so it was to be the 'Endeavour Express' for us. Dad was to take us to the bus station, but before he did so Gran came out and took me to one side.

'My dear Jo,' she said handing me a small locket, 'This will be your test. I have not mentioned it before but we have feared that such a calamity might occur at some time or other. Please give this locket to Uncle Joe when you find him. He will give you another in exchange. It is vitally important that you do because in doing so you may help to save the lives of many of our 'people' who have yet to see the light of day. You see, the Aoraki district is the main breeding ground for new Gondian life here on earth. When you get there you will hear of it spoken of as 'A Paradise for Stargazers,' due to the almost permanent clear skies over the turquoise lake and Mount Cook, a perfect habitat for our embryos. I am telling you this in the strictest confidence, so please be careful and bring his locket back safely to me. You will then have passed the test'.

I didn't know how she seemed to have all this planned presumably without any pre knowledge of the earthquake and I knew better than to ask, but I surmised that it was probably based on ancient forecast testimony somewhere in the 'Legacy.' I took the locket and kissed her.

'Don't worry Gran, I'll bring it back.' I said.

Now we were ready to board the 'Old Endeavour.' This was a double misnomer as it obviously alluded to Cook's ship whereas this was a rusty old tub, and it was also very far from 'Express.' Eventually after about 6 hours it rolled into Canterbury station to a scene that reminded of the evacuations that I'd heard about during the war. However in this case there seemed to as people coming as going. I suppose that the first group were looking for relatives, as we were, whilst the second group couldn't wait to get away for fear of aftershocks. We soon found a taxi with a very friendly driver called Magnus.

'You must be my hundredth customer today.' he said with a laugh. 'Everyone seems to want to go to St Anselm's today. That's more than at Christmas, Whitsun and Easter put together and I should know because Ingrid is a Catholic and she never misses holy days of obligation.'

His easy manner helped Duke and I to relax a bit so I ventured to ask him if his own family were safe.

'Right as rain,' he said, 'they're inside St Anselm's with everyone else because we've been temporarily evacuated. We expect to get back in as soon as they give the all clear, maybe in a few days.'

It only took 10 minutes to get to St Anselm's square which was a large area with the church on one side, flats on the other and a large crucifix in the centre.

'That's where Ingrid and I live with our little blonde bombshell Rosie. She'll be five in a few days.' he said and pointed to a block simply called Wellington. 'Number 503, 5th floor,' he said. 'Here take my card. You never know when you might need me again.'

With that he handed me his card and drove off. I looked at it and couldn't suppress a smile, handing it to Duke as I did so.

'Right up your street.' I said. He took it and read, 'Magnus Carlson. Swedish Taxi Sauna Service.' Someone had forgotten to place an 'ampersand' between Taxi and Sauna, so it seemed that one might enjoy a steam bath whilst travelling to a destination. The idea tickled us pink, and we fell about laughing on the pavement, but only for a moment, as the serious situation began to dawn on us. There were ruins everywhere but somehow the Church seemed to be untouched, and as I looked back at the Wellington block, I noticed that its neighbour was the 'Lancaster' and that is where Aunt Jess had said she lived. Both were, 'Closed until further notice.'

As we approached the church I had to admit that it seemed more like a busy railway station, a bit like St Pancras in London I thought.

But there the similarity ended, because there were no London cabs politely queuing up for fares, but rather a mad scramble of cars and vans and minibuses to get in and to get out. Inside I got a strange feeling of a 'referred' sense of déjà vu. I put it that way because I had never seen the London Underground during the Blitz, but I'd seen plenty of pictures, and I'd lived each moment as older relatives relayed their experiences every Christmas. It was a very large church and all the benches had been pushed to the sides and in their stead were rows and rows of beds. Another thought crossed my mind and that was of Florence Nightingale ministering to the sick, the wounded and the dying in the Crimea. Fortunately there were no patients here. I discovered later that those who had been hurt had been taken to St Mark's hospital, including some very serious cases from the Aoraki district where Uncle Joe lived.

We eventually spotted Aunt Jess and Uncle Desmond through the crowd and I called out,

'Over here. Over here Auntie Jess.'

She waved back and beckoned for us to clamber over the beds to get to them. 'No, come here,' she called out, 'we'll lose our place if we move and they're like gold dust.'

It was a bit difficult and we got some black looks as we negotiated our way through the throng, but eventually we got there to receive a big hug and a kiss from them both.

'It's so good of you to come,' she said, 'but actually there are so many much worse off than us.'

I said that I realised that, but that Duke and I had brought them some provisions anyway, to make life a little more comfortable.

'You are so kind,' she replied, 'but actually we're hoping to get back in the flat quite soon, once they give us the all clear. There's not much damage. These are lovely cakes dear.'

We sat amongst the crowd and enjoyed our 'picnic' on the bed that was their home for now, and after a while she stood up and said.

'Now you must meet Father Brendan to see how you can help.'

Like her sister (my mum) she didn't think to ask me, and the thought crossed my mind that some of my self- determination, (some called it wilfulness) might be another part of my family 'inheritance.'

Father Brendan O'Connor was sitting quietly at a desk in the corner of a back room that seemed to serve as kitchen and first aid centre as well as his office. He couldn't have been more than about 25 years old, but I did notice that he was (perhaps prematurely) grey. I'd noticed on my many visits to churches with Duke, on what he called 'Holy days of Obligation,' that Catholic priests seemed to be aged 25 or 75 with very little in between. Duke said that this was normal and there would be another tranche of novices soon. Well, I thought, on the evidence I'd seen it would be another fifty years before things picked up, but he wasn't worried.

'God always finds a way.' he said. 'I don't like to think of it, but take the case of poor Poppy in LA' he said. 'Look how many souls she captured there.'

I was annoyed at this remark. I considered it to be thoughtless and insensitive in the extreme but, given our situation in the church, I bit my lip and said nothing. The truth of the matter was that I really and truly had never understood why he saw every little thing in its relation to God, but I did know that it meant everything to him. When I'd questioned him in the past his stock answer was that he sometimes wished that he wasn't a Catholic at all, because life would be so much easier without his faith. But when I had suggested that there might be alternatives, he looked at me very oddly and said,

'Not for me there aren't. I just wish that there were.'

When Father Brendan saw us, he stood up and opened his arms as if to embrace us both but there was barely room for that, so it more of a gesture than a hug.

'Sit, please sit,' he said, 'have you come to volunteer? That's so kind. We desperately need people up in Araoki and we have an emergency bus leaving in an hour. Do you think that you could be on it?'

I must admit that I was somewhat amused. Just as Aunt Jess had done, he had immediately assumed that I would go to help those in trouble without thinking to ask me. I suppose I might have been offended at being taken for granted, but actually I felt a sense of gratitude that I was to be trusted again.

Naturally we took the bus with about ten other volunteers and after a rather rocky ride of about three hours we arrived at the foot of Mount Cook. As we had been told, the views over the sea blue lake and the mountain itself were spectacular, but closer to the eye was the town itself and this was in ruins. Fortunately there probably had not been that many tall buildings to spread damage far and wide, but most houses and streets that we saw had all been hit.

The bus headed for an old fire station out of town because this had been turned into a relief centre, and it has to be said, a morgue as well. Here we found Joe and his 'partner' Maggie and they greeted us very warmly.

'We're OK,' he said, 'but I hope you understand that others have not been so lucky.' Saying this he took my elbow and drew me to one side. 'Can we trust your friend?' he said, 'I'm afraid that Maggie and I have got to go to Lake Tekapo and deal with a rather messy business up there. Perhaps Gran has told you that Maggie is also one of the 'Chosen Ones' like you, so she feels very responsible for the embryos up there. Not many people here know about the incubation pools and we want to keep it that way. Do you think it best that he tries to help Sister Teresa down here, while we go to the lake? We can easily explain it as a division of labour.'

Actually I would have trusted Duke with my life but I did think that this task, as I imagined it, might be a bit much for him to take, so I agreed. Sister Teresa already had Duke helping with the supplies so I just said,

'I'm going off with Joe and Maggie for a bit. Will you give Sister a hand?'

He looked up from the heavy box that he was carrying and just said, 'Like this you mean?'

I waved, blew him a kiss and we left.

I will now find it very hard to explain the scene that greeted us when we arrived at the Church of the Good Shepherd on the shores of the stunningly beautiful luminescent turquoise Lake Tekapo.

Gran had not told me about Maggie but I was not at all surprised. It seemed only natural that 'new born life' would need the best of care and attention, and who better than one of their own to give it. Maggie was a hybrid, just like Gran and, so it seemed was I as well. Waiting for us was a small group small group of helpers gathered around the bronze statue of a Collie sheepdog, who in turn seemed to be watching over a long line of baby seals on the shore. I knew immediately that these were not seals but the carcasses of infant or embryonic Gondians. I was pitiful and everyone seemed to be crying. There must have been nearly one hundred of them. On our arrival I was taken to meet the leader of the group, a lady called Venta, I was told.

She immediately handed me a locket, similar to the one that Gran had given me and said, 'I wish that we might have met under more pleasant circumstances but now you must take this back and you will be told what to do.'

I handed her Gran's locket and she opened it and seemed to adjust something inside, then she gave it back to me.

'Good,' she said, 'please take this back as well.'

I thanked her and asked how I could help and she just shrugged.

'There have been no survivors,' she said, 'all we have to do is to place them in those black body bags over there and they will be disposed of.'

I had visions of many a war scene but immediately set to work with the others. Apparently the earthquake had damaged the Wataki Dam at the other end of the lake, thereby causing the Macaulay River to flood back in and contaminate any life forms there, including the hybrids that nestled in the deep. It was a sad scene but I was glad to have helped, and soon I was able to head back to Canterbury.

Unfortunately the scene that greeted me was no better, and in many ways it was far worse. St Anselms stood proud and victorious over all that surrounded it, but on the other side of the square, the 'Wellington' was a heap of ashes. Of course I rushed to see if Auntie Jess was OK and she was but she said that the block had tumbled just as some families were getting ready to move back in. I immediately thought of Magnus and his family as Duke came rushing up and grasped me so tight that I could hardly breathe. I could tell that he had been crying and it was I that had to comfort him.

'It's Poppy,' he said, 'it's Poppy. She fell from the 5th floor. She's dead. Poor little Poppy's dead and it's my fault.'

I turned to Jess and raised my eyebrows. 'What's he saying,' I said, 'he seems to be hysterical.'

Now she started to cry as well,

'No he isn't,' she said, 'but it wasn't Poppy. It was little Rosie Carlsson who fell from the block and was killed.'

My heart sank as I remembered that she had just had her fifth birthday and that her dad had been so proud.

Then I noticed that once more there were flowers strewn all around the crucifix in the middle of the square and a sign said.

DEAR ROSIE NOW IN HEAVEN, WITH ALL THE OTHER ANGELS.

I could tell that Duke was still thinking about Poppy in LA. It had all been too much for him and there was nothing to say except to hold each other; and we stayed like that in the square until dawn.

Our mission had been accomplished but for both of us I think that it was the most traumatic of our lives, and I was glad to get back to Queenstown where Mum made us both a 'nice cup of tea' as if to say 'there-there that will make it better,' but of course it didn't.

***

It took a few days, but eventually Duke seemed to recover a little and we got a chance to discuss our next moves as we sat out on the balcony.

'So how are we going to find Matlock?' he said.

'I was wondering about that myself,' I replied, 'but I've had a brainwave and it's all to do with schools. He has two kids and I'm pretty sure that one of the first things he would have done when he arrived here would be to enrol them in a local school. I remember just how serious he was about their education in the widest sense when he took them on all those trips to 'places of interest.' but in addition I also suspect that it would probably be a Church school of the Protestant variety, given his sojourn in Africa amongst the Afrikaaners so prevalent there. Probably Presbyterian I think and certainly not 'your lot,' I said with a smile. Fortunately he didn't take umbrage at my little joke and anyway he knew that I was right.

We then set about obtaining listings of all such schools in the area together with a surveillance rota for us both, and within a few days we were ready to implement it. I hoped that he had not changed all his identity documents to 'Spencer' because that might have made tracking him almost impossible. However he was a practical man and (I hoped) he would feel at ease enough in a new country to revert to Matlock. Now all we had to do was to wait and as it turned out, not for very long. It was my seventh school, the 'Martin Luther School for Boys' and as I sat waiting in my hired Holden, a Ford Galaxy pulled up and two small boys jumped out and waved back to the driver. My heart jumped. It was him all right. It was 'Bald Eagle' Matlock…… I'd have known him anywhere.

There and then I decided to follow his car from a safe distance. This was strictly against my agreement with Duke when we had agreed that such an idea would be too risky for me especially. Matlock knew me and just a glimpse of me might ruin our plans altogether, but seeing him just made my blood boil and so I decided to track him just the same. Fortunately I was not observed as he drove into a substantial property a few miles from the school. It was called 'Endeavour' presumably after Cook's famous ship, and I had to admit rather ruefully, somewhat appropriate for Matlock as well. Having pinpointed this residence I returned to tell Duke of my achievement but as I had anticipated, he was not happy.

'That's the trouble with you,' he said, 'you're always working off your instincts and that's going to get us into trouble one day.'

I knew that he was right but I managed to wheedle a smile from him when I said,

'You don't seem to complain about my instincts in bed do you?'

He laughed saying that there was a time and a place for everything, so I took this to be an invitation and said,

'Well now's the time and this is the place. Catch me if you can.' And with that I made a dash for my bedroom with Duke just catching me as we tumbled on my bed.

'Shush,' I said, 'Gran wouldn't like it and don't give me that corny answer; just kiss me, hold me, strip me and yes, fuck me, fuck me hard, go on fuck me!'

Funny I'd never used 'that' word before but there was something about a stolen illicit encounter that made the whole thing so exciting.

Duke felt it too as he began to whisper gently in my ear so that it tickled most delightfully, so much so that I guided his head further down. What was I doing? Sure we had been lovers for some time but today we both seemed driven to new heights and (most unusually) a simultaneous finale. As we lay back somewhat out of breath I asked Duke if he thought that the danger had contributed to the 'moment.' His reply was typically Duke,

'I haven't really thought about it, and I don't know and I don't care,' he said, 'maybe we should try 'al fresco' next time, what say here in the garden?'

Now he was going too far so I nudged him in the ribs and gently ushered him out of 'my' room.

'Fat chance' I said, 'I need a shower and so do you, but put your clothes on first in case you're seen.'

I then lay back 'very' satisfied with my day's work.

Later we agreed that we should tell Franks and Tucker of our progress so far and also that Duke should take up the watching brief on Matlock for now. I had other business to attend to and made my excuses claiming 'family duties' but really I wanted to find out more about Gran's Legacy, and what she had really meant when she had said, 'before it's too late.'

When Duke left to take up position at the Matlock house I took the opportunity to sit quietly in the garden and study Gran's book. I held it close to me in my lap, much as Gran had done when she had first met Duke. I touched the cover with my fingertips noting for the first time a rather uneven surface, but slippery rather than smooth to touch. It somehow felt like a dormant tuatara lizard likely to slither out of my grasp in seconds, and I shivered apprehensively as I opened it. Inside the front cover there was a note addressed to me from Gran and this is what it said.

My Dear Jo

This is your time. I was the chosen one and now you are now the chosen one. You are now the guardian of the legacy. You must contact your Uncle Leo at Arrowtown Hardware Stores without delay. He will give you further instructions but do not mention this to anyone else.

Good luck.
I love you.

Gran.

No one had mentioned an uncle in Arrowtown and Gran had asked me to keep my visit secret so before I read the book in detail I made an excuse at dinner that I wanted to see some of the old history of the region and wished to visit the old gold prospecting sites there. Naturally I had to resist offers from Duke and the family to come with me, but I just said that it would be good for me to have some time alone and by and large this was accepted. Mum and Dad thought I wanted some time away from Duke, and I didn't let on that that was far from the truth.

Duke on the other hand was feeling very responsible over his 'stake out' at the Matlock house so all he said was,

'Good idea, but don't be gone too long. Something might come in from HQ and we might have to move fast. And anyway,' he said, 'I'm looking forward to our 'al fresco' assignation that you promised.'

Had I promised? I don't think so, but maybe it wasn't such a bad idea I thought, just not in Gran's garden.

I planned to go Arrowtown the next day so that evening I opened the 'Legacy' once more and began to read. It seemed to be both a book of the past, a 'legacy' perhaps, but also a book of the future with guidance as to how that legacy must be protected and carried forward, generation by generation. I remembered how Gran had said 'Now it is your turn,' to me, and I suddenly felt the burden of history on my shoulders. Once more I wondered what my task was to be so I read on. As I expected the earlier chapters recounted tales from a long lost past when an ice Age on Earth attracted the first settlers from Gonda who arrived in space capsules adapted to survive in deep fresh water lakes. The occupants gradually morphed into creatures such as the Tuatara lizard that could survive in the lake without assistance then, after further adaptations, integrated with humans over many centuries and created a new hybrid race. However, hostilities from other humans, and a more benign climate on Gonda, resulted in a mass departure that nevertheless left many hybrids behind. This group called itself 'The Chosen Ones' being the ones to maintain the 'legacy,' which in part was to provide a home for Gondians in the future, should conditions on Gonda itself make it necessary.

There were separate chapters for each 'generation' and each contained coded instructions in the form of a riddle that would only make sense in that particular era as to how to accomplish the legacy. 'In the Age of the Sabre Tooth' was one, and another was called 'In the Age of the Flood,' and there were many more, none of which made sense to me. However I knew that there would be a chapter for 'my time' because Gran had said so, but before I found it I noted a long section about the future in which a scenario of a bright and beautiful future awaited 'those who were worthy.'

Worthiness was assured by adherence to a code of conduct that they called 'Alteri.' (Later I looked this up and found it to mean altruism, that concept that tends to put oneself last in any given situation,) in other words love of others, or 'neighbours' as the Christian Bible put it. This was not guaranteed however, and it had to be earned by each and every generation. This chapter was called 'The Light,' but another chapter warned of consequences if the guardians of the legacy failed. This chapter was called 'The Dark.'

I felt as if the whole thing was somewhat Biblical in outline listing as it did a distant past, whilst containing advice for the present as well as a promise for the future in 'The Light.' However, as in the Biblical Revelations, a warning was also given in 'The Dark.'

Now I finally had to acknowledge that I was not only a Gondian hybrid myself, but also a chosen guardian. How could I possibly explain this to Duke I wondered uneasily, but for now what was my task to be? Turning the pages I came to a section that was called 'In The Age of Var' and this is what the riddle for that age said.

> To the Chosen of the Star
> You have travelled very Far
> But only you know where is Var
> You must find it in the Dome
> And that will be our Home.

I knew at once that this was meant for me, that this was my age 'The Age of Var', because Var (the Variable Star) had only recently been discovered in a nebula of galaxies outside our own by Professor Hubble with the most modern of spectrographs. It seemed incredible that this had been foreseen so many centuries ago by the original 'chosen' who wrote the 'Legacy,' but there it was.

Now all (I say all, but that's a gross understatement), yes, all I had to do was to tell Duke and trust that he would trust me. There and then I decided to show him Gran's Legacy and hope for the best. I knew that it would be a difficult pill for him to swallow, but I had no choice and could only pray 'yes pray,' that I would not lose him, but on the bright side I was also beginning to think that there might be a silver lining in this after all. Indeed, just as he would have to acknowledge the reality of the existence of life outside our galaxy, so it seemed would I have to accept the existence of prayer (as in fact I had already done) and in that sense, the reality of God. Maybe we might be getting closer after all I thought; but my hopes were dashed for the time being as he was still out tailing Matlock.

I therefore decided to make my visit to Arrowtown at once to see what Uncle Leo had in store for me. (He ran a hardware store!)

As I drew up outside the 'Pots, Pans and Riddles' store in the main street (optimistically called Gold Avenue) I had to laugh at the 'double-entendre' in the name of the store, referring as it did to the old days of gold prospecting, but also, for those 'in the know' to that other form of riddle in the Legacy. Uncle Leo was sitting in a rocking chair out on a boardwalk veranda at the front and it seemed as if he had been there for centuries but was probably only about seventy. He was smoking a clay pipe and wore typical gold panning dungarees with a battered straw hat (I thought of the Beverley Hillbillies) but that was the extent of the similarity as he greeted me warmly with a broad New Zealand accent.

'Welcome to my humble home and help yourself to the gold.' he said and laughed. He then embraced me like a long lost relative, which I suppose I was.

He smelt of tobacco and linseed oil but there was also a kind of freshness about him as if he'd just stepped off the SS Earnshaw.

I liked him immediately and not only that, but I felt warm and safe as he guided me into the inner sanctum of the store.

'Most of our ancestors lived hereabouts,' he said, 'some panned for gold and some struck it rich, but most didn't.' he added ruefully. From time to time he got up as a cuckoo clock sounded from the shop, and a potential customer wandered in. He seemed very happy to tell such tourists the story of gold in 'them thar hills,' and usually sold them a small bag to prove it. Others were locals, and he seemed to take pleasure and smoke a pipe in their company as I waited. I noticed old mining bric-a-brac everywhere, much of which might be quite valuable, but I doubted that Uncle Leo was interested in that. At last he shut the shop, made coffee, gave me his full attention and said,

'Your Gran assures me that you are the 'Chosen One' so you must now take responsibility for our next generations. Next

Thursday is the Equinox, and at that time we are closest to both Orion and Syrius, and this is the only time that we can communicate freely outside our own Galaxy from here. On that day we will be able to exchange messages with Gonda and it is imperative that we are able to tell them what has been decided here on Earth, and that decision is now in your hands.'

Well naturally I was very interested at what he had to say about the Equinox but as for me being involved, well, to put it mildly I was dumbstruck. Fortunately he did not wait for a response but went on at length to describe what I must do.

'Within a few months Gonda will overheat beyond our endurance and we must find a new home without delay. We already have a number of seed pods here on earth in the Great Lakes and elsewhere but pollution has become a major problem.

'We had been hoping to re-integrate ourselves here on Earth with the help of our associates in Cerberus, but things have gone badly wrong in that respect. There is faction fighting within that group and even some of our most trusted leaders from our own Gondian heritage have betrayed us. As it stands they plan to make their attacks on the world's infrastructures within weeks, maybe because they know of our difficulties, but it has become obvious that there is going to no place for Gonda in their plan. We do not wish to collaborate in our own demise, but we have nowhere else to go and 'The Dark' will be upon us unless we act now and that is where you come in. We seek the Light and you must help us to locate Var.'

I didn't have much time to take all this in but I was thinking, maybe even hoping, that Matlock might be one of the traitors, and if he was to get his just deserts I'd be glad to deliver it myself; with interest.

'Tell me what I must do Uncle Leo,' I said, 'I confess that I didn't expect any of this, but I think I've known for a long time that I had some special insights over the years. I just didn't know that I was going to have to use them in this way; but maybe that was why I was given them in the first place. Go on, tell me more.'

Maybe I shouldn't have been surprised again, but I can assure you that I was when he told me what was expected of me in these terms.

'In times of crisis Gondian leaders will only negotiate with one of their own, in fact only with the 'Chosen One,' and that is you at this time. As you may know, previous attempts to make agreements with your governments have not been successful and now if Cerberus get their way, there is little doubt that a new nuclear conflict will become inevitable here on Earth, and we won't survive that either let alone our own global warming on Gonda You must therefore meet their leader in their deep water location at 'Doubtful Sound' and provide them with the coordinates for Var. They in turn will release all documents and timetables relating to the Cerberus plan. I will travel tomorrow to deliver gold from the ancient seams that still exist around Arrowtown as they need it badly as an alternative energy source to the diamonds that are now in short supply, and I want you to come with me. You see it's just not true that aliens always know best. They, that is, we, need your help badly. Locate the Star and that will be the New Home for Gonda as promised in the Legacy. Time is of the essence so please get the co-ordinates and return as soon as possible, and I will take you to there. Go now.'

He patted my arm and kissed me on the cheek as he ushered me out into a dark and gloomy night. I felt somewhat dark and gloomy myself at the prospect that awaited me. Firstly I didn't like the idea of a deep water location, secondly I wasn't too keen to meet up with 'actual' aliens and thirdly I didn't know how I could convince Franks and Tucker to make a deal on my say so, oh and yes there was also Duke to think about. I'd certainly need all my powers of persuasion to convince him. I needed cheering up, so as I drove home I put on a CD from the Wizard of Oz, and how appropriate it was; not only 'Over the Rainbow,' but 'I'm off to see the Wizard' as well. I laughed myself silly and nearly drove off the road, but I arrived home in a much more optimistic frame of mind.

The next morning Duke was quite excited himself as we chatted on the balcony after breakfast.

'Guess what,' he said. 'I think I know where they are. I followed Matlock way beyond the Cavell Hills, and eventually he wound up at the Homer Tunnel that leads to the Manapouri Power Station on Doubtful Sound. It's the biggest in New Zealand and I'm pretty sure that he has a base there. I think that we'd better contact Franks and Tucker to ask for further instructions don't you?'

Well I didn't know what to say at first. Of course I was pleased for him, and he seemed so keen to make further progress that I felt bad about having to tell him my own news, but there was nothing for it but to come clean. I needed the co-ordinates, and I needed Duke to help me get them, so I made a pot of coffee and told him the whole unlikely story.

He seemed incredulous at first as I related all the details, fixing me with a rather frosty stare as if I had stolen his ice cream; but he began to thaw after I handed him the 'Legacy.' It was as if the book had a magical power to convince, even though I might not. He touched the cover with his fingertips, turning it over and over as if it was a precious object (which of course it was). He opened it carefully and leaved through the pages assiduously as I waited nervously for his verdict. Fortunately it was a resounding 'Not Guilty,' as he placed the book down and stood up.

'Come here.' he said somewhat roughly, and as I did so he swept me up in his arms and cried out, 'Kiwi, darling Kiwi, how could I have doubted you? I love you so much and I hope it's not too late to make amends. Please let me help.'

I was overwhelmed. I had been worried that our love affair might be over but here it was, seemingly rekindled 'like a bright star' I thought to myself.

'Thank you Var,' I murmured in Duke's ear, but he just shivered with pleasure as he held me, now at arm's length.

'So you have got to deliver the Var co-ordinates to Doubtful Sound if Franks and Tucker will release them, and then you've got to meet negotiators from Gonda and they'll give you the Cerberus plans so that they might be thwarted. Have I got all this right and is there anything else that you haven't told me?' he said.

I smiled,

'Only that I love you Duke.' I replied.

'Well in that case,' he said, 'I'm coming with you, and I won't take no for an answer.'

I knew that this might be difficult, but I was pleased just the same.

As I expected it took some time to convince the 'powers that be' that this was maybe a once in a lifetime opportunity to kill two birds with one stone, namely to assist Gonda and to nullify the ever growing threat from Cerberus. I re-iterated that we did not have much time due to the imminent Equinox but they still dithered. Eventually I asked Duke to request that the CIA re-open the file on Senator Joshua Prince who had been murdered following his investigations into 'Aliens in Los Angeles Bay.' You may remember that this was one of the first things that he had mentioned before our investigation into Ward's disappearance. He did so and we waited anxiously for the next few days, but eventually the long awaited email arrived in cryptic code and this is what it said.

> Authority to proceed as outlined. Prince documents verified and prior meetings with Gonda also confirmed. Here are the co-ordinates.
>
> VAR is D 4371 L894 L370 T 712.
> Submit in reverse order.
> Do not divulge until you have the Cerberus Plan in full detail.
> Good luck to you both. The future is in your hands.
> Signed Tom Franks and Hilary Tucker, for and on behalf of the UN.

I suppose it was to be expected that the UK and US governments had not felt able to proceed alone, so I was very pleased to note that the authority was given in the name of the United Nations. Duke was also gratified that his hunch about Prince was right after all.

The next step was to phone Uncle Leo to tell him that I had the data and that I would be bringing Duke with me for the meeting. He wasn't too happy about the latter part of this information, but pleased to get confirmation that I had the co-ordinates. He told me to come to his store on the next Thursday at midnight. He would then transport us to the Lake for a 5am meeting, at which time he hoped that the early morning mist would have cleared, and that a direct communication with Gonda might be more easily achieved.

We had three days to spare and I thought that we might just relax for a bit until Duke reminded me that I'd almost forgotten about Matlock.

'I didn't track him down for nothing you know,' he said, 'don't you think that we should find out what he's up to?'

I knew that he was right and I apologised, saying that I was curious too, and that I was also wondering what his latest plan was.

I got my answer sooner than expected because when I opened my curtains the next morning, there were four cars with flashing lights parked right outside. Two white ones had QTP painted on the side and I recognised these are local Queenstown Police cars. The other two were yellow with the initials MPS emblazoned on the doors, and I later found out that these were from the Manappouri Power Station. All four cars had an officer in uniform spread across the bonnet with a gun trained on the house. Another man stood in front with a loud hailer and he seemed to be looking at his watch. I looked at mine. It was 6.50am and I deduced that he was waiting for 7am.

I rushed in to warn Duke and we both looked out of the back of the house but another two cars stood there as well. I quickly woke the family and told them the situation saying that Duke and I would go out to see what they wanted. I took the precaution to give Gran the co-ordinates saying (quite calmly I must say)

'Gran, please get these to Uncle Leo as soon as possible in case we don't get back.'

She held my hand warmly and I could see that she understood, but Mum and Dad were fretting so I just said, 'We'll be back soon there's nothing to worry about,' and then we walked out to the waiting cars.

We were told to lie down while handcuffs were fitted, and Duke got a kick in the groin for his trouble. We were then placed in separate cars and driven away. I was put in the back seat of one of the police cars beside a rather young WPC. I immediately thought of my own role back in Bristol and tried to strike up a conversation.

'Are you going to read me my rights?' I asked, but when she didn't reply, I added, 'or maybe you'd like to give me my last rites.'

I smiled at my own joke but she just looked straight ahead and said nothing. The cars then drove on for what seemed like hours through mountainous passes and dangerous ravines until we arrived at the entrance to a tunnel with MPS as a sign. The drivers all got out and an argument seemed to ensue, and I got the impression that the MPS employees did not want the police cars to accompany them inside. I was rather glad when all four cars did in fact proceed, because I did retain some small faith in the police even if they were in collaboration with MPS. By now I was beginning to realise that MPS must be a Cerberus front and that worried me a lot.

The tunnel was single carriageway with many narrow bends and the police cars seemed to keep scratching up against the sides. The expression 'bumping and grinding' came to mind but I agree that it was hardly appropriate. I was told later that the tunnel was two miles long, so at the rate that we travelled it took quite a while but eventually all four cars arrived at a small terminus and we all got out.

I looked across at Duke and noticed that his face was bruised and covered in blood. I realised that I had got off lightly, so far.

After passing through a control room not unlike Hinckley we were led into a small ante chamber at the back and told to sit down. It was quite dim which was surprising, given that we were in the middle of the biggest power generator in New Zealand. Everyone sat quietly around a table and then all stood as a tall man entered the room. It was very dark but I knew immediately that it was Matlock. He sat down at the head of the table and began to speak.

'Yes I am Alpha,' he said, 'and if I had my way neither of you would leave this place alive but unfortunately our friends in the police tell me that we only have you 'on loan' as it were and they will be the ones to press charges later.'

He pointed at Duke, 'You have broken the solemn oath and deserve to die.' he said and then looked at me repeating that I should die too for obstructing the 'rightful cause'.

'Today I warn you that your days are numbered,' he said, 'You will never sleep safely in your beds again because you will not have the arm of the law to protect you next time. Now take them away.'

We were both bundled into the same police car this time and were soon driving back through the tunnel. The WPC was in the front seat and this time she turned around with a smile,

'Nasty lot aren't they?' she said.

This broke the ice and Duke and I couldn't stop laughing, probably a little hysterically I think.

The family were quite surprised to see us back so soon and Mum said, (a little insensitively I think)

'Didn't they lock you up then?'

...and soon everything seemed back to normal. I told Gran that I would now carry the co-ordinates to Leo unless we were arrested but weren't so Duke and I set out for Uncle Leo's store at about 10pm the next day and arrived in Arrowtown at midnight.

He was waiting somewhat anxiously and bundled us straight into an old Station Wagon just saying

'Glad you're here. We have no time to waste so let's get moving. Good to meet you Duke. You drive, I'll give directions but Jo and I have business to attend to. We'll sit in the back seat to discuss the plan for when we get there. Just head off out of town that way and follow your nose until I say otherwise.'

We did as we were told and the big old car lurched forward as Duke tried to sort out the gears, and Uncle Leo mumbled something rude under his breath. Soon we were on our way and I relaxed (as far as I was able) in the back seat, and told Uncle Leo of the UN conditions.

'Seems fine to me,' he said, 'Now we only have to convince them.'

Eventually Duke brought the car safely through the mountain ranges, and there before us shining in bright moonlight was Doubtful Sound. I was struck by its beauty and I didn't really want to think about what awaited me in the dark depths. There wasn't much time to worry about that however, for as soon as we arrived at a jetty, Uncle Leo motioned us toward a very small rowing boat.

'There's your Mother Ship,' he said with a smile.

Duke responded with 'Beam me up Scottie' and we both laughed rather nervously. It seemed to break the ice a bit; but not a lot. At this Uncle Leo took his cue and said,

'Actually it should be, 'Beam me down Scottie' because you must row the boat out to the middle of the lake and face the prow to the North. You will have noticed that the vessel has a four sided lantern at the front, and that each side is a different colour. This is your signalling device and at precisely 5am you must switch on the lantern and point the blue quartile to the Moon. Hold it there for 10 seconds and then change to red for 10 seconds and then to Yellow for 10 seconds and then to Green for 20 seconds. Do this again and then wait.'

'So what will we be waiting for?' asked Duke rather impatiently, but Uncle Leo was not impressed and frowned as he replied,

'Just wait and see and you'll soon find out.'

It just might have been a romantic row out on the Lake on a lovely balmy moonlit night as dolphins manoeuvred around our little craft, but as I looked closely I could see that some of these objects were not dolphins at all, or if they were, they were the strangest dolphins that I'd ever seen, because some of them had a beam emanating from a singular eye at the front. I realised then that I was having my first sight of genuine extra- terrestrials.

I looked at Duke and felt like saying, 'I told you so.' but I could see that such a remark would have not only been a bit hurtful, but completely superfluous. I reached over, held his hand and said,

'Have you ever had the feeling that you are being watched?'

He gripped mine tight, smiled and just replied,

'Well I don't know what they are, but I think that we are definitely in for an 'Encounter of a Distant Kind.'

We huddled together, observing this phenomena and feeling rather insecure in our tiny boat when suddenly the lake all around us seemed to bubble as a large vessel emerged from the depths and enclosed us on all sides like a baby in a womb. Then as we waited nervously, a canopy began to cover the sky above thereby enclosing us completely. It rather put me in mind of the canopy at the Centre Court at Wimbledon but this was not the time for mixed double.

Now the vessel began to submerge with more bubbles but this time with us inside as it began its journey to the depths. I was even more scared now and gripped Duke's hand very tight. It felt clammy and I realised that he was just as terrified as I was. It had gone very dark but soon there was a bump as we touched bottom and all the lights in the craft suddenly came on and shone in our eyes. I was blinded for a while but as I became accustomed to our new surroundings I could see that we were in the middle of a large control room, not unlike Hinkley or perhaps a bit more like an operating theatre in a teaching hospital with us as the objects of interest. This notion was soon confirmed as a group of 'persons' in medical/laboratory dress soon surrounded us, Their faces were masked but they otherwise seemed to have the outward gait and manner of ordinary humans.

Then one of them stepped forward, bowed rather dramatically and removed his mask with a flourish, much as Errol Flynn might have done in a Hollywood film about pirates. To be fair though that was the only resemblance, for this particular 'pirate' had a long neck and an aquiline nose, to go with rather hollowed out eye sockets, from which tiny pinpricks of light served for eyes. His voice and manner however belied this rather sinister appearance, as he spoke slowly and carefully in English, with a slight Kiwi accent.

'Welcome Sister,' he said, 'come let's go to the lounge and have some coffee,' saying which he held out his hand to help me from the boat.

I noticed immediately that he had that additional finger that others had spoken of, but strangely I didn't feel scared any longer. The truth is that it was all so normal, if one ignored the fact that we were being entertained by aliens in the dark depths of Doubtful Sound. I turned around and smiled at Duke encouragingly, but I was wondering what he had made of Varta's reference to me as 'sister.' I knew of course that Gran and Uncle Leo and all the family, including me, had our roots in the Gondian hybrids of long ago, but what was Duke to make of it? I didn't want any questions there and then, so I decided that the best course of action was a coffee diversion.

'Would you like Black or White?' I asked rather cheekily.

He too now seemed more at ease and just replied, 'Make mine a Latte.'

Somehow the coffee lounge was much as I expected it to be.

They had done their homework and we could have been in a Hilton or Radisson anywhere in the world with neat tables, olives, cashews and fresh flowers on each. Our host served us the coffee and after a while introduced himself.

'I am Varta,' he said, 'please make yourselves comfortable and I'll be back in a moment.' He then left the table signalling to others in the room to do the same. I thought it extraordinary that his name resembled Var, the distant star that Hubble thought that he had discovered, but I realised that nothing about this extraordinary affair should surprise me at all.

I can't explain why exactly, but I felt as if I was on the same wavelength as Varta. It had been the same with Uncle Leo, and of course with Gran. The issue now was to test the extent of such telepathy, because I could not release the coordinates of Var until he had given me a complete dossier on the Cerberus plans. It was a game of cat and mouse but who would blink first I wondered.

He soon returned and sat down.

'Perhaps you are feeling more comfortable now,' he said, 'so let's begin with our business as there is little time to lose.'

'Certainly,' I began 'firstly I have been asked to give you this locket from Aoraki. I am told that it should match your own here, and all you have to do is to confirm that they match each other, and are compatible with the co-ordinates that I will give you. I have those here, but before I am authorised to release them to you I must be very sure that you are actually in a position to give us the full details of Cerberus planning so that this threat may be nullified at once.'

His reply was simple and to the point, but not exactly what I had hoped for.

'Thank you but I can't guarantee anything, but what I can do is to share all that we know about Cerberus, and I trust that this will be enough for us to proceed.' he said. 'You may know that we have been working with them for some considerable time in order to accomplish common aims, but recently we have become more aware of a private plan on their side to exclude us, once they have achieved their objective of world hegemony for the Aryan race. In short we may well be 'Turkeys voting for Christmas.'

At this we all laughed because that expression seemed so incongruous from an alien being.

'I must tell you now,' he continued, 'that we have observed chaos, death and destruction on earth for many centuries, and we fear that an Armageddon will not be far away if Cerberus proceeds with their plan. In that disaster Gondan hybrids will suffer along with everyone so now is the time to act. However we can't help you unless we can find our way to Var. That is our aim, and when we have triangulated the locket data from Aoraki with our own and integrated your co-ordinates, it seems that we will have enough information to proceed to our mutual benefit.'

He paused and looked at me somewhat studiously whilst ignoring Duke entirely. I think that Varta saw his presence as entirely unnecessary but I was having none of it for three reasons. Firstly because the CIA had to be right behind any deal that was made, secondly because I valued his input, but thirdly and perhaps most importantly I knew that Duke's strengths were closely tied up with his ego. I knew instinctively that he was having trouble with the whole situation in which he found himself because he perceived it as a threat, not only to the world, which it might be, but to the whole central platform of his Catholic faith. In his eyes the heavens were God's firmament alone, although I must say that he had been trying hard to square the circle given the evidence of his own eyes. I therefore made my position clear to Varta that Duke was a vital member of my delegation.

'My colleague here represents many on Earth who might have some difficulty in comprehending the reasons behind any agreement that we might reach. Many will always fail to believe in such things as alien life, but he has come here in good faith to listen to you and to assist you, so I trust that you will afford him the full respect that you have given me.'

At this remark I sensed that Varta acknowledged that he had ignored Duke somewhat, and he was quick to put it right by posing a question direct to him.

'Well Duke,' he said, 'If I give you an outline plan do you think that you can take it away and make sense of it. You will see that it is very detailed as to names, places and dates. Here let me show you.'

With that he opened up a lap top and began to enter a series of numbers before handing it over. 'There you are,' he said, 'see what you make of that. You will also observe that it is also delineated by economic as well as political scenarios.'

Duke browsed for a few moments but began to look increasingly puzzled and somewhat confused.

'There's so much here,' he said

'I'm afraid I'll have to send it to our Logistics Centres in London and Washington to see what they make of it. A full analysis could take some time.'

Now Varta looked deadly serious,

'But that's exactly what we haven't got, time that is. As I told you before, the contact can only be made at a specific date and time and that time is now.'

I sensed that he really meant it but I was truly on the horns of a dilemma. Yes I had been given the coordinates but I also knew that once I gave them to Varta we had lost any bargaining power that we might have had. I looked at our strange host closely. What was he thinking? What was he going to do and could he be trusted? Funny, but strange as it may seem, I seemed to receive a direct telepathic message from him as he stared back at me.

'Trust me.' it said, 'Trust me Sister. Our fate is in your hands.'

I looked over at Duke and smiled,

'Well if it's all right with you,' I said, 'I think that we'll get on with it,' and with that I handed him the precious co-ordinates as well as Gran's locket and Venta's locket from Aoraki. He checked the details much as a bus conductor might when he/she validated tickets, but instead of clipping them, he placed them all carefully in a jewelled casket and handed them to an assistant.

'Transmit.' he said rather dramatically, and looked at me. I nodded.

'Send the message.' I said, 'Let our people find their new home.'

Varta responded with a big smile and a kiss for me and then a big kiss for Duke as well. He himself seemed somewhat taken aback by this but whispered to me that it actually felt quite good. I didn't know if he was teasing, but it was comforting to think that he might be. That would mean that he was fully reconciled to the situation, but on the other hand it might mean that he, like me, had discovered that 'oranges are not the only fruit.' I looked at him quizzically but he just stared blankly and winked. Damn him I thought, what had happened to my powers of cosmic intuition? It was clear to me now that it was love that was getting in the way, but to be truthful that was a trade- off I was very pleased to make.

We bade farewell to our hosts, made our way back to shore in our small rowing boat and waited. Varta had said that the 'exodus' must be immediate if the constellations were to be aligned for their long journey. He had already sent messages to the four corners of the earth where similar craft in deep water lakes awaited instructions to leave. He assured me that for the most part, although hundreds of craft would be leaving, it was most unlikely that they would be observed due to what he called 'silence and invisibility phenomena.' This reminded me somewhat of the American 'Stealth' aircraft, but probably much more so. Anyway we didn't have to wait long before Uncle Leo arrived to take us home, greeting us warmly and settling down on the jetty beside us.

He looked at his watch and then said, 'Hush, here they come.'

The next few moments were the most extraordinary of my life as the calm moonlit waters of the lake suddenly begin to bubble, and what appeared to be many large dolphins appeared on the surface. They settled there for just a few seconds and then WHOOSH, they were gone and it was all over.

I won't bother you with all the checks and double checks that had to be made following our watery rendezvous, but Varta's data was beyond reproach. Within days comprehensive world- wide action was taken against Cerberus in all their bases, and against all their disruptive plans in the economic and political spheres. Within weeks they had been totally neutralised as a threat to society.

Only four issues remained after we had flown back to London.

Firstly, I wanted to know if Varta and the Gondians had reached their promised land, and I soon received an answer to that one.

> To Kiwi, 'Wherever you may wander, wherever you may roam, there's no place like home. Thank you friends and family. Please visit soon! All are welcome. Varta x'

Secondly, how was I now to explain to Duke what Varta had meant when he called me 'sister' and used the word 'family' in the message, and that I had referred, 'our people' in mine? And as for the kiss, Well! Would he really ever fully understand that Gran and Uncle Leo and indeed all of our family, including me, were part of a hybrid family of Gondians left behind over so many centuries? Fortunately he hasn't asked up to now, but I do know that he loves me and that I love him and that won't change no matter what.

Thirdly, I have some optimism that Gonda and Earth will find common cause in the future. 'Let there be love' is a Christian hymn but it's a concept that applies to all world religions, and the Gondian idea of 'Alteri' (altruism) is certainly in the same mould. I just hope that everyone (including Duke) will come to accept this over time.

The funny thing is that, just as I seem to have succeeded in leading Duke to a wider perception, I myself have been drawn to his own spiritual vision, and I've now begun to wonder if there's something real in the Catholic mysteries that he holds to so dearly, after all.

Fourthly, Varta had told us the names of the important hierarchy in Cerberus, and as I had anticipated it was Matlock himself that was identified as Alpha, the supreme leader of the whole enterprise. Apparently he had succeeded to this position within the last year and it was he who had been putting pressure on the Gondians.

I looked forward to hearing that he had been arrested during the massive clean- up operations but I was disappointed. Franks put it like this as we had tea on the balcony of his flat in central London.

'They seek him here they seek him there but they never did find that Damned Pimpernel did they?' he said. Of course I knew that he was right and with Matlock free as a bird none of us could sleep safe at night. The 'Bald Eagle Beast' would certainly continue to haunt our dreams until he was safely apprehended and put away for good.

There may be many 'Encounters of a Distant Kind' to come in the future, but I'm not worried as long as I have Duke and he has me.

FIN

ABOUT THE AUTHOR

Do you believe in love but wonder if it is ever enough?
Adam A. Masters does and he believes that it is.

In 'Encounters of a Distant Kind' he explores this quandary through the experiences of two intelligence agents caught up in a tale of murder and revenge set across continents and space. However the story is also about the choices that people make and the reasons that they make them. Sometimes these are ill defined, sometimes it might be revenge or greed and sometimes it's a kind of moral imperative.

But most of the time the reason is LOVE.

Adam A. Masters is now retired and in his seventies. This is his third novel but the other two were written under nom de plumes. Now he has distilled those prior works and his perceptions born out of personal experience, to produce this work. Like Truman Capote he calls it a work of 'faction' in which fiction sits comfortably with fact. Another important strand is the way in which he deploys very personal detail in the scenarios that he paints. This may be memories from the 'Blitz' in London during the war, or the Catholic roots of his mother's family/ 'He's always watching over you,' she would say, 'just make sure that you don't stray too far.' This was comforting in its way but maybe a bit of a burden too. A spell at a minor public school at Brentwood led to a career in the City and thence to the motor industry. At this time he married and had three children before accepting a post in east Africa that included the rather dramatic events of UDI in Rhodesia in 1962. On return to the UK he divorced and took a 2.1 History degree at Birmingham University and became a teacher. His wider interests include music and he is an accomplished jazz clarinettist. Politics are another abiding interest and he remains firmly out there on the left. His favourite authors include Asimov, Greene and Waugh and their moral themes continue to influence his work. 'Love is a mystery,' he says, 'be it earthly or transcendental it can never be ignored'.

Printed in the United States
By Bookmasters